JACK

A ROMANTIC COMEDY

GIULIA LAGOMARSINO

Jack
A Romantic Comedy
For The Love Of A Good Woman

Copyright © 2017 Giulia Lagomarsino
All rights reserved. This book or any portion thereof may not be reproduced or used in any manner whatsoever without the express written permission of the publisher except for the use of brief quotations in a book review.
Printed in the United States of America
First Printing, 2017

Self published through Kindle Direct Publishing

Cover Design courtesy of T.E. Black Designs
www.teblackdesigns.com

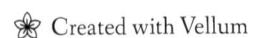

❋ Created with Vellum

For my husband, who inspired me to write this book.

CHAPTER 1

HARPER

"NO, NO, NO, NO!" I slammed my fists on the steering wheel as the car coasted to a stop on the side of the road. Of all days for my car to break down, it had to be today. Why couldn't it have happened when I was actually dressed properly? My mother had always told me to be fully dressed when I left the house. *"You never know what's going to happen,"* my mother used to say. I rolled my eyes as I heard her nagging voice in my head. I had never been good about listening to my mother. We didn't get along all that well. Or at all. I never took much stock in the advice my dear mother doled out. It looked like now would have been one of those times to listen.

I reached across the seat to grab my phone when I remembered that I had left it at home. Shit! I hadn't brought it because I was just making a quick trip to feed my friend Anna's cat. I had been looking after the little devil for the past week and we had an equal hatred for one another. He hissed, bit, attacked, and scared the living daylights out of me. I went once a day to feed the cat, change the water, and clean the litter box. Then, I got the hell out of there. I always snuck in as quietly as possible and ran for my life to escape the apartment. It had worked once so far.

Now, here I sat. Alone. I wasn't actually that far from Anna's apartment, but it was pouring outside. It was supposed to be a warm day, hence the inappropriate clothing, but it had cooled down considerably with the rain. Leaning over the seat, I scrounged around the backseat for something else to put on, but I had just cleaned out the car the other day. Glancing down at what I was wearing, a white, spaghetti strap tank, barely-there pajama shorts with pink flamingos, and flip flops, I realized I had not made a smart choice this morning.

Looking out the window, I huffed at the realization that if I was going anywhere today, I was going to have to walk. Taking a deep breath, I flung open the door and started running toward Anna's apartment. I got about ten feet from the car when my foot landed in a rain puddle that was actually a big hole. My foot twisted to the side and pain shot up through the top of my foot as I fell forward. I yelped as my arms flailed, hoping to grab on to the imaginary "oh shit" handles.

Crashing to the ground into the large puddle, my clothes were instantly soaked and I was shivering from the cool water coating my skin. I sat up and breathed through the pain. It was intense and I had to will myself not to cry. I took a deep breath in and counted to five, then slowly released my breath. Surely if I breathed through it the pain would recede, but as my luck of the day went, it did not. In fact, it felt much worse.

Seriously? I couldn't just have my car break down? No, I had to also try and break my foot while running in the rain wearing hardly any clothes. I swiped my soaking wet hair out of my face and held in a breath as I tried to stand on my injured foot. I was able to get up, but when I put pressure on my foot, I fell back in the puddle with a splash.

More concerned with my current state of distress than anything going on around me, I hadn't heard the vehicle pull up behind me or seen the man walk toward me, but when I heard his deep, incredibly sexy voice, I wished I had been paying more attention.

"Need a hand?"

My heart rate picked up at the sound of the steely voice. I looked up through my lashes and saw one of the sexiest men I had ever seen. I took stock of the man, my eyes trailing over his rain-slickened body, and couldn't help the breathy sigh that escaped my lips. I really did try to pull myself together, but I was mystified by his ruggedly handsome good looks.

I licked my lips as I stared up at him, panting internally as lust washed over me. God, he was so good-looking. He must be at least 6'2". *Purr.* I felt like a cat, wanting to rub up against her owner. That was only a slightly disturbing thought. I loved that stubble on his jaw. I rubbed my neck, wondering what it would feel like against my skin.

Mmmm. Chocolate eyes... not actual chocolate, but the color of chocolate. Dummy. You don't need to tell yourself that his eyes aren't actual chocolate. You're having a conversation with yourself and I'm pretty sure you knew what you meant.

I shook my head slightly, realizing that he had said something to me and I hadn't heard a word of it. I tilted my head, staring at him, hoping his words would somehow come back to me so I wouldn't just be staring at him, but the longer I stared, the more it became clear that I wasn't going to magically conjure up his words.

Get yourself together and stop staring! Say something! And wipe the drool off your face!

"You can keep staring, but maybe you should close your mouth. You do have a little bit of drool right here," he said as he swiped at his chin with a grin.

Apparently, I was speaking out loud. What an idiot!

"I'm Jack. You look like you need some help," he said as he held out his hand and pulled me to my feet. His arm snaked around my waist as he supported my weight with his strong, chiseled body. I leaned heavily into him as I reveled in the warmth of his body. I hadn't realized how cold I was until I felt his body heat through my soaked clothes. My hands perused his chest, feeling his rippling muscles under his t-shirt.

"Harper," I croaked out. Flushing bright red, I shook my head with a laugh. "I'm making a really bad first impression. I don't usually have to be hauled off the ground."

His fingers brushed against my cheek and I almost flinched, wondering what he was doing. He was petting me! No, he was just brushing my soaked hair off my face. God, he was so dreamy. Maybe he'd swoop me up into his arms and carry me off to his truck...

"Let's get to my truck, out of the rain." He started to pull me toward the truck, and my heart sank when I realized he wasn't going to pick me up. I wasn't sure what I was thinking. Men weren't actually that chivalrous.

Sighing, I started to follow him, but the moment I put pressure on my foot, I knew I couldn't do it. Pain shot through my foot and I let out a small whimper, hoping he hadn't heard. But he had, and an instant later, I was lifted in the air as he hauled me up into his strong arms and carried me to his truck. I felt weightless in his arms as he used his hand under my knees to open the passenger side door.

I immediately forgot about how he had just made every fantasy come true by carrying me when I saw his leather seats. I couldn't sit down on them when I was wet. I would ruin his seats.

"I'm soaking wet! Don't set me down in your truck," I yelled when he tried to set me inside on his beautiful, leather seats. He rolled his eyes at me and practically tossed me into his truck. Then he shut the door and climbed into the driver's seat a few seconds later.

"I'm going to ruin your seats," I argued.

He chuckled. "It's adorable that you think I would care about my seats when I just picked you up out of a puddle because you're injured."

My jaw hung slightly open as I tried to think of a response to that.

"Let me see your foot."

He had a very commanding presence and I found myself complying without batting an eye. As I started to lift my leg, I realized how short my shorts were and the fact that he would get a great view of my lady bits, seeing as how I wasn't wearing underwear.

Hey, don't judge. It's laundry day. I didn't know this would happen!

Well, obviously I couldn't lift my foot up into his lap like this. He would get a show that I was not prepared to give him. But as I glanced up to tell him just that, I saw his eyes were glued to my chest. I looked down, quickly covering my chest with my arms, mortified to see that I hadn't put on a bra and my nipples were poking through the thin fabric of my shirt.

Deciding that I was already well and truly embarrassed, I cleared my throat and raised my eyebrows in a disapproving glare. He didn't seem to care. He just smirked at me.

"What? I'm a guy and you have nice tits."

Then he reached down and adjusted himself. My jaw dropped at the blatant gesture, but I would only half admit to being turned on by it. This guy was majorly hot and he was getting hard from *me*. What rational girl wouldn't be flattered by that? Okay, maybe some girls wouldn't, but if they saw this insanely sexy man, they would be drooling over him just like I was right now.

"Now let me see your foot." He grabbed my leg and started prodding my foot and gently turning it to check for breaks. I grimaced when he turned it too far, but didn't make a sound.

"It looks like you just sprained it. What were you doing out there?"

"I was on my way to a friend's and my car broke down. I didn't have my phone, so I was going to walk there, but I didn't see the gigantic hold in the ground. I thought it was just a puddle."

I tried to shrug it off and play it cool, like I wasn't completely mortified of my current state. Meeting the man of my dreams like this was beyond embarrassing. I always assumed that when I met the man I would daydream of marrying, I would make a good first impression. My hair would be done perfectly and I would have makeup on, oh, and I would be wearing clothes. I felt that was an important part in this situation.

"Well, that's good to know. It looked to me like you were doing some kind of Indian rain dance, the way your arms were swinging around. I wasn't sure if I should stop at first, but when you went down, I thought I'd risk it," Jack replied with a smile.

That smile was to die for. A beautiful, full smile with a dimple in one cheek and a beautiful set of pearly, white teeth. I just couldn't stop staring. He was so beautiful. I swear I blushed from my head to my toes when he smiled at me. He was so sexy and I couldn't help staring at him. Did I mention he was sexy? Okay, I had to stop staring or I was sure I would jump across the seat and start humping him.

"Thank you for stopping," I said finally, my brain kicking back in just before I was about to make a complete idiot of myself. "It seems that walking in the rain is a dangerous endeavor."

I shivered from the cold and he reached into his back seat, grabbing a huge sweatshirt that I was sure would swallow me whole. It would be perfect to warm me up.

"Here. Put this on before you freeze to death." I took the sweatshirt from him and threw it on over my head. I didn't miss the way his eyes watched my chest as I lifted my arms or the disappointment when I was covered up.

"Thank you. Could I borrow your phone so I can call a tow truck?" I snuggled into the sweatshirt and sniffed his wonderful scent. Mmmm. Sandalwood. God, he smelled good. I stopped sniffing and glanced up to see if he had seen me acting totally weird. Luckily, he was looking out the window and I was pretty sure I was in the clear.

"I'll take care of it. I have a friend that can pick it up and take a look at it. Do you want me to drop you at your friend's house?"

"No. She lives in an apartment on the third floor and she isn't home. I'm just feeding her cat. He hates me and I am not staying the night with the spawn of Satan," I said emphatically.

He looked at me like I had grown a second head. "I can take you over there and protect you from the cat. Seriously, how bad can a cat be?" He rolled his eyes, which I didn't miss, and I wanted to tell him that he had no clue what he was getting into, but then he said, "Then, I'll drive you home."

He made it sound like this cat was a precious little kitten. Just wait until he met the tiger. He wouldn't be laughing then. I smirked at him and let out a little laugh.

"Alright, big guy." *Big guy? Did I seriously just call him that? Just keep talking. Blow through and pretend everything is normal.* "I'll take you up on your offer. Could you get my purse out of my car first? Oh, and make sure you lock the car doors."

I knew the car wasn't much, but I couldn't afford to buy a new-used car right now. Hopefully, his friend wouldn't charge me too much to fix it up. Maybe he could give a friends and family discount.

Jack glanced over at the car and laughed. "Really? You're worried about someone stealing it? No one would even steal it for parts!" I glared at his blatant disregard of my possessions.

"It's all I have, so please lock the doors," I said, trying my best to keep an even tone. He was helping me after all and I didn't want to piss him off before I could get my car towed.

He shook his head and went back out into the rain and was back just a few seconds later. He handed me my purse and started the truck, putting the heat on. He ran his fingers through his dirty blonde hair and shook off the rain. Good Lord, this man was sex on a stick. The rain water ran in tiny rivulets down the length of his neck and down the neck of his shirt. Was it wrong that I was jealous of rain?

I would give anything to be the one of those raindrops right now. I would run all the way down his body to his hard cock and wrap myself around him. Maybe I could go over and lick his neck. Just a little nibble. I bet his skin tastes salty. I could run my tongue up his neck and then nibble on his earlobe....

I was snapped out of my fantasy when he laughed and I could swear a blush was creeping up his neck. "Do you always say what you're thinking? Because what you're suggesting sounds pretty good to me."

I flushed bright red as I realized that once again my thoughts didn't stay that way. I couldn't look at his handsome face with those eyes boring into me, so I glanced away. No, not away. Down.

Oh my God! He's hard and *huge*.

My eyes popped out of my head and my mouth hung open as I saw the tent in his pants that made me want to reach over and take a taste.

"Again, not a thought," he said with a chuckle. "How do you not know you have verbal diarrhea? Not that I'm complaining. I kinda like knowing what you're thinking, sweetheart."

I would have been embarrassed, but he slid across the seat and hoisted me up to straddle his lap. I let out a surprised yelp as I settled into his lap. His lips came close to mine, but he held back, teasing me with the slightest brush of his lips against mine. My heart hammered as I anticipated what he would taste like. His tongue darted out and barely licked my lips as his breath huffed out against my mouth.

Then his lips were on mine in a bruising kiss that left me absolutely breathless. His hands came up to frame my face and he ran one hand along the back of my neck to hold my head where he wanted me. His kisses moved away from my lips and down my neck and I closed my eyes, enjoying the feel of his hot, wet kisses. I was vaguely aware of the strain this position was putting on my foot, but I couldn't find it in me to care all that much.

My heart was thundering out of control as my fantasies came to life. I had this hot, sexy man kissing me in his truck after rescuing me on the side of the road. It was insane and so perfect.

He ran his hands through my hair and down my sides, brushing against my breasts. My nipples tightened in anticipation of the feel of his hands on my breasts and I ground my throbbing clit against his cock. I could practically feel everything as I rubbed against him. If I undid his jeans right now, I could just slide my shorts aside and he would be fully seated inside me. God, it had been too long since I felt this. I needed more, but then he pulled away and rested his forehead against mine. Taking in deep breaths he said, "Now I'm hard."

I couldn't help the laugh that broke free. There was no use in feeling embarrassed by what just happened. He obviously wanted it just as much as I did. We sat there a few minutes letting our breathing return to normal. Then he kissed me lightly once and then again.

"Let's go take care of this demon cat. Then we'll see what trouble we can get up to." I nodded and slid off his lap. He slid over and put the truck in drive. "Where to?"

CHAPTER 2

JACK

I CALLED MY FRIEND, employee actually, at the shop and gave him the address where the car broke down. I asked him to take care of it right away and told him where I hid the keys. There was no way I was stopping to take a look at the car right now. We were pulled off to the side during a thunderstorm. People weren't as cautious as they should be when it was raining and I didn't want us to become another statistic. That's how my dad had died, and I was more careful now when stopping to help someone.

"Just turn up ahead at the light."

I nodded, but then saw the pharmacy off to the right and quickly turned in.

"What are you doing?"

"Stopping at the pharmacy."

"Why?" she asked, her brows furrowed in a cute little way that also made her nose scrunch up. It was adorable.

"Because we need an ice pack for your foot and some medicine. And probably a wrap."

"I can do that when I get home."

"I know you can, but we're right here, and I can take care of your foot and make you feel better now instead of waiting."

I parked and ignored her protests as I flung my door open.

"Jack! Seriously, I don't need you to do this! Let's just go."

I grinned as I stepped out into the rain that had lightened over the past few minutes. "Feel free to follow me and stop me."

She glared at me, her eyes narrowing at me slightly, but I could tell she wasn't really that upset. I slammed the door and hurried inside, shaking the rain from my hair as I made my way to the correct aisle. I wasn't sure exactly what to get, so I just started grabbing stuff off the shelf and made my way over to the medicine. I started to grab the ibuprofen, but then frowned. Was ibuprofen the one you weren't supposed to take on an empty stomach? I couldn't remember, so I grabbed some Aleve and Tylenol also, just to be on the safe side.

My arms were stuffed as I walked up to the register and dumped everything down on the conveyor belt. The cashier looked at me in surprise, like she couldn't believe I had this much stuff. "Someone injured?"

I stared at the woman with a bored expression. "Nope, just thought I would stock up in case."

She nodded and rang everything up, bagging it in one small bag that looked like it would rip. I paid and headed back out to the truck, handing the bag over to Harper. She started rifling through it, shaking her head.

"There's no way I need all this stuff."

"Better safe than sorry."

She sighed and leaned her head back against her seat.

"When we get to your friend's, I'll wrap your foot and you can sit down for a little bit. I'll take care of the litter box."

"Uh, yeah, that's not happening."

"Why?"

"Because it's litter and it's gross."

I nodded. "I'm aware, but it's not like I'm going to pick up the poop with my fingers."

"Still...you shouldn't be doing stuff like that. It's not your cat—"

"It's not your cat either."

Flustered, she shook her head. "Seriously, I can do it. My foot doesn't even hurt that bad anymore."

"Is that why it's swelling up?"

She glared at me, but I just laughed. I couldn't help it. She was so adorable when she was trying to be mad.

"How about this. We'll go upstairs, and I'll pretend to listen to your protests about me cleaning out the litter box, and you'll pretend to be really upset. I'll get your ankle wrapped up and you can relax while I take care of the cat. That way, you can still be indignant about the whole thing and pretend to be upset, and I can still take care of you. Sound good?"

She huffed and crossed her arms over her chest. "I make no guarantees."

I smiled, shaking my head. This woman was going to be the death of me. As I glanced at her out of the corner of my eye, I couldn't help but wonder what would make her think that leaving the house dressed like that would be a good idea. It was like she attracted trouble wherever she went. It was just one disaster after another with her. First, no proper clothes. Then her car broke down, and she had to walk. Next, she fell and injured herself on the side of the road...I had a feeling that if I dated this woman, life would never be dull, especially if she continued to say everything she was thinking out loud.

Although, I had to admit, the whole talking out loud thing was really sexy. I liked actually knowing what a woman was thinking. That's what had made me drag her across the seat. I just couldn't keep my hands to myself when she started saying everything she wanted to do to me. When she ground herself against my cock, I was sure I was going to come in my pants like a fifteen year old. I had never been so turned on by a woman before. Sure, I'd had women throw themselves at me. Some were fantastic in bed. Others were great at using their mouths for various activities. Never had a woman gotten me so revved up from making out. I had to pull back from kissing her to keep from ripping her clothes off on the side of the highway. I wanted to, but I didn't want to share her with anyone else when I unwrapped her. That would be for my eyes only. As soon as I was done taking care of this cat, I would take her back to my place and show her all the things I wanted to do to her.

We pulled into a small apartment complex with brick siding. This was obviously an older building and didn't have an elevator. The stairs were definitely going to be a problem, as she could barely stand up. How did she think she was going to do this on her own?

"You can just wait in the truck for me. There's no need for you to come in," Harper said as she tried to quickly jump out of the truck and leave me behind.

That just pissed me off. Why couldn't this infuriating woman just accept my help? There was no way she would make it up those stairs alone. I jumped out of the truck and was just coming over to her side when I saw her struggling to get her footing. I was by her side in an instant, my temper flaring.

"Are you crazy? I'm not waiting in the truck, and I'm not letting you hobble up the stairs by yourself. You'd probably trip, fall down the stairs, and break your neck."

She opened her mouth to say something, but I put my hand over her mouth to silence her. She stuck her tongue out and licked my hand, like that would gross me out. Visions of her wrapping those pretty, full lips around my cock swirled in my brain. I licked my lips as I thought of her licking and sucking my dick while I gripped her hair and fucked her mouth. Shit. I was hard again.

"Just lean on me and let's get this demon cat taken care of. I have plans for you and they involve that pretty, little mouth of yours."

She gasped and I could see the desire in her eyes. I smirked at her and wrapped my arm around her waist and she put hers across my shoulders. Reaching into the truck, I grabbed my bag of supplies and slammed the door. We made our way over to the entrance and I was already irritated at how long this was going to take. I was a firm believer in doing things the quickest and easiest way. There was no point in making things difficult. I stopped walking and gestured to my back.

"Hop onto my back and wrap your arms around my neck."

"You can't be serious," she said incredulously. "We'll fall down the stairs and then I'll have more problems than a sprained foot. You'll break me in half when you land on top of me."

"Harper, look at me. I'm a pretty big guy. I lift weights heavier than you. Just lean into my back. Besides, I would never bruise my ego by letting a woman I'm carrying fall."

She assessed the validity of my statement for a moment before motioning for me to turn around. I squatted down and she climbed on. I gripped her legs and we were on the move before she could get comfortable. We were up the stairs and at her friend's door in a matter of minutes.

"What's your friend's name?"

"Anna."

"So why are you taking care of Anna's cat?"

She tapped my shoulder, so I lowered her to the ground so she could climb off. She started digging through her purse that looked more like a tote bag. Her whole arm was inside and I instantly thought of how much she looked like Mary Poppins and wondered if she would pull out a lamp. She finally pulled out her hand and held a key up in triumph.

"Ah ha! That would be really horrible if I came all this way and forgot the key. Anna had to go home to visit her grandma. She's been sick and the doctors don't think she has too much longer. Her grandma is the last of her family."

I nodded. I didn't know what to say in these situations. I was never good at reading emotional cues and always ended up saying the wrong thing. So I did what any normal man would do and kept my mouth shut.

She paused and drew in a deep breath. "Okay. I am going to very quietly put in the key and turn the knob. It is very important that you don't make a sound. Don't breathe loudly, and don't shuffle your feet." She looked at me and then down at my work boots. "Better yet, hold your breath and remove your shoes."

I just stared at her. This woman was nuts, but I was really turned on by her quirky attitude. When I didn't immediately remove my boots, she shrugged and said, "It's your funeral."

She slowly put in the key and started to turn it. I swore, if she went any slower, the lock would rust shut. She turned the knob very slowly and inched open the door. Apparently, she was satisfied with what she saw because she motioned for me to go forward. I walked through the door and stood in the living room. There was an armchair to the right, a coffee table directly in front of me, and a couch beyond that. I heard her closing the door and was just turning around when a huge tiger cat jumped off the bookcase that was at the side of the door and leapt onto Harper's back. I wanted to warn her, but the cat was on her before I could say anything. She was so startled that she screamed in surprise and shifted her weight onto her bad foot. She lost her balance and fell forward into me. I wrapped my arms around her to catch her, but I stumbled backwards into the coffee table and fell on top of it, splitting it in two.

The cat, which had held onto Harper for the whole ride, calmly got up off the floor and walked away. Harper groaned next to me and I reached over to start checking her to make sure she had no more injuries. This woman was a walking disaster. "Damn, Harper. Are you okay?"

"Yeah, I'm good." She sat up and winced, making it obvious she was not as good as she wanted me to think. "Nothing I haven't been through already with this cat. I told you he was the spawn of Satan. You didn't believe me and just had to come up and *protect me*." We both got to our knees, and when I tried to help her up she brushed me off with an *I got it*. Then two seconds later, collapsed onto me when she tried to stand.

"You sure you're okay? Seems to me like you need some help, but I can let you go if you've got this," I said while trying not to laugh. She glared at me and I let loose the laugh that was building in my chest. I couldn't wait to get this woman into the bedroom. She was going to be feisty, and riling her up was so much fun. I hadn't even known her for that long, but I knew she was different from the other women I had been with. The women I dated were either too aggressive or completely lackluster. Harper was obviously attracted to me, but she didn't throw herself at me. Yet, the way she kissed was with all the hunger and passion that I was looking for in a woman.

She flopped back on the couch with a groan and I immediately moved to place a pillow under her injured foot. Then I went to the kitchen and got a glass of water for her and grabbed the spilled contents of the bag from the floor, handing her the ibuprofen.

"Here, take these, and I'll get you some ice for your foot. It already looks twice the size it was at the pharmacy." I went into the kitchen and found a bag of frozen veggies in the freezer and returned to her, placing the bag on her foot. "This was all I could find. I hope Anna doesn't mind, but considering the circumstances, I think she can deal with the sacrificial peas."

Harper sighed in relief, leaning back against the cushions.

"Okay, what do I need to do and where are the supplies?"

Harper told me where I could find everything and I set about my chores. When I finished, I walked back into the living room and saw Harper relaxing with her eyes closed. I took a minute to study her face. She really was beautiful. She was very natural. She wasn't wearing makeup and I really liked that. I had never realized how much better women looked when they didn't cake all that shit on their faces. Now that her hair was drying, I could see it was dirty blonde and wavy. She was a good foot shorter than me. Her tiny body looked like she could get lost in my sweatshirt if there weren't arm holes to guide her. She looked like she skipped meals, and based on the comments she had made about her financial situation, I guessed it wasn't a choice. She was fiercely independent and didn't like to take help, so wining and dining her may be the only way to help her out.

My gut churned at the thought of Harper skipping meals to pay rent or put gas in her car.

Staring at the vulnerable woman before me, I couldn't help but feel protective of her. She was definitely a heap load of trouble, but everything I knew about her so far made me want to get to know her better. That was something I didn't do very often. I was always working or hanging with the guys. I didn't do relationships because they didn't seem to be worth the trouble, or maybe I just hadn't found the right woman.

I wanted to take her back to my place, but given the circumstances, she might just want to go home. I walked over and sat down next to her. She didn't move. "Harper," I said quietly. I ran my hand through her wavy locks and she still didn't stir. I didn't have the heart to wake her after her morning, so I pulled a blanket off the back of the couch and covered her legs. She had to be cold. I laid down next to her and tucked her into my side and closed my eyes. An afternoon nap sounded pretty good right now.

I must have been having a really good dream because I felt a hand on my crotch, rubbing and stroking me. Then I heard the moaning and blinked a few times, coming fully awake. This was definitely not a dream. Harper was obviously still sleeping and having a dirty dream. I just hoped it was about me. I tried to slide away from her, but she just nuzzled in closer and stroked me harder. My cock was rock hard now and I wanted to take advantage so badly, but she would be mortified if she knew what she was doing in her sleep.

"Jack," she whispered. Shoot me now. How was I supposed to do the right thing when I knew she's dreaming of me?

I pulled my arm from behind her neck and started to move away, but she started kissing and licking my neck as she stroked me. I decided the best thing to do was wake her up and pretend like nothing happened. I turned my face to her and called her name.

"Harper."

"Yes, Jack. Oh, God yes," she moaned.

"Harper, wake up sweetheart." Her eyes flew open and she

turned bright red. She looked fucking gorgeous. I could see the desire and the uncertainty in her eyes. Her hand was stalled over my dick, so there was no pretending this didn't happen. My dick chose that moment to twitch and a rueful smile crossed her face.

"You are so fucking sexy. That was the most gorgeous thing I've ever seen. Now I can't wait to see you come. But sweetheart, if you don't remove your hand from my cock, I'm going to fuck you on your friend's couch."

"Oh, God. Please do," she seemed to say to herself. I chuckled because I wasn't sure if she meant to say that out loud.

Harper quickly snatched her hand back, seeming to realize she had been stroking me just moments before. She sat up suddenly and screamed, "I'm not a slut. I swear, I don't go around grabbing men and...and...I swear I'm not some crazy slut out to devour you!" I couldn't help but laugh. She was so damn cute.

"Honey, I never said you were a crazy slut. I just don't want to fuck you on your friend's couch, because what I plan to do to you is going to be very dirty." I dipped my head and nuzzled her neck, running my tongue the length of it and biting her ear. Then I whispered in her ear, "Now, would you like me to take you home or are we going back to my place?"

She blushed even redder and simply nodded. "You do realize that was not a yes or no question. I need an answer from you," I said laughing.

"Let's go to your house." She started to stand and I was ready to run out of the building with her on my back when she said, "Oh shit! I have a shift in an hour. I have to go back home and get ready." She started hobbling over to her purse and throwing the spilled contents inside. I had to adjust myself to keep my hard on from breaking my zipper. It looked like I had a cold shower in my near future.

"What kind of shift?"

"I'm a waitress at O'Malley's." She stood and turned to look at the broken table. "What are we going to do about that?"

"We'll come back tomorrow and take care of it." She stared at me with a stunned expression.

"Why? Why would you do that? We just met and you're offering to help with the cat and clean up messes that have nothing to do with you." She looked at me curiously.

"Well, technically, I broke the table, so it's only right I come back and clean it up. Besides, it guarantees I get to see you again and have a shot at seducing you." I walked over to her and pulled her in for a kiss. She melted into my arms and I had to pull away before I mauled her. "Okay, well let's get you home and off to work. Are you sure you should be walking around on your foot? How are you going to balance a tray and wait tables?"

She shrugged. "I'll figure it out. I'm pretty resourceful when I need to be. Besides, I need the shift. Bills to pay, ya know?"

I had a feeling that she did a lot of shit she shouldn't have to just to pay the bills. That didn't sit so well with me, and I really wanted to do anything I could to help her out. I could already tell she was fiercely independent and I would have to work hard to get her to accept my help.

"Alright, well, let me give you a lift downstairs." We walked out the door and locked up. Then, she hopped on my back and we headed back downstairs. I got her situated in the truck and she gave me directions back to her apartment. When I pulled up outside I had to hide the grimace on my face. I knew this wasn't the best part of town, but this place was a dump. There was litter everywhere outside and junked cars in the parking lot. The building looked like it hadn't been cleaned in years. I got out and helped her out of the truck. When I went to take her inside, she stopped me.

"That's okay. I've got it from here. Thanks for the lift...off the ground. And the ride. Wrapping my foot. And taking care of the cat. And carrying me up the stairs." I could tell this was going to keep going so I cut her off.

"Anytime. You don't have to keep thanking me. How about I walk you in? I want to make sure you get in safely. My mother would kill me if I didn't at least walk you to your door."

With that I picked her up bridal style and started walking to the front door. I wasn't lying. I really did want to make sure she got in safely. With her luck, she would injure her other leg getting up there or be attacked by a drug dealer. The place looked that bad.

CHAPTER 3

HARPER

TO SAY that I was embarrassed to have him see my apartment was an understatement. My own apartment was fairly clean, but the building was a disaster. I was afraid the staircase would collapse if we were both on the same stair at the same time. I wasn't sure what was more embarrassing, me groping him in my sleep or where I lived. I tried not to be too self-conscious of where I lived. After all, I was making it on my own and trying to do what I loved. There was no shame in that and I had to stop judging myself for where I was in life. Still, having him see this dump was a bruise on my ego.

My dad was always trying to help me out, but I wanted to do it on my own. My mother relied on my dad to take care of her, and when he didn't provide her with the lifestyle she wanted, she left him for someone better. She was divorced from husband number two now, and I was sure she was on the prowl for her next victim. Sorry, husband. She wanted to be kept in luxury and she would use any man to do that. I wasn't independent because I wanted to be a strong woman that could prove myself against the world. I just didn't want to ever rely on someone else for my happiness and well-being.

Not taking help from my father meant that sometimes my life

was difficult. I was an aspiring writer that worked as a waitress to supplement my income. I could usually grab a cheap dinner at the restaurant and pick up cheap breakfast items. I loved to cook, but food was expensive, and I was on a budget. I really only cooked once a week, and I tried to make something that would get me through a few meals. It worked for me, and food was easy enough to spend less on if you knew what you were doing.

I sighed at my wayward thoughts and limped over to my mailbox to pick up the endless bills that were no doubt piling up inside. Jack, once again, carried me up the stairs, and since I was on the second floor, I let him. As he set me down outside my door, another door opened down the hall and I had a sinking feeling it was my neighbor.

Great. The creepy guy is back to hit on me. Maybe he won't try anything with a big, hunky man here looking like he's going to ravage me.

"I'll ravage you anytime you want, sweetheart," I felt him say behind my ear. I could feel his hot breath on my neck, sending shivers down my spine. I was definitely going to have to change underwear before my shift. Well, if I were wearing underwear. I ignored the fact that once again my thoughts were vocalized. It seemed to be the norm around him now, and he didn't seem to mind.

Jack wrapped an arm around my waist and started kissing my neck. He drove me wild when he kissed me. I could feel my whole body melt into his touch. This was insane. I had met Jack just hours ago, and I already felt like my body was in tune with his, ready to let him have his way.

"Let's send a message that you're taken," he whispered. Then he whipped me around and crushed his mouth to mine. He hauled me up by the waist and I immediately wrapped my legs around him. My arms wound around his neck and my fingers ran through the silky strands of his hair. He kissed me fervently and his tongue slid in to duel with mine. I was so turned on that my hips started grinding against him again. I needed him right now. I was never like this, but I had never connected with anyone like this before.

His hands were latched on to my ass, so I reached behind me and turned the knob to let us into my apartment and we practically fell through the door. He caught us and slammed the door shut. Then he whipped me around and slammed me into the door, his mouth on mine once again.

I started desperately tearing at his shirt to rip it off over his head. As I pulled up, I yanked too hard and smacked him in the face. He grunted, but moved his head to allow me to finish taking it off. My fingers grasped his belt buckle as his lips latched on to my neck. He was sucking so hard, I was sure to have a hickey. I couldn't force my hands to work as his mouth worked its magic on my neck. My brain seemed to be malfunctioning, and I couldn't remember what I was trying to do.

God, if he kept doing that, I was going to come. He sucked harder and then made his way down my neck. He set me down and ripped the sweatshirt over my head, *not* smacking me in the face. He stared at my breasts for a second and I thrust my chest out toward his body. It was instinctual, like my breasts were being drawn to his body. He pressed me back against the door and started kissing his way down my chest and over the fabric of my tank top. I could feel his warm tongue on my nipple and then his whole mouth was covering it and his teeth started to nip at the peak.

"Oh, God, Jack. Don't stop." I was moaning and could feel my legs start to quiver. He moved over to my other breast, and then I felt his fingers slide under my shorts and start stroking my pussy. When he touched my clit, I lost all my senses and started writhing in pleasure. His name was torn from my throat as he made me come on his fingers. He continued to stroke me as I came down from my orgasm. My chest was heaving with the intensity of the pleasure I felt. I took in a shaky breath and looked up at his sexy face. He had a grin that said he knew just how hard he made me come, and I couldn't help but want to do the same for him.

I started to kneel and the grin slipped from his face. It was replaced by desire and his eyes looked molten. I reached forward and undid the button on his jeans. I was going to unzip his pants, but hesitated because I was afraid I would get the zipper caught on his hard cock. He reached down and did it for me and I pulled his jeans down. I gulped as I saw him sticking out through his boxers.

"You're huge!" I bit my lip, wondering how he was going to fit in my mouth, but when his hips jerked forward and the head of his cock brushed against my lips, I found that I liked the idea of him shoving his cock in my mouth and fucking me hard. Before I could think too much about it, I leaned forward and sucked as much of him into my mouth as possible. I ran my tongue along the length of him and tasted the salty moisture on the tip of his cock. I started to take him deeper and deeper until he was all the way at the back of my throat. I was on the verge of gagging and was going to pull back when I heard him moan in pleasure. I relaxed my throat and took him deeper. My pussy was throbbing with need and I slid a hand down my body to touch my clit.

He threaded his fingers through my hair and grabbed on tight. Then he started thrusting his dick into my mouth and quite literally fucked my mouth. It was the sexiest thing I had ever felt, and I started moving my own hand faster, pushing myself towards orgasm. After a minute, he pulled back and practically growled at me.

"I fucking love your mouth, but right now I need your pussy."

He picked me up and pulled my shorts down. In one swift move, his cock was inside me. He didn't stop for me to adjust to his girth. I could feel every thrust deep inside, and with every punishing drive, I felt my back hitting the door with such force that I would probably bruise.

"Oh, God, Jack. Don't stop. Fuck me hard."

I was never very vocal during sex, but he seemed to bring it out of me. He kept pounding into me and I could faintly hear a creaking and the door slamming against the frame. I heard wood snapping and almost told Jack to stop, but I was on the verge of another orgasm. He reached down between us and started pinching and massaging my clit.

"Come for me, baby. I want to feel you come on my cock." I started to come and he thrust faster and harder. "Fuck yeah," he shouted as came inside me. Then I felt myself falling backwards as the door frame splintered and the door gave way. We fell in a crumpled mess into the hallway with him still very much inside of me. We looked at each other, both panting heavily and started laughing. "Oops. Looks like I just fucked you through the door," he said between huffs. "I guess we have another mess to clean up."

"What the fuck?" a voice screeched from down the hall. "This is a fucking family place and we don't need to see you fucking in the hall. Not to mention your fucking cock and her cunt. Her tits are practically hanging out of her fucking top. Have some fucking decency and cover your tits before the fucking kids see that shit."

A short, fifty something woman came walking towards us wearing a hot pink vizor around her strawberry blonde hair. She was wearing a blue and purple leotard with a pink mini skirt. How did I know it was a leotard? Because her skirt was that short and I was on the ground.

"We'll keep the fucking in the hallway to a minimum if you control the fucking fucks. Sound good?" Jack replied. "How about you turn around and let me get my woman covered up?" Though it wasn't really a question.

He leaned forward and gave me a swift kiss on the lips before trying his best to cover my nudity as he dragged me back inside my apartment. I hobbled over to the couch and grabbed a blanket to cover myself as he pulled his jeans back on, covering his gorgeous ass. I admired his perfect body as he picked up the door and tried to stand it back in place.

Now that he was only in his jeans, I could see his gorgeous six pack with a tiny trail of hair that worked its way down the v of his body. His jeans were slung low on his hips and my libido picked up again as his muscles contracted. I could feel the burn on my neck where the scruff from his jaw rubbed against me. His hair was on the shorter side, but still long enough that I could run my fingers through it. He was the sexiest man I had ever seen, and I had just had amazing, door-shattering sex with him. My face flushed as I replayed what had just happened. I had to fan myself to cool my heated face.

I watched as Jack pulled out his phone and called a friend to fix the door. Then he turned to me with a sexy smirk and told me to go clean up. I was in a lust-filled fog and found that my limbs obeyed him on command. I stumbled back to my bedroom, partially from my injured ankle, but mostly from the jelly-like state my legs had taken on. I stepped into the shower and couldn't wipe the smile from my face at the most soul-shattering sex I had ever had.

As I came down from my high, I finally had enough sense to wash my hair and body. My ankle was starting to throb and I needed to get off it soon. I turned off the shower and grabbed my towel, drying myself off. I made my way back into the bedroom and glanced at my clock on the nightstand. Shit. There was no way I would make my shift tonight. I had spent too much time fucking around. Besides, my ankle was hurting so bad, I knew there was no way that I could work more than a half hour before I would be in too much pain to walk.

I grabbed my phone off the dresser and called into work, explaining to my boss that I had hurt my ankle and that I wouldn't be able to work tonight. I apologized for the last minute phone call, but Shelley was awesome and told me to let her know if I couldn't work any other shifts.

I sat on my bed for a while and replayed the day's events in my mind. It had been a shitty day that ended quite well. I was exhausted now and found my eyes drifting shut. I needed to take something for the pain before I went to sleep, otherwise it would keep me up all night. Right now, I just needed a warm bed and an ice pack for my foot. I hobbled over to the bathroom and got a pain pill out of the medicine cabinet and used a little paper cup of water to wash it down with. I heard some talking in the other room and decided to go check out the damage.

CHAPTER 4

JACK

I WATCHED Harper hobble her sexy ass over to her bedroom and tried to shake the grin from my face. No such luck. That woman was a wet dream come true. The way she wrapped those lips around my cock was enough to fill my fantasies for the next year. I felt myself growing hard and pulled out my phone to get down to business before I went into her bathroom and had my way with her again.

"Ryan, I need a favor."

"Sure, what do you need?"

"I have a door that needs to be fixed. Can you swing by?"

"Yeah, no problem. I'll bring Logan with me."

"It's not at my place. It's over at West Side Apartments. 2C."

"Give me ten minutes and we'll be over."

I glanced around the room at the mess we had made and decided to start cleaning up before they got here. I found the broom and dust pan and started cleaning up the splinters from where the door broke and picked up stuff that was knocked over when we pushed through the door. It's funny because I didn't even hear anything fall over in my lust-fueled haze. The door was propped up as much as possible, but there was still a gap since the frame was busted also. I heard a low whistle behind me as the door was shoved aside.

"Dude, what happened here? Was it a break in?" Logan was standing in the doorway checking out our handiwork.

"No, man. The door is busted from the inside out. Definitely not a break in. So what happened?" Ryan asked as he turned to me.

"Um, well..." I rubbed the back of my neck, trying to figure out what to say. I didn't want to embarrass Harper. I really liked her and didn't want my friends making shitty comments to her. "We sort of broke it."

They both stared at me, waiting for further explanation. When I didn't say anything else, Logan spoke up. "Dude, that's all you're going to tell us is that you sort of…. Oh my God. Was this a sex accident?" He had an awe inspired look on his face and then broke out laughing. "Oh, shit. What, were you banging her against the door? You actually fucked her through the door?" I looked up at the ceiling trying to figure out how to end this conversation so that Harper didn't hear any of it. It would sound like I was bragging, and that wouldn't help convince her to give me a shot.

"Logan…" I glared at him as he continued to laugh.

"That door is a piece of crap, but still, you must have been fucking her good and hard to break the damn door down," Logan continued.

I heard a gasp behind me that signaled Harper had just overheard my loud-mouthed friend spewing his shit for all to hear. My eyes closed and I counted to five before turning around to see Harper's bright red face filled with a mix of rage and humiliation. I was about to walk over to her when Ryan punched Logan in the stomach and stepped forward.

"Hi, I'm Ryan, and that jackass is Logan. Jack called us to help fix your door. By the looks of it, I'm gonna need to come back tomorrow. There are a few things I need to pick up. I'll secure it the best I can for tonight, but you might want to sleep somewhere else."

Harper looked grateful that he was ignoring his friend and talking about repairs. Then, Logan stepped forward, and I was considering whether or not to deck the dickhead. His outstretched hand had me holding back.

"Sorry about that. Jack hasn't said a word. I just sort of figured it out and…well, I can be an asshole." Harper seemed to accept that and took his hand for a short handshake.

"Thank you for coming over here. I really appreciate anything you can do. I'm sure it will be fine for me to stay tonight."

Say what? She seriously thought she was going to stay here where anyone could walk in? The door didn't even close all the way or give the impression that it was shut. Before I could think better of it, I turned to her and let the words fly.

"Are you fucking crazy? Your door is busted in and you want to stay here? Remember the creep down the hall?" At that, Harper flushed bright red, no doubt remembering what happened as he walked past. "Look, you're coming home with me tonight. I'm not gonna let you stay here, and I'm pretty sure you don't want to go stay with Satan. I can bring you back tomorrow after we go to your friend's place. Go pack a bag and we'll get out of here."

I should have seen it coming. After every word I said, I saw her face grow angrier. Her inner bitch was about to be set free like a hurricane. The smart thing to do would be to shut my mouth and ride out the waves. I was about to pay big time for my stupidity.

"Excuse me? You won't *let* me stay here? Am *I* fucking crazy? I think I would be fucking crazy to allow a guy I just met today boss me around and tell me what I was going to be doing for the night. Frankly, I'd rather take my chances with Satan!"

Ryan and Logan tried to act like they weren't paying attention, but decided instead to go get supplies. I heard them mumble something about being right back and Logan threw out some comment about being handed my balls. Now I was all alone with a pissed off woman that would rather sleep in an unsecured apartment than come home with me. I was going to have to do some groveling if I had any hopes of her coming with me. Unfortunately, I'd never been in the position of groveling and what came out just made it worse.

"Look, I didn't mean to order you around, but I'm not gonna let you stay here to be attacked by a creep in the middle of the night. Be smart about this. You can't be stupid enough to think this is safe." Her jaw dropped. Yeah, it didn't sound good to me either when I said it. "I mean...what I mean is...I'm just looking out for you, and..." I started to run my hands through my hair, trying to figure out how to make this better. With every word, I heard the hammering of nails in my coffin.

"Please, do tell me what you are *actually* trying to say. I would love to hear some more about how stupid I am."

She crossed her arms over her chest, just begging for me to spew more word vomit. Her eyes bore into me, and I swore my balls curled up inside my body. This woman had so much attitude, but it was a hell of a turn-on. I had to get it together and fix this because there was no way I would be letting this vixen go. My instincts were telling me to stalk over to her and claim her as mine, but after all the shit she had been through today, I thought a more cautious approach would work better.

"What I was really trying to say is that I like you, and I would love to see you again. Ever since I saw you sitting in that puddle, I've felt protective of you. You seem like you could use someone to help you out. Not that you can't help yourself, but maybe a helping hand would be nice. I just don't want anything to happen to you, so I would appreciate it if you would allow me to help you out by coming to stay the night with me."

It was like battery acid in my mouth to be so nice about it when what I really wanted to do was drag her down the stairs and make her come with me. She huffed, but a small smile crossed her face.

"Next time, start with that, and then tell yourself to shut up." I breathed a sigh of relief that I seemed to have chosen the best course of action. "I'll go pack a bag. Be right back."

I released a long breath and thought maybe I should send her over to Sebastian for a job. He ran a security firm and Harper might make a great interrogator. Her glare was enough to make a grown man piss himself.

The guys came back a few minutes later, extremely happy that the argument was over. They quickly did a makeshift fix for the door and said their goodbyes, promising to be over first thing in the morning to fix it. Harper came out several minutes later with an overnight bag and her laptop case. I noticed that she seemed to be favoring her ankle a little more than before. I grabbed her bags from her, knowing she was hurting when she didn't fight me on it.

We slowly made our way downstairs, and I had to bite my tongue every time I saw her struggle. I quickly ran out to the truck and threw her bags inside. When I got back, she had only made it down a few steps. I hauled her up in my arms, which she put up a very small fight about, but in the end, she wrapped her arms around my neck and allowed me to carry her out. By the time we were at the truck, her head was resting heavily on my shoulder, and I saw her eyes drooping when I set her down. I buckled her in, and when I closed the door, her head hit the window with a soft thunk.

My house was a good twenty minutes outside of town, and I could tell she would be asleep by then. My house used to be my dad's hunting cabin, but when he passed, I decided to update it a little and make it my home. It wasn't anything big, but it was peaceful and a great escape after a long day. The guys usually came over once a week for poker night. We didn't have to worry about how loud we were, and we could just relax and have a good time.

I glanced over at Harper as we approached the driveway to my house to see she was in fact asleep. My driveway was a bumpy, dirt road, and I didn't want to wake her, so I drove slowly. I shouldn't have worried because she didn't even stir when I pulled her out of the truck and took her inside. She could sleep like the dead.

I took her straight back to the bedroom and laid her down on the bed. I grabbed her stuff from the truck, but she was still passed out on the bed when I returned. I contemplated getting her in her pajamas, but it looked like too much work in her current state. I unzipped her jeans and pulled them off, then pulled back the covers and tucked her in. Her head flopped around as I laid her down, my brows furrowing as I wondered how the hell she was sleeping so hard.

I went through my nightly ritual of turning off the lights and locking the doors. I didn't really worry about much out here. Our town was pretty safe, but still, it was a habit to lock everything up tight. I took a quick shower and then joined her in bed. Normally I slept nude, so I climbed in bed, figuring it wouldn't be a big deal since we'd already had sex. She was turned away from me, so I pulled her back into me and wrapped my arms around her. It didn't take long before my eyes drifted shut and I was asleep.

I was awoken sometime in the middle of the night by a loud scream, and then a hard hit to my face. The punch landed pretty close to my eye and was throbbing painfully. I grabbed my eye as I rolled to the edge of the bed to stand up.

"Shit!"

That fucking hurt. What the fuck was going on? I stood and looked over at Harper who was staring at me with wide eyes and wielding the lamp from my bedside table. She leapt across the bed and came at me, swinging the lamp and screaming like a banshee. I swiftly grabbed the lamp from her and threw it to the ground as I grabbed her wrist with my other hand. She was about to swing her fist at me again, so I grabbed her other wrist and pushed her back onto the bed, then climbed on top of her.

"What the fuck, Harper? It's me. Jack." I stared into her angry eyes and saw recognition dawn on her. She let out a laugh, so I took that as my cue I could get off her.

"Whew. I about beat the shit out of you. Where am I, and why are you naked in bed with me? What is going on?" Her voice rose with every word she said. How the hell did she not remember what happened? I was beginning to think that she really was crazy. Figures that I would have a thing for a nut job. Of course, I should have seen this coming when I literally picked her up out of a puddle wearing the skimpiest outfit possible.

"What's the last thing you remember?" I asked tentatively.

"Umm. I remember the crazy bitch in the hall and going to take a shower. Oh, then I took a pain pill and called into work. After that, it's kind of fuzzy."

Well, that explained it. She took a pain pill. Usually, those had some side effects, like drowsiness. Now it made sense. I picked up the discarded lamp off the floor and walked over to the other side of the bed to plug it back in. When I turned the light on, I heard her moan. When I turned around, she was staring at me like I was her next meal. I very gladly would be, except I had been punched in the face, and after her brand of crazy, I was ready to call it a night.

"You came back here to my house because my buddies couldn't fix the door tonight. And I'm guessing you don't remember that because you took a pain pill." Harper seemed to be trying to concentrate on her thoughts. She looked up into my eyes and gasped.

"Oh my God, Jack! Did I do that?" She pointed at my face in horror. I gingerly felt around my already swollen eye and smirked at her.

"Nah, this is how my face always looks. You just decorated it a little." A small smile crossed her lips. "Come on, let's get back to bed. I have to work in the morning. You can stay here, and I'll come get you at lunch to take you home." We climbed back into bed, and I wrapped my arms around her and pulled her into my chest. She was definitely a nut job, but I found I kinda liked her that way. She sighed, melting into my arms, and soon we were asleep.

CHAPTER 5

HARPER

DREAMS WERE terrific because your mind took you places that you desired most and let you live out your fantasies. My current dream had a roughened hand massaging my breast, making me wet and ready for a romp in the sheets. The hand trailed down my skin and slipped beneath my underwear. My heart started pulsing faster and faster as fingers slid through my wet folds and started spreading my desire up to my clit, stroking me in small circles. Lips spread hot kisses over my neck and nibbled on my ear. A hot tongue flicked at my lips, and I opened immediately. Moans of pleasure escaped my lips as the hand fondling me pushed me over the edge into the most orgasmic experience of my life.

"You are so sexy when you come," Jack whispered in my ear. He licked and nibbled at my ear as he continued to spread my release around my swollen pussy. His hands disappeared, and my legs were spread wide. Cool air hit me, and a moment later, his cock was sheathed to the hilt inside me. The force of his thrust brought me out of my haze, and I opened my eyes to see that this most definitely was not a dream.

"Morning, pretty girl." I didn't have time to say anything as he pulled out of me and slammed back in a moment later.

"Oh," I cried as he continued to ram inside of me, my body shifting further back with every thrust. He leaned forward and started kissing my neck, down over my t-shirt that was riding up my body. He pulled my t-shirt up with his teeth so that it was above my breasts. He nipped and licked my perky nipples, giving little tugs that made my pussy clench around his cock. Wet kisses trailed down my stomach from one hip to the other, and a laugh escaped my lips as I curled into myself at the sensation.

Jack looked up at me in confusion. "It's never a good thing when the woman you're pleasuring starts to laugh."

"Sorry. My sides are ticklish."

"Really?" A huge grin appeared, and then he was tickling me so hard I thought I would pee. His cock slipped free of me as I struggled to get away, but he pinned my arms above my head with one hand while his other hand attacked my sides.

Gasping, I tried to get him to stop. "Please. Please! I can't take anymore. Stop. Stop!" I continued laughing until he moved swiftly down between my legs and his mouth was on my pussy. He slowly ran his tongue up my lips to my clit and started sucking hard.

"Oh, God! Oh! Please don't stop. Don't stop!"

He continued to suck my clit and flick his tongue over me until it was too much and I didn't think I could take anymore. My legs were quivering for the impending orgasm that was about to take over my body. I tried to close my legs, but he rested his arms on my inner thighs and held them open. The sensations overwhelmed me, and just when I thought I couldn't take anymore, he slid a finger into my pussy and began pumping.

"Holy shit!"

I came hard and begged him to stop, but he continued to draw out my orgasm. When he finally slowed, my legs fell to the bed and I took long, deep breaths to slow my pounding heart. When I finally looked at him, he had a hunger in his eyes, and I knew this morning was just beginning. He crawled back up the length of my body and kissed me. I could taste my arousal on his lips, and his erection was prodding at my entrance.

"We didn't get a chance to talk yesterday after...I didn't use protection. Are you on birth control?"

"Yeah, we're good."

He nodded. "I'm not usually that out of control. I always use protection, but something about you had me acting like a caveman. I couldn't wait to get inside you, and everything else just flew out of my head."

Hearing how much he wanted me made my heart soar and gave my ego a huge boost. For once in my life, I felt like a desirable woman with a sexy man bowing down at my feet. With my new found confidence, I reached down and grabbed his hard cock, guiding him towards my entrance.

"Stop talking and fuck me."

An evil grin appeared on his handsome face. "Gladly." Then he slammed into me so hard I was sure I could feel him in my throat. He withdrew slowly and slammed back in again. His strong hands gripped my hips, lifting me up as he shoved a pillow under my ass, and then thrust into me again. The angle was different and a little more comfortable. He could fuck me harder this way and so much deeper. He leaned forward and pulled a nipple into his mouth. His hips slowed as he pumped tantalizingly slow, in and out.

His movements were slow and sweet, reminding me of making love. I couldn't look away from his beautiful face as he thrust slow and deep into me. The way his eyes stared into mine, I could swear I saw something different there, but as I tried to uncover what it could be, his eyes shuttered and all I saw was lust. Then the moment was broken when he pulled out and flipped me over to my stomach. He pulled me up to my knees and entered me from behind. He pumped into me hard and fast, as he spread my ass cheeks and his balls slapped against my pussy.

"Oh, yes! Fuck me harder," I shouted.

"Harper, you are so fucking sexy. Tell me what you want, baby."

"Touch my clit." The words fell out of my mouth before I could think about it. His hands moved to my clit and started massaging. I moaned and screamed his name as I started to come. His cock pistoned in and out of me as his fingers dug into my skin to grip me as he fucked me hard. I heard him moan my name as he slammed into me one last time. I felt his body curl around mind as he laid his head on my back.

"Oh fuck, Harper. You've ruined me for other women."

The sentiment should have been flattering, but instead it felt like a splash of cold water. The reality that he would move on and find someone new washed over me, but also saddened me that this meant so much less to him. No, I needed to keep perspective here. This was a good time, an excellent fuck, but I couldn't let myself think it would be more, or I would get hurt. After all, if I expected more, I shouldn't have slept with him the first day I met him. I rolled out from under him and collapsed onto my back, staring at the ceiling trying to catch my breath.

Jack kissed me, then got up and went to the bathroom. He returned with a warm washcloth and wiped me clean. "I have to go to work. I'll be back about noon to pick you up."

"Jack, that's really not necessary. This was great, but I have to get home. I have work to do and deadlines to meet. So, thanks, but you don't have to do any more."

He looked stunned that I was giving him the brush off. Had I misread him?

"Look, I know this is happening kind of fast, but I never do anything I don't want to. So if I tell you I'm going to do something for you, it's not because I feel I have to. Besides, your apartment door won't be fixed this early in the morning. It should be done by lunch, and then I'll take you home, but don't mistake me, I will be seeing you again."

I was completely stunned. I was not expecting that from him. I knew he liked me, but I had assumed it was just a good time.

"Just lie down and take a nap. Relax. I'll call you when I'm on my way home so you can be ready. Speaking of, I need your number."

He left the room and came back with his phone. He programmed my number into his phone, then went to take a shower. I laid back and recalled the last twenty-four hours and how much things had changed. This man was super sexy and he seemed to really want me. I didn't want to get my hopes up, yet he seemed pretty adamant that we would be spending more time together. I had to admit, I really wanted that too. We had this chemistry that was off the charts and I'd really never had this kind of connection before with anyone else. Waking up this morning to him exploring my body had been amazing, and I could definitely deal with more of that.

I woke up a few hours later feeling completely rested. My foot was propped up on a pillow with a warm ice pack resting on it. It was throbbing again, so I headed into the living room to grab my purse. After getting some ibuprofen, I headed into the kitchen to grab some water. Jack had left me a note on the counter.

Harper,

I can't stop thinking about how you taste. That was a great way to start my day. Dinner tonight- 6? Like an actual date? Your foot was pretty swollen, so I put an ice pack on before I left. There are more in the freezer. Ice it a few more times before I get back. Towel and washcloth on the sink. Hope you slept well.

Jack

I smiled and went to the freezer to grab another ice pack. After propping my foot up on the couch, I turned on the TV and watched the news before heading off to take a quick shower. My curiosity got the better of me as I started rummaging through his cabinets—you know, in case he was really a psychopath. Everything in his medicine cabinet appeared normal. No sedatives were stashed there or little baggies of white stuff. So far, so good. Then I went through his drawers and came up empty again. I huffed in annoyance. I was a little disappointed. It's not that I wanted to be dating a serial killer, but I was expecting something interesting. He was generally a pretty tidy man, not a whole lot out of place and nothing interesting to speak of. It looked like I would be going on a date with a normal man. Well, you can't win them all. I found the towel and washcloth he left out for me on the counter and took a quick shower. He didn't have any girly shampoo or body wash, so I would smell like him the rest of the day. That was definitely not a bad thing.

After getting dressed, I went off in search of food. I made some fried eggs and toast, then did up the dishes. I really needed to get some work done on my book, and after yesterday and this morning, I had plenty of new material to spice up my book. I was lost in writing for a couple of hours and only stopped when I heard my phone ping with a message from Jack. He was on his way and I had to hurry up and get ready, so I saved my work, shut down my computer, and then packed up my stuff. By the time I was done, I heard him pulling in the driveway. I hauled my stuff out to the truck and hopped in.

"Hi. I didn't lock the door."

"That's okay. I need to run in and grab something anyway." He went back inside and returned a minute later. He was covered in grime, and he looked so sexy. Who knew men covered in dirt would be sexy?

"So, where do you work?" I asked as we headed back into town.

"I, uh, I own the auto shop on 7th." He didn't look at me when he said it. It was almost like he was embarrassed or trying to hide the fact that he owned the shop. Then I realized that he was the one who was taking care of my car. I couldn't help but wonder why he didn't tell me yesterday.

"So, you're a mechanic." He nodded. "So, why didn't you look at my car yesterday? Not that I'm not grateful for all you did, but you probably could have told me what was wrong with my car in two minutes."

"The shop I own was my dad's. His name was Graham. He was a great mechanic, and he really liked to help people. He was always seeing people broken down and would pull over to help. He stopped one day on the side of the road to help a stranded woman. There was a car coming, and the driver wasn't paying attention, went into the gravel on the side of the road and lost control. My dad was killed. So, now when I pull over, I try not to spend too much time on the side of the road. Accidents happen, ya know?"

That was horrible, and I felt terrible that he had lost his dad that way.

"I'm sorry about your father."

He shrugged. "It's been five years. You can't dwell on what could have been. It was an accident, and he wouldn't want me being pissed off five years later. I took over the business, and it's been going great. I miss working with him, but I still work with some of the guys that worked with him. We tell stories from time to time and joke about the old days." Jack was smiling, and I found myself thinking how great it would be to see that smile every day.

"So, I'm assuming my car is at your shop? Do you know what's wrong with it?"

"My guys looked it over yesterday and ordered the parts. There were a few things wrong, so we're just fixing up anything that needs it."

He said that like it was no big deal, but it sounded like a lot of money—money that I didn't have. Fixing whatever was wrong with it would be enough to drain my savings for sure. I didn't have a lot saved up, and I didn't really want to spend it on repairs. My only other option would be to take the bus, and I really liked having a car. I'd just have to pull some extra shifts at the restaurant to get some extra money.

"Jack, I really appreciate you taking care of that, but I can't afford a whole lot. I really wish you had talked to me about it first." I did my best not to sound bitchy, but I needed him to understand that I wouldn't tolerate that kind of high-handedness.

"There's no charge. I want to do what I can to fix it up. No major repairs; I just want to be sure it's safe for you." I sat there speechless. The only person who ever wanted to take care of me was my dad, and I was trying really hard to prove I didn't need help.

"Jack, I understand what you're trying to do, and I appreciate it, but we just met. I can't accept that kind of help. It's just too much. Let me know how much the repairs are, and I'll take care of it." He was quiet for a minute as he considered what I said.

"I'll let you pay for the parts, but not the labor. As you said, I didn't talk to you about it first. I can't in good conscience ask you to pay. It wouldn't be ethical." It seemed to be a good compromise, so I accepted.

"Fine, but I want a list of all the work that was done to ensure that I'm paying for all the parts."

"Of course."

We drove to Anna's place first, and he insisted on running upstairs and taking care of the cat himself. He told me I would slow him down, and that by the time we got upstairs, he could have it done and be back in the truck. Fifteen minutes later, he was back and we were headed to my apartment. He hauled my stuff upstairs, and when I wasn't fast enough, he came back and carried me the rest of the way. As we approached the door, I blushed at the memories of what happened yesterday. I would never be able to walk into this apartment and not think about the amazing sex we'd had.

The door was completely fixed and seemed to be a lot thicker than the last one I had. There was a brand new deadbolt, chain lock, and a second deadbolt. Did he think I was preparing for war?

"The last door wasn't that thick. How did you manage that? And why are there so many locks?"

He gave me a quizzical look and spoke slowly, as if I was having a hard time understanding him. "We broke your door while fucking. That shouldn't happen." I tried to say something, but he held up his hand to stop me. "The guys rebuilt the frame. It was busted anyway, so they adjusted for a heavier door. The extra locks are because you have some strange characters in this building, and I want to know you're safe. More than that, I want you to feel safe."

I stood totally dumbfounded for a moment. This man was amazing. The independent part of me was saying that he was going overboard, but the girly part of me was going gaga over how this man was taking into consideration my safety and feelings.

"Sorry, it's just... that's the sweetest thing anyone has ever said. Or done. Thank you. I really apprec-"

He cut me off with a wave of his hand. "I know you really appreciate it. You don't have to keep thanking me. I told you, I only do what I want to do. I have to get back to work, so let's get you settled on the couch. I'll get you an ice pack, and I'll be back to pick you up at 6."

I went over to the couch and put my foot up on a pillow. He came back with an ice pack, then gave me a panty melting kiss that I was sure would hold me over for at least an hour.

Good Lord, that man can kiss.

"There's a lot more I can do than kiss. I'll show you again tonight," he said. Then he was out the door.

I had to fan myself as I watched him walk out the door. Not only was he an excellent lover, he had a gorgeous backside that made me want to squeeze every delicious inch of his tushy. After a few minutes of staring at the door, I came to my senses and decided it would not be productive to stare at the door all afternoon. I spent the afternoon writing, and at four o'clock decided to start getting ready for our date. I wanted to allow extra time to look really nice for him. I started to get a little nervous the closer it came to the time he would pick me up. Everything was moving fast, but had also been very sexual. What if we didn't have anything to talk about at dinner? I had never liked someone as much as I like Jack, and I hoped that all went well tonight. I was already falling for his charms, and I had to be careful that I didn't take it too fast.

CHAPTER 6

JACK

IT HAD BEEN A CRAZY DAY, and I wasn't even sure if I could make my date with Harper. There was so much to do around the garage, but in the end I decided to delegate. That wasn't something I was very good at. I always felt the need to be in charge of everything to do with my garage. She was my baby and my dad's legacy. I wanted the garage to succeed, but I also needed it to succeed to make sure my dad's good name lived on. So, I ran my garage the way he did. I was the first in and the last out.

The guys at the garage often gave me a hard time about not dating and being married to my job, so when I told them I was leaving early for a date, they let out a round of wolf whistles. They were all telling me that *it was about time* and *I needed to find a good wife*. I was relieved that no one was pissed they had to work later than me. The guys usually all worked until the work was done. There were no set hours and the guys seemed to appreciate it. It gave them a chance to make some extra money, and because of their willingness to work as long as needed, I was generous with vacation time.

I checked the clock as I pulled in my drive, noting that I had just enough time to shower and change before hitting the road to pick up

Harper. I made reservations at Luna tonight. It was a new, swanky restaurant in town and had great reviews. The chef had been part of a cooking show contest and had come in second. Even though he didn't win, the offers for him to run a kitchen came pouring in, and he had settled here.

I arrived at Harper's apartment just before six. I was a little out of my element tonight because I was comfortable in jeans and t-shirts, but the restaurant demanded I wore something nicer. I had on black dress pants and a black button down shirt. It felt too suffocating for me, so I left the top two buttons undone. I didn't have time to shave, so I had scruff on my jaw, and I hoped she didn't think I was a slob for it.

After Harper let me in, I walked up the stairs and knocked. When the door opened, I stood there gawking like an idiot. She looked stunning. She had on a tight, black dress that hugged her ass and had a scoop neck that showed just a hint of cleavage. It was sexy as hell. Her blonde hair hung in waves down her back, and she was only wearing enough eye makeup to make her eyes stand out. My gaze roamed down her long legs to the strappy, high heeled shoes that begged to be wrapped around my back as I fucked her. Shit. I was getting hard.

I heard a throat clear and I finally dragged my eyes up to meet hers. They were dancing with humor that I had been caught daydreaming. I cleared my throat and stepped inside.

"You look beautiful. Are you ready to go?"

"Sure. Let me grab my purse." She turned around and I stayed in the doorway or I might drag her down the hall to her bedroom. She locked the door and we started down the stairs. She was walking slowly and I grabbed her arm, afraid she would fall down the stairs. Then a thought crossed my mind.

"Should you be wearing heels? I mean, is your foot up to that?"

"I iced it all afternoon and it feels much better. Besides, flats do not work with this dress." I shook my head in disbelief. Of course, it always came down to fashion sense with women. I helped her into the truck and we headed to the restaurant.

"I made reservations at Luna. Have you been there?"

"No, I haven't, but I hear the food is excellent. I love to cook and try new recipes, but I love getting to eat a meal cooked by a professional. Then I go home and see if I can replicate my meal."

"So, I have some homemade meals in my future," I teased. She pretended to think about it.

"If you're a good boy and give me what I want." She flushed immediately, seeming to realize how that sounded. My dick hardened at the thoughts running through my mind.

"Baby, I will always give you what you want."

She glanced away and looked out the window the rest of the drive, but I caught the smile that she tried to hide. I had to keep it under control tonight. I wanted us to have more than sex, and in order for that to happen, I had to make it through our date.

We pulled up to the restaurant and were seated at a small table in front of the window. The lights were dimmed in the restaurant and there were candles at every table. It was the perfect setting for a romantic evening. We looked over our menus and placed our orders. Luckily, the waiter paired a red wine with our meals. I didn't know jack shit about wine, and frankly would rather have a beer, but this wasn't really the place to order beer.

"So, what did you do with your afternoon?"

For once, I actually wanted to know more about my date. Most of the women I dated were so superficial and I found it hard to have a decent conversation with them on a date. They were only interested in sex, and that was fine, but I actually wanted to have a conversation with Harper and find out more about her.

"I was writing. I'm working on a book right now. I'd actually been stuck, and then yesterday inspiration struck," she said with a slight grin. "So, thank you."

Huh? She was thanking me? I looked at her a little confused. "Uh, you're welcome? I don't understand why you're thanking me."

She blushed and ducked her head. "Okay, don't laugh. I write romance novels. Until yesterday, I was stuck on my story, and it felt stagnant. I needed something to put some spark in the book. Let's just say our meeting and certain events that occurred inspired me."

She had a gleam in her eyes and a bright smile on her face. I smirked at her reference to *certain events*. They had definitely been noteworthy.

"So, I'm going to be in your book?"

"Well, not you personally, but one of the characters does take on some of your attributes and... skills."

I wasn't gonna lie, I was pretty flattered. I didn't want to personally be in a book, but the fact that she thought my skills were bookworthy inflated my ego a little more than necessary.

"So do some of our escapades from yesterday occur in your book?"

"Some do. Some of it, I elaborated on. After you left..." She looked like she was embarrassed to say something. I motioned for her to continue. "After you left, I started daydreaming about what we had done and maybe fantasized about some things I think we should try. I incorporated that into my book."

Fuuuuck. I was hard as a rock. The thought of her fantasizing had me calculating if I had enough time to drag her into the bathroom right now and give her more material to work with. I was going to have to steer this conversation in another direction to get my cock under control.

"I think we need to see your book when I take you home. I think we definitely need to try these things. For your readers, of course. We need to make sure the details are accurate."

"I think you might be right. We should test a few of my fantasies and see if they're accurate. I would hate to write about something that isn't physically possible to do. Right. So, we should definitely go back to my place and have sex. For the sake of research." She finished with a sharp nod.

The waiter returned with our meals, and I inhaled my food. The faster I ate, the faster we could leave and get back to Harper's. It seemed, however, that Harper had other plans. She seemed to be practicing the art of seduction. She would cut up a piece of filet mignon, slowly open her mouth, and practically suck the steak off her fork. Her eyes were smiling the whole time, and I swore I had drool hanging from my mouth. What killed me though, was when she took a sip of wine and then slowly licked her lips. I could see the red tinge of the wine left on her lips. It had me yearning to reach across the table and taste those delectable lips.

Is it acceptable to whip my cock out in a restaurant for you to suck?

"Only if we're in the bathroom, but let's wait until we get back to my place." Harper winked at me.

What the fuck? I shook my head and laughed. I was turning into Harper. I couldn't believe I had just said that out loud. Christ, I was going to hell. I waived over the waiter and whipped out my wallet. We had to leave.

"I need the check now. Get it here in two minutes and there's an extra twenty in it for you."

Harper's eyes widened. Apparently, she didn't realize how good she was. I had the check paid and we were out the door within two minutes. I practically dragged her back to my truck. I spun her against the truck door and kissed her hard. My hands had a mind of their own, roaming over her body. My cock was straining against my zipper, so I pulled back from her to distance myself. Taking a deep breath, I let out a chuckle, running my hand through my hair. I was on the verge of sexual collapse. I got her in the truck and headed toward her place. I didn't know how long I was going to last, and Harper seemed to realize this because as soon as we were away from heavy traffic, she undid her buckle and got up on her knees to face me. My heart was thudding as I considered what she was going to do. Her hands were on my zipper and undoing my pants before I could tell her to wait. I was going to crash the truck for sure if she got her hands on me.

"Harper, maybe you should wait until we get home. I'm pretty sure if you do that, I'm going to crash into another car."

She didn't stop. My dick was now out of my pants and being jerked off by the sexiest woman I had ever met. I had to get off the main road so I didn't get us in an accident, so I took some side roads and headed out of town to my place. I had to slow down to a snail's pace so I didn't get in an accident. She must have sensed the change in direction.

"Where are we going?" she asked, but then sucked me into her mouth and pretended she was a vacuum cleaner.

"Holy fuck," I groaned. "We're headed to my place."

Goddamn, this woman was going to be the death of me. I couldn't even speak coherently as all the blood had left my brain and was now in my dick.

"Better to be... off the road. Ya know...people and...things... shit...that we could damage. Oh fuck, Harper...Just cows and...fences..."

Fuck, I sounded like an idiot. I couldn't even put a sentence together while she was sucking me. I pulled sharply over to the side of the road and grabbed her hair, then thrust up into her mouth.

"Fuck, I love fucking your mouth. Shit. I'm gonna come."

She sucked me deeper into her mouth, and I exploded into the back of her throat. That was by far the sexiest thing that had ever happened to me.

Two out of three holes tested and approved.

"Do I get a stamp saying *Jack tested and approved*?"

"Shit. Did I just say that out loud? Damn. I'm turning into you."

I took in a deep breath and let it out slowly. "Alright, sweetheart. Let's get back to my place. I have plans for you. They involve me sucking and fucking your pussy. We've got a busy night ahead of us."

I threw the truck in drive and headed home, then spent the whole night doing exactly what I promised. We had a few hours of sleep here and there, but I couldn't seem to get enough of her. I would fall asleep holding her, but my cock knew she was there for the taking and would wake me up for another round. Finally, around three in the morning, we fell asleep completely exhausted. I couldn't have fucked her again if I wanted to.

When I woke in the morning, Harper wasn't in bed with me. I climbed out of bed and went to the bathroom, then made my way to the living room where I saw Harper in an upside down v. What the fuck was she doing? I leaned against the door and watched. She was wearing my white t-shirt and her black thong from last night. Her ass looked magnificent up in the air. I could probably walk right up behind her and be fucking her in just a few seconds.

She stood up and then moved into some weird pose, which I recognized. She was doing yoga and was in the warrior pose. An idea sparked, and I decided to have a little fun with her. I crept up behind her and wrapped one arm around her waist under the t-shirt and the other lightly around her throat to hold her in place.

"Good morning, pretty girl. Want to play a game with me?"

She nodded, and I slid my hand from her waist up to massage her breasts. I lightly teased her nipples and tugged them until they were hard peaks.

"Here's what we're going to do." I started kissing her neck and continued to play with her breasts. "I'm going to do what I want to you, and if you can stay in this pose, you get to choose what we do today." My hand slid down and cupped her mound. "But if you can't stay still, I win and I get to choose. I can guarantee you, you'll be sore by the end of the day." I nibbled her earlobe. "Want to play?"

I could feel her heartbeat hammering in her neck, and I slid my fingers under the tiny scrap of fabric that covered her pussy. She was soaked already, and I had no doubt in my mind that I could win in under three minutes. She nodded frantically and barely croaked out a yes.

"Good girl. Now make sure you stay still."

I continued to run my hands over her body and I placed wet kisses on her neck and shoulder. Then I removed my hands and sat down between her legs. She glanced down at me, but held her pose.

Her breathing picked up in anticipation and I could smell her desire through her panties. I rubbed my face into her panties and inhaled her scent. God, she smelled good enough to eat. It really was a delicious way to start the day.

I moved the thong aside and gently massaged her clit with my thumb as I watched her features. Her breathing was erratic, and her eyes had slid shut. I ran my tongue the length of her seam and started sucking her clit as I spread her plump lips. Her juices started flowing, and I could feel her legs shaking around me. I needed more of her and wrapped my arm around her ass to pull her closer to my mouth. I licked and sucked, but it wasn't enough. I would never be able to get enough of her. I was already addicted. Her hands were threaded through my hair, and I felt sharp tugs as she moved my head where she wanted me. I felt a flush of liquid hit my tongue as she called my name. I sucked harder and harder, wanting to draw out her orgasm as long as possible.

Enough of that shit. I grabbed her around the waist and flung her down to the ground. I grabbed a pillow from the couch and shoved it under her ass, then started eating her pussy again. She came screaming my name a few seconds later. I shucked my pants quickly and was seated inside her a few seconds later. I stalled for a minute to get my dick under control, and then I fucked her hard and fast. She was clenching around me so tight that I knew I wouldn't last long. I threw her legs up over my shoulders and pounded into her, harder and faster. The only thing I could hear was our harsh breaths and my skin slapping against hers. I came undone when I looked into her eyes and saw the same desire I felt. I thumbed her clit, needing to push her over the edge one last time before I found my release.

"Come for me, baby. I want to hear you scream again."

She came hard as her legs squeezed my neck. A few moments later, I slammed into her one last time and jerked my cum into her sweet pussy. Her legs collapsed, but were still scissored around my neck, causing me to fall on top of her.

Her arm was thrown up over her eyes as she took a deep breath.

"I'm sure this is uncomfortable for you, but I don't give a shit. You're just gonna have to stay there until I can feel my legs." She was panting heavily and my weight was probably adding to her erratic breathing, so I untangled myself from her and laid down next to her.

"Next time you need a workout, just call me. No need to do yoga."

We continued to lie there looking at the ceiling until our breathing slowed to a normal rate.

"So, who won the contest?"

CHAPTER 7

HARPER

WHAT I HAD ASSUMED WOULD BE a day full of sex was actually a day of hiding from enemies and dodging bullets in a sweaty jungle. This was his idea of fun? Go to war? Okay, we weren't actually at war. We were playing paintball, but I had no clue how to play, and was more likely to shoot myself in the foot than any player standing within five feet of me.

When we had finally dragged ourselves off the floor to take a shower, we argued for a good ten minutes about who won. Technically, Jack had won. I didn't stay standing, but did it really count if you were thrown to the floor? Somehow it didn't seem fair, but I was interested in what would make me sore by the end of the day. I just hadn't realized we would be getting dressed today.

"So, who are we meeting?" I asked as we drove through what looked like the backwoods of Pennsylvania.

"A few of my friends. You've already met Logan and Ryan." I nodded. "And then my friend, Sean. He's a police officer in town."

"How do you all know each other?"

"We went to school together. I actually thought Sean might join me at the shop, but after we graduated high school, there were a string of murders in the area—"

"I remember that," I cut in, remembering all the missing women. Of course, I was younger than him. I was still in high school at the time, but I remembered all the teachers warning us of strangers, and the special protections that had been put in place to make sure we all got home safely.

"His sister was one of the victims."

I covered my gaping mouth with my hand. I couldn't believe it. "That's terrible."

He nodded. "She survived. In fact, she was the only woman to survive."

"Oh my gosh. I can't believe it."

"That's why he became a police officer. He wanted to catch the guy. He's working to become a detective now."

"Good for him. I hope he catches the bastard."

He grinned slightly. "That's what we're all hoping for. We all knew Cara. It's really hard to see her the way she is now. She doesn't really see anyone anymore. She just stays inside all the time."

"I can imagine. I'm not sure I would want to leave the house if that happened to me. I would be too scared."

"Don't get me wrong, she's still feisty as hell. Just terrified to go anywhere. I'm actually surprised that Sean hasn't had Sebastian put a detail on her."

"I'm sorry, a what?"

"A security detail. Sebastian, one of the guys you'll meet today, owns a security company."

"And you think she needs protection?"

He shrugged. "I don't know. Maybe? I would probably do that if it was my sister. But then again, the murders stopped, so maybe he thinks he has it handled."

I shook my head in disbelief. "That's just crazy. I mean, you hear these stories, but you don't ever think you'll actually know someone that went through that stuff." Not wanting to think about it anymore,

I decided to switch gears. "So, who else are we meeting? No one else with a tragic past, I hope."

I thought it would be funny, but Jack winced.

"Oh shit, I've stuck my foot in my mouth, haven't I?"

He cleared his throat. "My friend, Cole...He's an ex Marine Scout Sniper. He returned two years ago from a deployment and he hasn't been the same since. I'm actually surprised that he's joining us. He's kind of against weapons now."

"Why?"

He shook his head. "I think he's just had enough of war. But Sean's been doing everything he can to drag Cole back to the land of the living. He had it pretty bad for a while. He wouldn't even leave his bed. Sean was the only one that was able to help him."

"Maybe because of Cara," I surmised.

"Maybe...Anyway, he's come once or twice before, but I didn't really think he would keep coming. This is a good sign. Maybe Sebastian will be able to convince him to work for him."

"Do you think that'll happen?"

He was quiet for a moment, and then shook his head. "No, not really. I think he was serious when he said he never wanted to hold a weapon again."

"But isn't a paintball gun the same?"

He shrugged. "I don't understand it. Maybe it's because it's not deadly. Maybe it makes him feel slightly normal. I don't know."

We pulled down a gravel drive where several other trucks were parked and got out. I was nervous to meet everyone, and wished there was just one other woman here that I could talk to. All these guys looked intimidating as hell in their gear.

"Guys, this is Harper. Harper, you've met Logan and Ryan. This is Sean, Cole, and Sebastian." Jack gestured to each of them as he introduced them.

"So, Harper, you ever play paintball?" Sean asked. The guys seemed to be analyzing me. They would see soon enough that I had absolutely no skills when it came to this kind of stuff.

"Nope. I'm probably horrible at it. I'll probably be the first one out."

"You can be on my team, baby. I'll protect you from these ruffians." It was sweet that he wanted to help me out, but I had a feeling the guys would respect me more if I could hold my own.

We got all geared up and split up into teams. Cole, Jack, Sean, and I were on one team, while Ryan, Logan, and Sebastian were on the other. They must have realized that I would be useless and I didn't really count. Which was most likely true. We had been out playing for an hour, most of which, I spent hiding out next to Jack. He would tell me when to move, duck, crawl, and run. I basically followed orders. We were getting ready to move again when Jack got hit three times.

"Harper, you're gonna have to make it across the opening to that hideout over there." He pointed across the woods to a wooden hut. My heart started to race. It was only a game, but I was so nervous. I started sweating profusely at the idea of running over an open area to shelter while paintballs whizzed around my head.

"Just run hard and fast. The guys will do what they can to help you out."

"Okay," I nodded. "I can do this."

I took in a deep breath and started to get up when I heard paint splattering all around me. I checked myself over and found that I hadn't been hit, and probably would have felt it if I had. Cole shouted to me that he would cover me. I steeled my nerves and decided I was going out fighting. I took in a few quick, deep breaths as I jumped out from my hideout, letting out a banshee cry. I swung my gun around and started running as I sprayed paint balls at anything that moved. My warrior cry echoed around us, and my throat was raw, but I continued on. I saw a gun aimed at me, and I leapt to the side and rolled like I had seen in the movies. Then I got up to one knee and popped off a few shots.

My breathing was coming fast and heavy, but I refused to give in. I got up and sprinted as fast as I could toward the hideout. I was so close I could almost taste it. With a final breath, I leapt over the short wall and yelled, "You'll never get me!" I landed on my feet, and then rolled toward the safety of the hut. Pain stabbed my side and I was breathing hard. I felt like I was going to throw up after all the energy I expelled. Spots were appearing in front of my eyes and my whole body felt like jello.

I glanced down to see that I didn't have any paint on me. My head flopped back against the ground as I stared up into the trees, trying to calm my racing heart. Had they let me get across so that I wouldn't feel bad? Or maybe they were taking it easy on me because I was a girl. I heard footsteps approach, but I was done. I had no energy left to get up, let alone hold my weapon. I wasn't even sure where it was at this point. Whoever was coming wasn't being very quiet.

"I surrender. Don't shoot me. I can't fight anymore. I'm done." Was that my voice? It was croaking and barely understandable.

"Baby? You okay?" I looked up into Jack's laughing eyes. I could tell he was trying to hold back, but soon all the guys were looking down at me and laughing. Okay, that just pissed me off. I didn't want to come out here and play their stupid game anyway, but I did, and I tried my best. They didn't need to laugh at me.

"Shut the fuck up. I told you I had never played before! You don't need to laugh at me." I tried to sit up as I said it, but my body was too tired, so I flopped back down. I shot a glare at every one of them for trying to make me feel like shit.

Cole was the first to speak up. "Darlin', you just kicked their asses."

Huh?

Logan stepped forward and pointed to his chest. "When you came running and screaming from the hideout, we were all so shocked, we just stood there. Then you started shooting, and you hit all of us." He started laughing and then mimicked my face and screamed like I had as I jumped from the hideout.

Sebastian held out his hand to me. "If I had known you were

gonna go all Lara Croft on us, I would have insisted you be on my team. You've got some big lady balls."

I was shocked. I won? They thought I was good? "So, I took all of you out? Like, the game is over?"

"Sweetheart, you took all three of them out in under fifteen seconds. Cole didn't even have to lay down fire for you." Jack had a big grin on his face and I finally relaxed, feeling like I might have earned a little respect from the guys today.

We headed back to the truck and I made Jack carry me since I couldn't work my body if I tried. Thankfully, the guys didn't give me a hard time about it, and they each gave me a hug as we got ready to leave. As soon as I sat in the truck, I felt exhaustion setting in. I had to work tonight, so I would have to nap on the way home so I could make it through my shift. No problem there. I couldn't keep my eyes open if I tried. I fell asleep within minutes of leaving and slept the whole hour ride home.

Jack walked me up to my apartment and kissed me goodbye at the door. I only had an hour to get ready for work. I stripped my clothes off and scrubbed the dirt from my body. A bath sounded great, but I didn't have the time to soak my sore body. I got dressed in my work clothes and scoured my cabinets for something to eat. Nothing looked good, but then I remembered I had lasagna from the other night. I quickly ate and then headed off to work.

As the night dragged on at work, I could feel every muscle in my body ache. Shelley could see I was hurting, obviously thinking that I was still in pain from the other day.

"Are you okay, Harper? Do I need to get someone to take over for you?"

I shook my head. It was my own fault that I was this sore. I needed the money after taking off a few days from my ankle sprain, so I was going to have to push through.

"Remember I told you that a guy helped me out the other day? Well, we kind of hit it off, and he took me out with his friends today. We played paintball. It was pretty uneventful until the end. I made this mad dash across the woods and shot them all. It was pretty intense, and now I'm paying for it." Shelley had a shocked look on her face.

"You won paintball against a bunch of guys? Oh, that's great! Ha! I wish I could have seen that." Shelley was laughing hysterically, and people looked over to us, curious as to what was so funny.

"Anyway. I just have to make it through my shift and go take a nice long soak in the tub."

I saw someone's hand shoot up in the air and smiled at Shelley as I walked over to help. I was about halfway through my shift when two older couples walked in. They were seated in my section and I went over to help them. One man stared adoringly at his wife as she told a funny story. He laughed at what she said and joined in on her conversation. The other man talked over his wife and seemed to have no social graces. I made my introductions and took drink orders. When I returned, I started telling them about the specials for the evening. The man that appeared rude started snapping his fingers at me. I was a little surprised by the behavior and stood there in astonishment for a minute before recovering and putting a smile on my face.

"Excuse me, miss, but what can you tell me about the filet?" I was an experienced waitress and knew how to hold my own with these questions.

"Well, the filet is the most tender slab of beef. It's served in a 6 oz portion with a mushroom sauce served on top. We can cook it however you prefer, but the chef recommends it to be served rare."

"Where does the meat come from?"

Oh, I so wanted to say it. A cow. Yes, that would be rude. *Don't say it. Don't say it.*

"All of our meat comes from local farmers."

"Grass fed or are they shot up with hormones?" He didn't seem genuinely concerned. More like he was trying to show off for the others at the table. His wife sat politely next to him, while the others looked at him like he was going off the deep end.

"The cows are grass fed."

"Are they certified organic?"

"Yes."

How long would this go on?

"When were they killed? I don't want to eat meat that's been sitting around for a month." Really? Christ, couldn't he just order already? I was about to lose it. I was a professional, but this guy was getting on my nerves. I noticed some of the other patrons starting to stare, and I knew I needed to wrap this up quickly.

"All the beef is fresh."

"How did the cow die?"

I lost it. I may lose my job, but I couldn't help it. This guy was a jerk, and after my long day, I just wanted to go home and relax. I was tired of dealing with customers all the time. This wasn't what I wanted from life. Sometimes, you just had to let it fly.

"Well, the farmer took a cast iron pan, marched into the field, and whacked the cow over the head with the pan. The cow was pretty big, so he may have had to hit him a few times. Then, the farmer threw him in the back of the pickup truck and brought him to the back door of the restaurant where our chef slit the cow's throat and cut him to bits. This all happened yesterday. So the cow died quickly, and didn't feel a thing since he was unconscious. The meat is very fresh, and when we examined the contents of his stomach, we only found partially digested grass."

The man seemed satisfied with the answer and went back to perusing the menu while the rest of the table silently laughed. Patrons at other tables seemed equally astonished, and were whispering about all that had occurred. After they placed their orders, I went to the back to turn in my ticket, fully aware that my smart mouth could very well have gotten me fired, but instead I saw Shelley laughing.

Relief flooded through me that I hadn't just totally screwed myself over. Shelley told me that it was the funniest thing she had ever seen, but thought maybe it was best as a one time show. I went about checking on my other tables, and was speaking with some guests about wine when I noticed everyone staring at the table of four. I glanced over and saw the rude man holding his wine glass high in the air as he continued to talk to the others at his table. The other couple was looking at him like he was nuts.

"I'll be right back with your wine," I told the people at the table. I made my way over to the table of four. "Sir, is there something wrong with your glass?"

"Yes. It's empty. I need a refill." I rolled my eyes and took the glass from him. "Of course. I'll be right back. Can I get anyone else anything?"

They all shook their heads, and I went back to the kitchen to fill the orders. I carried on with my night, but dreaded it every time I had to go to that table. I returned with their appetizers shortly after and continued on with my night. When I brought them their entrees, I immediately wanted to throw up. The rude man had his soup spoon against his ear and was trying to scratch his inner ear.

Please don't put that back in your mouth. Please don't put that back in your mouth.

He started talking to me, but I was completely mesmerized by the spoon in his ear. I knew he was talking to me, and I should pay attention. I finally forced myself to listen to him and did my best to keep the disgust off my face.

"We'll be wanting dessert also, so come back in exactly fifteen minutes for us to place our orders. I don't want to be waiting around all night."

Then he did it. He placed the spoon back in his soup and started eating. I felt a look of disgust cross my face, and no matter how I tried, I couldn't make it go away. I had seen some crazy stuff as a waitress, but this topped them all. I handed out the food and then took my tray back to the kitchen.

Fifteen minutes later, I went back to the table to take their dessert orders. "Are you ready to order dessert?"

"Why would you assume we want dessert? We haven't even

finished our meals yet. Come back in five minutes and we'll let you know."

He dismissed me with a wave and I headed off to check other tables, heaving a sigh. As I was taking orders at another table, I heard a snapping sound. At first I ignored it, but then a woman at the table spoke up.

"Excuse me, dear, but I think that gentleman over there is trying to get your attention."

I turned to see a hand in the air snapping rhythmically.

"Let me finish taking your order and then I'll go check on him." I smiled at the lady, and she seemed to appreciate that I hadn't run off. When I was done taking their orders, I walked over to the table.

"How can I help you, sir?"

"We're ready for our check."

"Of course. Let me go get that for you."

Thank God that was over. I dropped off my previous order with the kitchen and totaled up the bill for the other table. I returned it and left before they could say anything further. When the bill was settled, I took the receipt back to the register. There was a note with a hundred dollar bill inside.

Thank you so much for dealing with that asshole. You deserve more than this for your night with him. I especially liked the story of how the cow died. Have a great night.

I smiled at the fact that I earned a hundred dollars off one table, even though I had to deal with that douchebag. My night ended at eleven o'clock. I helped clean up the dining area, and then I headed home. I plugged in my phone to charge and ran a bath. As the tub was filling, I checked to see if I had any messages. There was one from Jack.

Miss you already. I'll be at work late tomorrow. Text me sometime tomorrow, and I'll respond when I can.

I smiled at the text. It felt so good to come home after a shitty night and hear from someone. I took my bath and then got into bed. I had a long day ahead of me tomorrow. I needed to finish my book and get it off to the editor this week. It didn't take more than a few minutes to fall asleep.

CHAPTER 8

JACK

I SWORE as I got off the phone. It had been a shitty day. I was up to my neck in auto repairs, parts were coming in behind schedule, and I had two guys call in sick today. On top of all that, I hadn't seen Harper in three days. She had barely responded to my texts, something about finishing her book. I knew she had to get her book done, and she was working nights waitressing, but damn I really needed to see her. I got up from my desk and got back to work. These cars wouldn't fix themselves.

It was after ten at night before I took another break. I sent the guys home two hours ago. They all had families to go see. I sat at the desk eating my sandwich and looking over orders that I still had to do. The paperwork for Harper's car was sitting on the desk with a note attached.

Tried to pay. I told her I couldn't find the paperwork and to check back with you later in the week.

-Sal

. . .

That little sneak. When did she find time to come over here and check on her bill? And why didn't I know about it until now? I set it aside and went through the rest of the paperwork. Payroll had to be done for tomorrow, so I waited on the rest of the orders and got to work writing checks. We didn't have a fancy payroll system on the computer. I had bought it, but I hadn't had time to learn how to set it up and use it. I really needed to hire an office manager, but there weren't enough hours in the day to do that. By the time I finished up with payroll and balancing the books, it was well past midnight. This was why I didn't date. No sane woman would want to put up with my work schedule. I hauled my tired ass into my truck and headed home.

"Fuck it," I said as I turned the truck around. I headed over to Harper's and grabbed my bag that was in the back seat. I always carried an extra set of clothes with me just in case. I had a dirty job, and I lived too far out of town to run home quickly. I got out of the truck and rang the buzzer to her apartment, sure I was going to wake her up, but I didn't care right now. When she didn't answer, I sent her a text.

Downstairs. Let me up.

Two minutes later, Harper appeared at the door in her pajamas and a robe. Her hair was up in a messy bun, and she looked like she had been sleeping. I felt bad, but I needed to at least hold her tonight.

"Hey, sorry to wake you, but I had to see you."

She immediately looked concerned. "Is everything alright?"

"Yeah, I've been so busy, and I know we won't get to see each other the rest of the week, so I decided to come here."

She held the door open for me and we walked up the stairs together.

"Just so you know, I'm exhausted and I'm going right back to sleep." She yawned and walked into the apartment.

"I'm just gonna grab a shower and I'll be in."

I started toward the bathroom and took a quick shower. When I came out, Harper was already asleep in bed. I walked around the apartment and checked the doors and windows, then went back to the bedroom and set my alarm. I pulled her back to my front and went to sleep.

Harper didn't wake when my alarm went off in the morning. I was very happy about that, since I had woken her up last night. She had to be exhausted, and I didn't want to feel any more guilt than I already did. I snuck out of bed and left before she woke. I had a shit ton of work to do, and I had to get on it before business started suffering.

I didn't hear from Harper the rest of the week, and didn't really think to contact her. I was so busy playing catch up after my guys were out sick, that I didn't have time to stop and think about it too much. I decided that I couldn't be selfish anymore and ring her bell in the middle of the night. She needed sleep, and I wasn't going to take that from her. I kept telling myself that I would call her during the day on my breaks, but I was always bombarded with phone calls and new orders coming in. I ended up working all weekend to make up for my previous weekend off. I didn't even think to text her until Sunday afternoon when I got off work.

How's the cat? Is your friend home yet?

I waited for a response, but never got one. That seemed odd, but then again, I didn't know her that well. She must have been busy. I had hoped to see her sometime this weekend, but it just didn't work out. Since it was still early in the night, I decided to call the guys and head into town for a beer. We all met up at The Pub. Yes, that was the name, very straightforward and hard to misunderstand what kind of place it was.

I walked into the bar and started looking around for the guys. They were all at a table with their heads together, and when Sean looked up and saw me, his face saddened. I made my way over and sat down.

"What's up with you guys? You look like you just got some terrible news." They all looked at each other, and then, finally, Sebastian spoke up.

"Look man, we don't want to be the ones to tell you this, but your girl is here, and she isn't alone." His head jerked to the other side of the bar where Harper sat at a table laughing with some douchebag. I watched as she put her hand on his arm, and then leaned in to give him a hug and kiss on the cheek. What the fuck? Rage consumed my body at the realization that last weekend only meant something to me. I thought after she spent the night that we both wanted the same thing, but apparently, she was already out looking for someone new.

I stood up and stalked over to Harper, my anger building with every step. Her laughs were supposed to be for me. Her bright smile was supposed to be for me. All of her was supposed to be for me. That was why women weren't worth the trouble. You thought you had something, and they turned around and shit all over you. In public. She didn't even have the decency to let me know she had changed her mind. I told myself I was going to be calm and collected, but when I got to her table, shit flew out of my mouth.

"Hey, Harper. Who's this asshole?"

I tried to sound friendly, but it came out as more of a growl. Her face flushed, and she glanced over at the dickhead. Yep. She was caught. He was looking between the two of us with confusion, and I almost started laughing because it was becoming clear to him that she was screwing us both over.

"Am I missing something, Harper? Who is this guy? You never mentioned you were seeing someone." The douchebag had hatred in his eyes when he looked at me, but he held back.

"This is-" I cut her off before she could finish.

"Jack. I was seeing her, but it looks like she's just as much a slut as she was the first day we met."

Okay. That was a little harsh, but come on. Moving on to the next guy without so much as a word to the one she was seeing? Slut.

Harper stood abruptly and took my hand, dragging me to the door. I glanced over to the table where my friends were to see disappointment on all their faces, but they were glaring at me. Yeah, I was being a dick. I called her out in front of the whole bar, and that wasn't cool, but I was pissed. As soon as we were out the door, Harper whirled on me.

"What the hell was that? I'm a slut now? How dare you say that shit to me. I thought we had something happening between us, but trust me, that is so over now."

"I thought we had something too, but you're in there rubbing up against that prick, and you haven't even bothered to contact me all week. Is that why you said you were tired the other night? Didn't want to sleep with me because you were already moving on to someone else?"

My eyes drilled into her with accusation. She didn't even try to look sorry. She looked pissed at me, and I couldn't figure out why she would be pissed at me when she was the two-timing slut.

"Is everything okay here?" A petite brunette walked up and laid a hand on Harper's shoulder.

"Everything's fine, Anna. Luke's inside waiting. Congratulations on the engagement, but I can't stay. Have a good night," she said with a hug. Then she turned around and headed to her car. I watched her walk away, and only felt slightly better that I had gotten that off my chest. But then I started replaying her words to her friend in my head as I walked back into the bar.

Did she just say....?

I glanced over to where Harper had been sitting and saw Anna kissing the guy. Oh fuck. I was such a dip shit. Harper was here to celebrate with her friend, and I had called her a slut and accused her of cheating on me. I ran my hands down the back of my neck and cursed myself for being such an asshole.

"Uh, dude, what happened?" Ryan asked.

"I'm a fucking idiot, that's what happened. I need to find a way to make this up to Harper".

"Good luck with that. You just called her a slut in front of the whole bar. You'll be lucky if she doesn't cut off your balls the next time she sees you," Logan replied as he took a swig of his beer.

"I need to take care of this now. I really fucked up. Shit!"

I banged the table with my fists and stood. I walked out the door and headed to my truck. We hadn't been dating long, so the odds of her taking me back weren't good. Even if I apologized, that wouldn't change the fact that I had called her out in front of a crowd of people without talking to her first. The only excuse I had was that I was exhausted and wasn't thinking straight, and I was pretty sure that wouldn't fly with her. I headed over to Harper's place and tried the buzzer, but she didn't answer. I continued to ring it for five minutes with no response. I tried calling her, but she kept sending me to voicemail. The only thing left for me to do was send her a few texts to apologize and hope she read them.

Please call me back.
I am such a fucking idiot.
Please let me explain.

When she didn't respond to any of them after five minutes, I sent one last text to her.

If you think you can ever forgive me, please call. Give me a chance to explain and make things right.

. . .

I got back in my truck and sat there for a half hour more hoping she would respond. She never did, so I started up my truck and went home. I waited a week and heard nothing from Harper. She stopped by the shop several times when I had been gone to check on her bill. Every time she was told a different story. The last time, Sal told her to contact me directly, but she absolutely refused. Her refusal to speak to me was the final nail in my coffin. I went from being depressed to being downright angry. I was an ass to everyone I came across. I had something really good with her and I blew it. She was a funny, down to earth girl, and the sex was amazing. How often did you meet someone that you connected with right away? I prayed that she would eventually forgive me, but I didn't hold out hope.

The guys came over the following Saturday night for poker. It had been two weeks since I had last spoken to her and it was becoming clear that I would never hear from her again. I pulled into my driveway at six and started to get set up for the game. I wasn't in the mood to play poker, but the distraction would help. When the guys all got there, we ordered pizza, and I passed around the beer.

"Have you heard from Harper?" Logan asked.

Shit. I was hoping for just one night that I didn't have to think about her.

"Gee, don't beat around the bush. Let's get right down to it."

"Someone's got to, man. You look like shit, and you're not gonna fix it by moping around. Man the fuck up and get your girl back," Cole replied as he took a swig of beer. Everyone stared at Cole for a minute. "What? We were all thinking it. I just said it."

"And what exactly am I supposed to say that fixes calling her a slut?"

"Dude, I'm not a fucking girl. I don't have the first clue, but sitting around here moping isn't gonna do a damn thing." He paused as everyone looked around for someone to speak words of wisdom. "Alright, poker night cancelled. Let's sit down and devise a plan for getting Harper back. Logan, you take notes. Ryan, get more beer. Sean, find out her friend, Anna's number. Sebastian, start doing backgrounds on candidates for an office manager. Jack, sit your ass in the chair. Let's get this shit worked out, boys."

"I'll get the nail polish," Logan smirked. He got several funny looks.

"What? Are we not doing each other's nails at this sleepover?"

CHAPTER 9

HARPER

I HAD BEEN miserable the past two weeks. How had I been so wrong about Jack? He seemed to genuinely care about me, but then he didn't call me for a week. He stopped by, but he was gone in the morning without saying goodbye or leaving a note. I knew he was busy, so I gave him space. When I didn't hear from him over the weekend, I decided to make other plans. Anna was back from her grandma's, and she brought great news. Luke had finally proposed. I had known Luke since we were kids, and he was like an older brother to me. He didn't take too kindly to Jack calling me a slut, but he always tried to not interfere.

I had introduced Anna to Luke a few years ago, and they had hit it off right away, but they were both trying to settle into their careers and wanted to be stable before getting married. They had been talking about getting married for over a year now, so it was inevitable, but I was over the moon when she told me. We were supposed to get together that night and have a celebratory drink. Anna was running a few minutes behind, so I sat and talked with Luke, telling him how happy I was for him. I had never considered that I would run into

Jack, or that he would automatically assume that I was cheating on him.

Then again, we had never discussed being exclusive, so even if I had been hitting on Luke, he couldn't be upset. What hurt the most was that he had called me a slut without even letting me explain. I had never been promiscuous. I always waited an appropriate amount of time to sleep with any guy. With him it was different. There was an energy between us. I didn't feel guilty about sleeping with him so fast because it all felt so right. It really hurt to have that thrown in my face.

He had tried to get ahold of me later that night, but I didn't want any excuses. If he would go off on me for something like that without talking to me, how did I know he wouldn't respond that way in the future? The fact was that I couldn't trust him. No matter how intense the attraction, I needed to feel safe and secure and I didn't feel that with him.

I decided the next day that I needed to cut all ties to him. I drove past his shop and stopped in when his truck was gone. I tried to pay the bill, but the man, Sal, said that the computer was down and to come back another time. The next time I stopped in, Sal told me that the computer wouldn't pull up my file, and they had already shredded the paper copy. The third time I showed up, I demanded to speak with someone else, but Sal told me there was no one else that could run the computer. I waited for him to pull up my receipt, and he made up an excuse that the parts were listed at the wrong price and he couldn't give me a bill. He gave me a card with Jack's name and number and told me not to stop in again unless I talked to Jack first. Unbelievable! I just wanted to pay a bill! There was no way I was contacting Jack. If he wanted me to pay for my car repairs, he would have to send me a bill.

I needed a distraction from my loneliness, so I threw myself into finishing my book. The editor had sent back my book with changes that needed to be made. I made the changes and checked one last time for anything that needed an edit, then I sent off the book to the publisher. I had a few ideas swirling around in my head for a new book and started making notes on what I wanted the book to be about and background on the characters. I was a romance author, and frankly, after what I just went through with Jack, I was having a hard time finding inspiration. Most of my thoughts revolved around a woman falling for a man and then wanting to take a hunting knife to his balls. Not very romantic. Or a couple that goes skydiving, and the woman pushes him out of the plane...without a parachute. I came up with the idea for a young couple in love, and then the man gets a disease and suffers a slow, painful death. The more I thought about it, I realized that one might be offensive to people that were actually suffering from a slow-moving disease, and thought I would steer clear of anything to do with that. Except maybe Ebola. Hmm. Interesting idea. Just something to keep in mind.

Shelley had let me know they needed to hire another waitress at the restaurant part time. I insisted that I could take on the extra hours because I was between books and I could use the extra income. For the past week, I had been working a shift and a half every night. When I got home, I was exhausted, but it helped me sleep. I was so depressed when I was home because all I did was think about Jack. I had to leave the apartment to write, going to the coffee shop or the library, otherwise I sank into a funk. My appetite had vanished, and most days I could barely stomach crackers. I had lost at least five pounds in the last two weeks. My cheeks looked sunken in and I had dark circles under my eyes. I got a few hours of sleep every night, but I always woke up early because my brain couldn't shut down. I was a wreck.

By the end of the third week post-Jack, everyone seemed to be worrying about me. Shelley had asked me to slow down and told me if I didn't start eating and getting sleep over the next week, she would take away the extra shifts I had been given. Anna stopped by most days with an excuse of needing help with wedding planning. She never had a whole lot to work out. She always seemed to know what she wanted already and only wanted confirmation from me. The last time Anna stopped by, I told her to save it all for one visit next week or I wouldn't be helping her anymore. I didn't need to be babied, I just needed some time to get over it.

Anna called Wednesday and made plans for the two of us to go out Friday night. No excuses. Anna said she really needed the break, and I needed to clear my head. I was all dressed up in a tight, red dress with my hair and makeup done. Sadly, the clothes didn't fit as well as they used to, but it would have to do for tonight. I ran downstairs and met Anna, and we were off to our destination. Anna said she would drive because I needed to drink more than she did. We started heading out of town, and Anna told me we were going to a country line dancing club in the country. I wasn't really dressed for it, but I was more concerned about drinking tonight than dancing. Halfway there, I realized this route looked very familiar.

"Where are we going?"

"To that new club I was telling you about. It's about another ten minutes away."

I sighed. "Would it happen to be anywhere near Jack's house?"

"Listen, Harper, I know that you think you're handling this breakup well, but you really aren't."

"I'm doing just fine."

"Really? Then why are you wearing two different shoes?" I glanced down at my heels and frowned. "The other day when I came over, you had Cheetos stuck in your hair and drool on your face."

"I had just woken up," I said indignantly.

"It was two o'clock in the afternoon! You've lost at least ten pounds, and let's face it honey, your boobs are not the place for you to lose weight." I stared at my friend in shock. "Your boobs were perfect and now they're small. They're called fun bags for a reason."

Who was this person? What happened to sweet Anna? It didn't feel very good to be told you looked like shit. I thought we were in for a fun night, but instead, I was being ambushed about my appearance and forced to see the one man I never wanted to lay eyes on again.

"Can you drive me back home, please?"

"Sorry, honey. I can't watch you do this to yourself anymore. You and Jack are gonna have it out and end it properly or get back together, but either way, I am getting my friend back."

We pulled up outside Jack's cabin and he was standing there waiting for me. This was all one big setup and I had fallen for it. I glared at Anna as the car came to a stop.

"If you need a ride home, call me in the morning, but not before eight. You two need a while to hash it out, and I won't be coming before then."

She shooed me out the door, and I reluctantly stepped out of the vehicle. I didn't have much of a choice. I supposed that I could have sat there, but right now, I wasn't sure whose company I would rather be in. She pulled out with a cloud of dust trailing behind her. I stood there staring at the retreating car, vowing that I would not forgive her for a very long time. At least a week. Maybe I'd even pick out a hideous dress for her wedding and drink myself silly, giving her the most embarrassing maid of honor speech. I smirked at my evil plan when I heard Jack behind me. I immediately wanted to punch him.

"Harper. Are you coming in or staying out here with the coyotes?"

I stomped up to the house and shoved past him, making sure to shove my shoulder into him. If he wanted me here, fine, but I wasn't playing nice. I took off my shoes and made my way over to the fridge. If we were gonna have it out, I was gonna need liquor. I whirled around and started my inquiry.

"So, how did you manage to get Anna on your side? Did you tell her about how you called me a slut and accused me of cheating on you with her fiancé?"

I glared at Jack. He had his hands shoved in his pockets and he glanced away. I could see that he wasn't doing so well either. His hair hadn't been cut and he had quite a beard growing. His clothes were wrinkled, and he looked like he hadn't slept much either. Good. At least this wasn't easy on him.

"I said some pretty shitty things to you the last time I saw you.

There's no excuse for what I did, and I know saying sorry isn't enough. I talked with Anna at the beginning of the week and explained to her what happened. She told me if I wanted you back, there had to be changes."

He looked back at me, and I felt his eyes bore into my soul. It was intense and if he kept staring at me like that, I might lose my nerve and fall into his arms. I squared my shoulders and stood taller, refusing to give in to him.

"I'm not used to being held responsible by someone else in my life. I always come home when I want, and I don't think much about contacting other people when I'm busy. I know that was part of the problem. I wasn't there and even though we were new, that's when I should have been present the most if I wanted this to work."

"Jack, there is no us to get to work. We're done."

He continued on like I hadn't just told him we were over.

"I hired an office manager at the garage. Now I can spend my days working in the garage and not on office shit that's backing up. This last week, we've been out every night at six. I know that we're both busy, me with the garage and you with writing, but I am making the effort to be more available."

"That's really sweet, but not what the main problem is. You're an asshole, and I don't want to be with you."

"I know. I'm...overprotective and domineering. I like things to go my way, and I don't like to be second-guessed. That became pretty clear the first day we met. I overreacted when I saw you with that guy. I didn't stop to think that he was a friend, because I just assumed you didn't want me since I hadn't heard from you. I hurt you and made you feel like you were trash, when you are the furthest thing from that. The guys knew it right then that I had made a huge mistake. I just couldn't see past my jealousy."

He looked down for a minute and I just stood there unsure of what to say. He sounded so sincere, but I wasn't sure I could give in. He was saying this now, but would his jealousy always take over? I didn't want to be second-guessed all the time. When he looked back up, I could see in his eyes how much he wanted me back. His eyes were fierce, and he spoke with such determination that I was inclined to believe every word he said.

"I promise, if you give me another chance, I will never hurt you that way again. I can't promise I won't fuck up, because I am a guy after all. I'm sure I'll say something to piss you off. I promise to treat you with the respect you deserve. I promise to always give you the benefit of the doubt. Most of all, I promise to give you the love you deserve because I know I was falling before we broke up."

I tried to hold back, but a small smile escaped before I could stop it. He was trying his best to be sweet, but I wasn't a sap, so I did what I do best. I pierced him with my best glare that said no one would ever find his body if he crossed me again.

"Don't fuck up again."

I stepped forward into his arms and kissed him. His hands trailed down my back and then lifted my dress up over my hips. He grabbed me by the ass and I instinctively wrapped my legs around his waist. He set me down on the table and pushed me back so I was lying down. He pressed hot kisses over my ankles and up my legs to my inner thighs. He lightly kissed over my panties before kissing down the other leg. I was getting wet and he continued to give hot, wet kisses to my inner thighs, teasing me and leaving me wanting more. My pussy was pulsing with need, but he still wouldn't touch me. Enough of this shit. I grabbed his hair and pulled his face up to look at me.

"It has been three fucking weeks. I don't want sexy and slow. I want you to put your mouth on my pussy and make me come."

"The lady gets anything she asks for tonight, but she is going to have to ask," he said with a grin.

"Just fuck me."

"Yes, ma'am."

The panties were ripped from my body as Jack leaned in and licked my pussy. There was no way I would last with him licking my clit like that. I exploded in his mouth, but he wouldn't let up. He continued to suck on my tender flesh until I was shaking uncontrollably. He stood up and looked at me with heat in his eyes. Then he licked his lips and moaned so indecently that my pussy trembled.

He yanked me up by the arm and wrapped me around his body. I could feel his erection pushing against me as he carried me out of the kitchen. I needed him badly, and my body had a mind of its own as my pussy started grinding against his erection. I kissed him with all the need I was feeling, and he started bumping into things in the living room, not paying attention to where he was going. Having had enough, he finally just threw me down on the couch. My dress was ripped from my body, and his gaze locked onto my breasts. I was suddenly aware of how small they had gotten and I covered myself as I flushed in embarrassment. He pulled my hands away and started suckling my nipples through my bra.

"God, I love your tits. Have I ever told you how perfect they are?"

He ground his hips into me until I couldn't take anymore.

"Take your pants off and fuck me."

"All you had to do was ask."

"I did," I said indignantly as I smacked him.

He quickly undressed, and I noticed that he had also lost some definition in his body over the past three weeks. It looked like I wasn't the only one suffering. He quickly erased those thoughts from my head when he dragged me over the side of the couch. He bent me over and spread my legs, then thrust his hard cock inside me.

"Oh, God. That feels so good," I moaned. He thrust in and out, slowly at first, but then started to build speed. "Yes! Fuck me hard, Jack. I want it hard."

He started pounding into me, and then I felt his thumb brush the entrance of my ass. I shuddered at the feeling. I had never been touched there, and I was a little nervous about it. He moved his fingers to my clit and started to massage, then he brought my juices to the tight ring of my ass and slowly inserted his thumb. The pain made me gasp and I moved forward to get away from it, but he continued to push his thumb in and out. I got used to the sensation and after a few minutes, the pain went away, and I found myself wanting more. I pushed back against him and felt his thumb push deeper inside me.

"Do you want my cock in here?"

Part of me wanted it, but the other part of me was still nervous. He continued to play with my ass, and I moaned at the pressure.

"Yes, Jack."

"Have you ever had it before?"

"No."

"Okay. We'll go slow."

He removed his thumb and then shoved his cock back inside my pussy and fucked me hard. His hands made their way back to my nipples. The pinching and pulling had me clenching around him as I started to come. Moments later, he came shouting my name, and then collapsed on top of me. When his breathing returned to normal, he pulled out, and I could feel him leaking down my legs.

He picked me up and carried me to the bathroom where he cleaned me up. My legs were boneless and I was grateful to him for doing the heavy lifting. My eyes grew heavy and my energy was completely sapped. The last few weeks, followed by makeup sex, had finally taken its toll on me. He laid me down in the bed and held me, rubbing small circles on my stomach. The window was open and I could hear the crickets outside. It was calming, and I found it quite easy to drift off to sleep, thinking it would be nice to have this every night.

CHAPTER 10

JACK

THE NEXT FEW weeks were filled with lots of sex and many sleepovers. There was hardly a night that we didn't see each other. Most nights, Harper came to my house after work since she got off later than I did. I used those nights to catch up on any extra work that had to be done at the garage. Harper had started writing a new book, and usually worked on it at my house in the morning while I was gone. Her stuff had started to take over my closet, but it made sense. Otherwise, she would be hauling a bag back and forth.

We were getting ready to go to The Pub on a Saturday night she was able to get off. We were meeting the guys, Anna, and Luke down at the bar. Harper came out of the bedroom dressed in tight jeans, a white t-shirt, and cowboy boots. Her hair was in loose waves down her back. She looked damn sexy.

I had been thinking about asking her to move in with me, and I knew that I had to tread carefully or she would shut me down. She was very independent, and I didn't think I had a good chance of her saying yes, but I had to try to get her out of that shit hole she called home. It wasn't safe, and I hated her staying there.

"So I've been thinking, maybe we should consider you moving in here."

"Um, thanks, but I'm gonna keep my apartment."

She smiled at me and went back to the bedroom. She hadn't even thought about it, just brushed me off. She was supposed to at least consider it. She came back out a minute later putting in earrings. I wasn't backing down that easily. She needed to at least hear me out.

"I think we need to talk about this some more."

"Talk about what?"

I looked at her incredulously and started to fume.

"You know what." I was getting pissed. "You practically live here already. Your shit takes up over half my closet. This is the next logical step. Besides, your place is a shit hole, and I don't like you staying there. It isn't safe." With every word, my voice grew louder until I was practically shouting at her. She very calmly walked over to me, but I could see the anger brewing in her eyes. Shit. I fucked that up.

"That shit hole is all I can afford. I'm working double shifts so that I can live there. And in case you've forgotten, you put three locks on my solid oak door, so I'm pretty sure it's safe."

Her hands were on her hips and she was breathing heavily trying to control her temper. She never looked sexier than when she was pissed.

"Look, if you gave up your apartment and moved in here, you wouldn't have to work so much and you could focus on writing. You wouldn't have to work at all if you didn't want to. I can take care of you. I make enough money for both of us to live comfortably."

"So now I need to be taken care of? Pretty soon, I'll be staying here ironing your socks and cooking all your meals for you!"

"I wouldn't say no to that."

I had meant it as a joke, but based on the look on her face, she didn't find it funny.

"So, let's say I give up my apartment. We've known each other for two months. What happens if we get in a fight, like right now, and we go our separate ways? Or you become a huge ass, and I decide to cut off your balls? Or a car falls on top of you because someone, maybe me, lets the jack down with you under it? Then where do I go? What do I do for a job?"

"Okay, I'm going to take that comment sarcastically and assume you wouldn't actually try to castrate me or murder me at my job."

"Take it however you want. I'm just throwing out some 'what ifs'. Jack, this is still too new and I'm not going to change my way of life to live with some guy that I met two months ago!"

Coldness seeped into my bones. I was trying to move forward with her and she was thinking of things that were going to pull us apart. She didn't give a fuck about me. I got that moving in might be too fast, but *some guy*? I guess I didn't really know her all that well. I put my hands in my pockets because I was about two seconds from hitting something.

"*Some guy*, huh? Is that what I am to you? Just some guy you're fucking? Ya know what, how about we table this discussion for now. The guys are waiting on us."

I turned around and walked out the door, not really caring if she followed at this point. She did follow me and climbed into the truck, slamming the door. The drive to The Pub was uncomfortable, but I wasn't going to try to fix that. All I wanted to do right now was get a drink and forget that conversation. I walked right up to the bar and ordered some drinks. I drank down a shot and then carried my other drink over to the table where the guys were sitting.

"Did you get me a drink?"

Harper looked around for her drink and then at me. I sneered at her. She could get her own fucking drink.

"Nah. I wouldn't want you to think that I'm taking care of you. Ya know, you have to be able to order your own drinks in case we get in a fight and I leave you."

I downed my drink and slammed it on the table. Everyone at the table fell silent and stared at the two of us. This had not been my intention. I didn't want to drag others into our fight, but my head was itching for a fight. Harper walked over to the bar and ordered a drink. Anna left to go talk to her.

"What the fuck was that, man?" Luke looked over at me in disbelief.

"I asked her to move in with me, and she basically told me no, because we were gonna end eventually."

The whole table sat in stunned silence. They all knew how I felt about her, and I didn't think they were too happy about it either, but they were trying not to say anything. Harper and Anna returned a few minutes later with some drinks. Harper set one down in front of me. I couldn't help the comment that flew out of my mouth.

"Do I need to worry about this being poisoned?"

Harper turned to me with a glare. "Excuse me?"

"Well, I mean, you already told me that you had plans to murder me at work. Figured maybe this was a sneak attack."

Sean turned to Harper. "Seriously? You told him you had plans to murder him?"

"No, I was posing a scenario in which we wouldn't be together anymore."

"And one of those scenarios was you murdering him."

Harper started to get flustered and couldn't find the right words to say. I inwardly laughed. The guys were just busting her chops, but I thought it was hilarious. She got herself into this, and she could get herself out.

"I was just... I was saying that people break up, and it's not smart to move in together."

Cole was the next to speak up. "So, he asks you to move in, and you plot to murder him?"

I tried to hold back the laughter. She was making a total ass out of herself. I could jump in and try to help explain, but she kinda deserved this. When she got mad, she made some pretty crazy comments. It was one of the things I loved about her, but right now, it made her sound crazy as fuck.

Sebastian handed me his business card. "Just in case you decide you need some extra security. Remember what she can do with a paintball gun."

"Look," Harper snapped, obviously not enjoying their banter as much as I was, "this ass suggested that we move in together and that he 'take care of me'. I was just saying that it wouldn't be smart because if something happened, it would leave me out in the cold."

Logan looked at me with a baffled expression. "Total asshole move, dude. What were you thinking, offering to take care of your girlfriend?" Logan turned to Harper. "If you ever do decide to take care of him, you give me a call. I have plenty of places to bury a body." The whole table erupted in laughter and Harper stalked off toward the bar.

Anna turned a glare on the entire table. "You don't have to be such assholes. That conversation was taken out of context. You guys sure know how to make someone feel like shit." She turned and stormed off, and we all looked at each other, then broke into laughter again.

Later that night, Anna and Luke challenged Harper and me to a round of darts. Harper was pretty good. Apparently, she used to play in college quite a bit. We were on our second game, and I had just gone to remove my darts when I suddenly felt a sharp pain in my shoulder. I glanced over my shoulder and saw a dart sticking out of my back.

"What the fuck?" I pulled the dart and glanced over at Harper to see an innocent look on her face. Or as innocent as Harper could pull off. That woman was the devil.

"Oops. Looks like I missed the board. My bad."

"My bad? You threw a fucking dart at my back. Is this another scenario where you would accidentally get rid of me?"

"It just slipped. Maybe you shouldn't be standing in front of the board."

I stalked over to Harper, grabbed her hand, and pulled her down the hallway toward the bathrooms. I was seriously pissed off, and this shit was going to end one way or the other. Either she changed her attitude or I would change it for her. I pushed her up against the wall and pushed my leg between her legs. Her attitude, as shitty as it was, turned me on, and I was ready to fuck her up against the wall. I grabbed her knee and pulled it up against my hip, drawing her body closer to mine. I leaned in and scraped my teeth along her jaw.

"Is that what this is coming to Harper? Throwing darts at me? Do you really not want me anymore?"

I kissed down her neck and back up to nibble on her ear. My thumb was rubbing against her knee, itching to move further up her leg. Her breathing was harsh against my skin, and I could feel her heart thumping wildly against my chest.

"I want you to be with me, Harper, and I'm not gonna apologize for wanting to take care of you." I leaned forward and kissed her hard, then pulled back and whispered in her ear. "But you've gotta make up your mind. Either you're in this with me or you're out. No more giving me scenarios or what ifs. I want all of you. Now you have to decide if you want me too." I rubbed my nose against hers. "What's it gonna be, pretty girl?"

She clutched my shoulders and her breath tickled my face. I could see that she was struggling with my demands, but I knew she wanted me as much as I wanted her.

"I want you too."

That was all I needed. The rest could be worked out later, but for right now, I needed this woman in my bed, and she would stay there if she knew what was good for her. She could keep running from me, but I would always find a way to drag her back into my arms.

"Let's get outta here before I fuck you against the wall."

I grabbed her hand and dragged her out the door. We headed back to her place because it was closer, and spent the whole night making up. The next morning, I woke before Harper and went to the kitchen to make coffee. Since Harper had been staying with me, there wasn't really anything to make for breakfast. I found some breakfast bars and set those out. As I sat in the kitchen, I looked around at Harper's stuff. We were going to have a long talk about living together. It was ridiculous to keep shuffling back and forth.

Harper came out a half hour later and shuffled over to the coffee pot. She gave me a kiss and sat down at the table.

"Good morning."

"Morning, baby. You ready to talk about this?"

Harper nodded and took a long drink of coffee.

"I want you to move in with me. I know you want someplace to go that's yours, but baby, it's ridiculous to keep a separate place for yourself. I'm not leaving you, and you need to get that idea through your head. If you moved in with me, you could cut back on work. Just imagine how much time you would have to write if you didn't have to work so much. I'm just asking you to lose the extra shifts you've been picking up. Then, down the line, if you need more time for writing, you can stop working and just write. We could spend more time together and we wouldn't have to try and work out whose place to go to every night."

"Jack, that's all great, but I like that I have my own space that I can come to."

"Baby, we can add on to the house and give you your own home office or chill room. Whatever you want. Besides, if you're not paying rent, you can afford to buy a better car and I won't be worrying about you stuck on the side of the road in that death trap. There are so many positives to this."

She thought about it for a moment and she looked around her place.

"If I agree to this, you need to give me space when I need it."

"Agreed. I need to be able to hang out with the guys also. Living together doesn't mean we spend every moment together."

Harper drank her coffee in silence for a few minutes while she thought it over. "Okay. Let's do this."

CHAPTER 11

HARPER

THE NEXT SATURDAY, Anna came over to help me start packing. During the week, I had slowly moved over the rest of my clothes and bathroom supplies to Jack's house. Jack and I had gone through all of my kitchen stuff and decided what to keep and what to put in a garage sale. Then we went through the living room and bedroom. Logan decided to have a garage sale at his house that all our friends were contributing to. We were going to have it in a week, so I had to hurry up and pack up whatever was going to Jack's.

"So how did Jack convince you to move in with him?" Anna asked as she loaded another box.

"I don't know. He just seemed to genuinely want me to be with him, and he wanted to help me achieve my goals. I guess I just needed him to show me that it wasn't just about having a good time. He said that we could build on to the back of his house to give me an office or some space that was just mine. I don't know if he was serious, but that would be pretty cool."

"Sounds like love to me." Anna started making kissy faces at me.

"I don't know that we're there yet. I mean, I really like him, and I'm sure I'm not far off, but I'm in no rush to say it. We have this explosive chemistry, but sometimes he makes me so mad I want to take an axe to his balls."

"Is this where all the murdering came into play?"

"Yes, we were arguing about things that could happen to make us break up, and I may have taken things too far. They were some pretty creative ideas, if I do say so myself."

"So, he's gonna build you a room to write in?"

"Well, after I stubbornly agreed to move in, we sat down and talked about how to make this really work so we aren't in each other's space. He suggested building a room for me that could be for me to work in, but would also function as a getaway for me. It could have a reading nook or a cozy area for friends to come hang out. That way if we both have friends over, we aren't talking tampons while he's trying to watch the game."

"I hear ya there. It's totally different living with a man. Women are all alike, for the most part. I will never understand how men bond over football and beer. There isn't actually any conversation that has any meaning. I mean, sure they talk about the game, but the most in depth answer a guy will give is *I'm doing good, man,*" Anna mimicked in a deep voice.

I laughed, "Yeah, men don't do talking very well. I think that's my biggest reservation about moving in with him. We get along great, and I really, really like him. I just don't feel like we ever talk about anything. I asked him the other night to tell me something he really wanted to do and he said *travel*. I asked him to elaborate and he looked at me all confused. Like why would I need more explanation?"

"Well, maybe now that you'll be living with him, you'll just pick up on stuff and then eventually he'll share more with you." We both burst out laughing at the absurdity of the statement. Yeah, because men were so simple.

I set to work on unloading my bookcase into smaller boxes and marking them. Then, I moved on to photo albums, paperwork, and knicknacks. By the time we finished with boxing up the smaller items, it was lunch time. We went down to the sub shop and were climbing the stairs to my apartment when Anna stopped in her tracks.

"Harper, you locked the door when we left, didn't you?"

I looked at the door, worry swirling in my gut. This was why Jack didn't want me living here. It was a shady building, and there had been quite a few robberies here. I was just shocked that it hadn't happened before now, but I was amazed it had happened since Jack had the door reinforced.

"Yeah, I did." I started to approach the door and Anna grabbed my arm.

"Wait! You can't just walk in there. Whoever broke in could still be there," she whisper-hissed.

"I don't hear anything. I'm sure it's fine. You stay out here and I'll check it out."

"Yeah right. You know what's worse than Jack finding out you went in there? If I let you go in alone."

We pushed the door open and were relieved to see an empty apartment. Nothing appeared to be out of place, but we couldn't see into the kitchen, the bedroom, or the bathroom. Anna tiptoed through the living room toward the kitchen. She peered stealthily around the wall and saw the kitchen was empty. Anna shot me some hand signals, pointing with her fingers and making various hand gestures. I mouthed back to Anna that I didn't understand and threw out a few of my own hand gestures. We kept going like this back and forth until we heard a noise from the bathroom. My heart ramped up, and I grabbed the first thing I could find, which was a rolled-up poster. I clutched it in my hands like a baseball bat. Anna grabbed the dining room chair and held it like a lion tamer. We headed toward the bathroom, arms raised, wielding our weapons.

"Really? A poster? That's what you're going with?" Anna whispered to me.

"What are you going to do with a chair? Politely ask him to sit down and explain why he's trying to rob me? Maybe make him some tea and scones?"

It was a little habit of mine to become extremely sarcastic when I was in an uncomfortable situation or when I was scared. I didn't want to appear weak to others, so that's how my fear manifested.

As we were whispering back and forth, the door creaked open and it didn't register until a large figure stepped out. We both screamed and I swung the poster with all my might at the intruder's head. Anna lifted the chair over her head and smashed the chair to little bits over his back. Even after he fell, I continued to assault the man until I was sure he wasn't moving. We both stood there heaving for several minutes, arms still raised until we were sure he wasn't going to move.

I looked over at Anna and saw that all that was left of the chair was one of the legs. Then I looked down at my poster and saw it was all bent and mashed up.

"Aww, man. I mashed my poster. I'll never be able to use this again," I whined.

"You're never going to be able to use this chair again either."

"You really beat the shit out of him with that chair."

"Don't be too hard on yourself. I'm sure you gave him quite a few paper cuts with that poster. Those hurt like a bitch," Anna said fiercely.

"You bet your ass I did," I said triumphantly. We looked at each other and then burst out laughing. Anna had tears shooting from her eyes, literally. I clutched at the pain in my side from laughing so hard.

"I mashed my poster," Anna said mockingly. We were caught up in another round of laughter when there was a pounding on the door, followed by a few large men entering the apartment.

"Police, freeze! Put your hands in the air. Drop your weapons!"

We whirled around at the command, and I really tried, but when he told me to lower my weapon, I started laughing again. Did a poster really count as a weapon? We were both still poised for an attack when I finally calmed down enough to realize there were guns pointed at us, and the officers weren't looking too jovial. I slowly lowered my arms and whispered for Anna to do the same. Anna dropped the chair leg to the ground with a thud, and I cursed her for making the loud noise. I didn't really want to get shot because someone was trigger happy.

"We got a call about a possible break in. Is this your residence?"

That came from the hunk of beef standing in front of me. He was extremely sexy in his uniform, and my mind drifted to Channing Tatum. I perused his body, wondering if he ever did a striptease in that uniform, but then remembered Jack. Hey, a girl could look.

Hands still raised, Anna pointed a finger at me.

"Mind telling me what happened here and who the man on the floor is?" the first officer asked as he lowered his weapon.

I told the officer what happened from the beginning and watched the officer's face take on a look of disbelief.

"You came in here knowing there was someone inside?" That came from hunk of beef number two. Also a very good looking guy that could also do a Magic Mike for me at any time.

I rolled my eyes. "Of course we didn't know someone was in here. I didn't want to call the police if there was no one here. Besides, we handled it."

The second officer walked over to the man and checked his vitals, called it in, and put him in cuffs.

"Ma'am, in the future, please call the police and let us handle it."

I heard a ruckus in the hall, and heard Sean announcing himself before he and Jack entered. Jack was calling to me before he entered the apartment, and I looked at the ceiling, knowing this was going to be bad. This just proved his point that my apartment was unsafe. I would never hear the end of it.

"Harper! What the fuck?" They stopped inside the door when they saw the police officers and the man on the floor.

"Hey, Jack," I responded nonchalantly.

"Hey, Jack? I got a call from Sean saying there was a break in reported at this address. I was freaking out."

Jack walked over to me and pulled me into a tight squeeze. This wasn't the reaction I had been expecting. I thought he would come in and start lecturing me about how stupid it was to enter and how it wasn't safe for a woman to live here alone. I liked this Jack a lot better.

"We're okay, Jack. Anna beat him over the head with a chair."

"Yeah, and Harper beat him with a poster." Jack's head swiveled from me to Anna and then back to me.

"A poster? You couldn't find something....harder?"

I could tell he was trying not to fume, but he was also trying to disguise the fact that he thought I was an idiot. Yes, I beat up a man with a poster. In hindsight, I should have found something else, but at the time, I grabbed the first thing I saw.

The second police officer that was kneeling by the man spoke up. "This guy has quite a few paper cuts. That's gonna hurt like a bitch when he wakes up."

I glanced up and saw Jack glaring daggers at him. I couldn't help the grin that spread across my face.

"Why didn't you call me? Or the police? Anna, what were you thinking letting her come in here?"

And there it was. Caveman Jack was coming out in full force. He was practically shouting at Anna, and that really pissed me off. We were almost attacked by a robber, and we fought him off. I was still coming down from the adrenaline rush, and I had plenty of pent up anger to unleash.

"Please tell me you did not just ask why she *let* me come into my own apartment." I crossed my arms and glared at Jack.

"Dude, just shut the fuck up. It's not worth it right now," the first police officer whispered out of the corner of his mouth. Jack blew out a breath and took a minute to collect himself.

"Alright, baby. We'll talk about it later. Are you two alright?"

We both nodded, and Jack guided us over to the couch to sit down. After the ambulance came and collected the man, Anna and I gave our statements to the police officer. Jack told us we were done for the day and had me call off my shift for the night. Luke came by to pick up Anna and Jack took me home to have a stiff drink. He got on the phone to Cole and asked him to finish packing up the rest of the stuff with the guys, after he explained what happened. Then he called Sean and asked him to look into the robber and find out anything we needed to know. After that, he called Sebastian and asked for the number of the guy that trains police dogs. Jack had just finished up by the time we got back to his place.

I was exhausted and just wanted to relax in the bath. I soaked for a good hour and then got out and put on some comfy pajamas. When I came out, Jack had dinner waiting on the table. It was sweet because I usually did all the cooking. We ate in silence, and then I took a glass of wine and snuggled into the couch. Jack came and sat by me, and I knew he was about to start.

"You okay?"

"Yeah, I'm good. I'm just tired." I finished my glass of wine and set it on the coffee table.

"Harper, you scared the shit out of me today. Please promise me if that ever happens again, you will walk away and call the police."

"I promise."

I turned toward him and kissed him. I had to remember that it wasn't just me anymore, and I needed to consider Jack. Giving this promise would make Jack feel better and I would do anything to put him at ease.

"A friend of Sebastian's is coming over tomorrow with a protection dog. We'll see if he fits in here, and if he does, he'll be your dog."

"I don't take him everywhere with me, do I?"

"Not to work, but if you're going somewhere they allow dogs, I would prefer it."

I had never been a dog person, but decided I'd tested Jack's patience enough tonight. I was exhausted and wanted to go to sleep. The easiest way to achieve that would be to agree to his request.

"Okay, babe. If it makes you feel better, I'll do it."

CHAPTER 12

JACK

IT HAD BEEN a few months since the break in and everything was going great. The guys had helped me move the last of Harper's things to my place. We were now the proud owners of a German Shepherd protection dog, Hooch. He immediately took to Harper, and had been going everywhere with her ever since. We had spent the last few months settling in to a new routine around the house and working on plans for building an addition onto the house to make space for Harper to write. Her last book had done well so far, and I had been trying to convince her to leave her job waitressing to write full time. I hadn't had much luck yet, but I wasn't giving up.

Thanksgiving was approaching in the next few weeks, and I always did a celebration with my mom, Agnes. The first time Harper met my mother, she pulled Harper into a hug and told her she was so happy Harper had straightened out her son. They had gotten along well ever since and even set a lunch date for every Tuesday. Harper told me she was happy to get together with her, especially since she didn't get along with her own mother.

"Jack, I want to have a big Thanksgiving this year with all our friends and your mom. I have a schedule written out here with all the foods I want to make, prep times, and cook times. It's going to be flawless. I may have to start the night before to cook for that many people, but it will be so worth it."

"Baby, you know my mom will help in any way she can. She loves to cook as much as you do."

"I know, I've already enlisted her help. How do you think I came up with all the recipes? We've been working on it for the past month." Harper glanced down at what appeared to be a to-do list and checked off an item. "Now, I just need you to talk to the guys and see who's coming and if they're bringing someone with." She looked up at me expectantly.

"Like, right now?"

"Well, not right this minute, but soon. I want to be as prepared as possible for this. If this goes well, imagine what we could do at Christmas." Her eyes lit up as she spoke, but I wasn't a huge fan of celebrating at Christmas. "We can decorate the house and put up lights all over the place. It'll be so magical." She was smiling like crazy, and I really didn't want to wipe that smile from her face. God, I hated Christmas. Dad had died right around Christmas and it sucked. I didn't hold onto the anger anymore, but it was hard to be so happy when my dad wasn't there to celebrate with us. We had so many great Christmas traditions that just weren't the same without him.

"Maybe we don't have to think about Christmas yet. It's such a pain in the ass to get all that stuff out. Why don't we just put up a tree and leave it at that."

"What?! Just put up a tree? Are you crazy? I'll do all the work. You don't have to do a thing," she pleaded with me.

"No. We're not doing it," I snapped at her. "Look, I get that you like all this shit, but you aren't doing it by yourself because you'll fall off a ladder, and then I'll have to do it, and I don't want to do it. So the easiest solution is to not do it."

Harper stood there stunned, and I didn't miss the look of hurt on her face, but I couldn't deal with it right now. I wasn't used to sharing this crap with someone else. I always did my own thing, and I didn't think about anyone else. My mom didn't care that we downplayed Christmas, and that was all that mattered. In the back of my head, I knew it didn't work like that anymore, so I decided to take a breather and get my head on straight.

I grabbed my keys and left the house without another word. The final plans for the addition were over at Ryan and Logan's office, so I decided to go over there and make sure we were all set to start building. The whole way there, I thought about what an ass I had been, but shit, if I didn't want to do something, I shouldn't have to. That was the problem with relationships. All the sudden, what you wanted didn't matter.

I spent about an hour at the office working out the final details. They would be over to start work Monday morning. I had Ryan work with his interior decorator to come up with some sketches to show Harper. I was really excited to be able to do this for her. Maybe this would convince her to stop waitressing.

I wasn't ready to go home yet, so I ran around town doing errands for the garage, got some new work clothes, and picked up some stuff for dinner. When I got home, it was dark out and there was just a single light on in the house. As I approached the house, I heard Hooch whining, like he was in distress. When I opened the door and looked into the living room, I saw Harper on the floor in tears. Shit! Had I done this? I ran over to her and started rubbing her arms, trying to calm her down.

"Hey, baby. Tell me what's wrong."

I lifted her chin and saw tears streaming down her cheeks. A pain shot through my chest at the thought that I did this to her. Harper never cried. She was so strong.

"Baby, is this because of what I said before I left?"

She shook her head no, but continued to cry. She must have gotten horrible news. Had someone died?

"It's gonna be okay, honey. Just tell me what's wrong, and we'll figure it out together."

I leaned in and hugged her while placing kisses on her temple. Harper's breath started to hitch as she tried to talk, and I could barely make out what she was trying to say.

"I was....doing laundry...and the phone rang....Oh, God!" Harper started sobbing some more, and I knew this was going to be bad.

"Okay. What happened? Who was on the phone?"

"It was my mom. She said... Imgonnabea...." She started sobbing so hard I couldn't make out the last thing she said. I started rubbing her back in soothing circles. "She said I'm gonna be a sister." She was trying her best to stop crying, but the tears kept coming. I didn't know much about her mom, but I had a feeling that this meant she felt wronged or something.

"You don't want to be a sister?"

Her crying slowed and she looked up at me in confusion. "What? No that's fine. I don't really care about that. She...she married some rich guy that has a couple of kids."

"Ah, so you're upset because she didn't invite you to the wedding."

I got it now. She had been left out. That had to really suck because she was an only child and was now being shoved aside.

"No, I don't care about that either."

"Harper, if that isn't the problem, then what is?"

I was starting to lose my patience. I wanted to be there to console her, but spit it out already. *Just say what the problem is so I could fix it.*

"I was on the phone with her, and I decided that I was hungry. I made a sandwich, and the tomato slipped out of the sandwich and down my shirt. My favorite white shirt. It's completely ruined!" Harper started sobbing again.

What. The. Fuck. Had I come back to a different house? I had been gone, what, four hours? How did Harper go from my happy-go-lucky girlfriend to a sobbing mess on the ground over a tomato?

"Harper, seriously? It's a shirt. Throw it in the wash and put something else on."

She exploded off the ground. "It's a shirt?! How can you be such a moron? It was my favorite shirt, and now it's ruined. Ruined! Don't you see?"

I didn't see. Not at all. Who was this batshit crazy woman? Why would she be flipping out over a stain on a shirt? And then it struck me.

"Harper, is it that time of the month?"

"Oh, that's rich! I'm upset about something, so automatically I must have my period. Fuck off, jackass." She stormed out of the room and slammed the bedroom door. Looked like I would be sleeping on the couch tonight. Then she opened the door and yelled, "And you can forget about coming to bed tonight. Sleep on the couch, and if you even think of coming near me, I'll twist your balls until they turn blue, yank 'em off, and shove 'em down your throat!" She slammed the door again and I felt my balls crawl up inside my body, seeking protection.

Why did she always have to threaten my balls? Seriously, I had received more death threats from this woman in the four months I had known her than I had in my entire life. I walked back to the laundry room and looked at the stained shirt. I took out a bottle of Shout and sprayed it on the spot, then rubbed it in. While I let that sit, I threw in a load of laundry and unloaded my truck. I thought I would need to do some groveling, so I brought home Mexican for her because it was her favorite. It turned out that I needed it more than I originally thought. I chuckled to myself at how quickly this day had gone from bad to worse. I laid out the food on the table and decided it would be against my best interests to knock on the door. I did what any rational man would do when confronted with a crazy woman—I texted her that dinner was on the table.

A few minutes later, Harper came walking out of the room, stopping when she saw what was on the table. She ran over to me, and I flinched when she leapt toward me. She wrapped her arms around my neck and started kissing me. Seriously, this woman was bat shit crazy. She flew from one extreme to the other in a matter of minutes, and I didn't know how to handle her sometimes. I didn't dare touch her as she laid kisses all over my face. I wasn't sure what was going to happen next, and I wasn't sure I wanted to know. She pulled back with a huge smile on her face. My body slumped in relief at her reaction.

"You're the best, Jack. I can't believe you knew exactly what would make me feel better. You are amazing!" I stood there in stunned silence contemplating how to react. It was almost like she was a scared kitten. Make one wrong move and your eyes get clawed out. She sat down at the table and started eating. I took a seat across from her warily, watching her every move in case this was a trick. We ate in silence, and afterward, cleared the table. I brought out the plans I had picked up and laid them out on the table.

"What are these?"

"These are the plans for the addition. I had an interior designer come and look at the layout and put together some ideas for what we could do with the room."

Harper looked over the plans and smiled up at me. "Thank you so much. This is perfect." And just like that, I had been forgiven.

CHAPTER 13

HARPER

IT WAS the day before Thanksgiving, and I was running around to get last minute stuff done. There had been a slight miscommunication between Jack's mom, Agnes, and me. I thought Agnes was bringing the turkey over this afternoon, and Agnes thought I had bought a frozen turkey earlier in the week. So, with only a few hours to spare in my busy schedule, I ran out to the store for a fresh turkey. The first store I went to only had a frozen turkey, and I didn't think I could thaw it in time. The second store only had game hens left. So, here I was at the last store searching for a fresh turkey. I made my way over to the meat department and found one fresh turkey left. I was just picking it up when a little old lady put her hand on the turkey.

"Oh, dear. Is that the last one? My Alfred just loves turkey for Thanksgiving. He'll be absolutely heartbroken if I don't bring one home to him."

I felt bad, but I really needed this turkey.

"I'm really sorry. I would give this to you, but I have a whole house full of people coming over tomorrow." I started to put it in my cart when the little old lady spoke again.

"My Alfred and I have been together sixty-five years this Christmas. It may very well be our last Christmas together. The doctors have only given him a few months to live. Oh, you know doctors can be wrong, but I want to make every holiday count. I just want to have some good last memories with him." She wiped a tear from her eye, and I felt a pull at my heartstrings. I could figure something else out. I couldn't take away this woman's final Thanksgiving with her husband.

"Here. Why don't you take this turkey." I handed over the turkey, and I was sure the turkey would sink the old lady if she was in the ocean.

"Oh my. What a dear you are. I know God is smiling down on you. Such an angel." She turned away to put the turkey in the shopping cart. I started to look at what was left for buying. I could try to thaw a frozen turkey or I could buy a couple of turkey breasts and cook them. As I stood there deciding, I watched the little old lady hobble away and join a younger version of herself.

"Sucker. It works every time, dear. You just have to know how to pick 'em. I bet I could have gotten a whole Thanksgiving dinner out of that one." The little old lady told her daughter.

"That bitch!" I stormed over to the lady and yanked the turkey from her cart. "I'll be taking my turkey back now. Next time you want to scam someone, wait until you're out of earshot before you brag." I started to turn around when the little old lady started to cry out.

"Help! Help! This woman just stole my turkey from my shopping cart." I looked around and saw people sneering at me from all around the store. This was mortifying, but I wasn't going to be scammed by someone playing the sympathy card.

"Nice try, lady. I'm not giving it back." A store manager walked over to me and started to inquire about the disturbance.

"Excuse me, ma'am. Is there a problem?"

"Yes. This young gal just took my turkey that I planned to make for my poor, dying husband."

She started to cry and I narrowed my eyes at her. Oh, she was good. I wasn't about to be beaten though. Little old lady or not, I would win the battle.

"Actually, I had the turkey first, and this lady told me this sob story about her husband, but when she turned around she was laughing it up with Bonnie over here about scamming me out of a turkey."

"Hey, my name's not Bonnie."

"Well, you might as well be! Ya know, Bonnie and Clyde? You're the accomplice and she's the brains."

The store manager stepped in. "Look, I know things always get out of control at the holidays. Can we please work out an agreement over who is taking the turkey home? Let's not cause a scene in the middle of the store."

"It was my turkey first and I'm taking it home."

I started to step away from the woman, but the little old lady grabbed tight to the turkey.

"No, you will not. This turkey is for my dear husband." She yanked the turkey back towards her body.

"Give me my turkey back, you old hag!"

I yanked one final time and the turkey slipped from the old lady's grasp. However, I wasn't prepared, and I fell back a step and the turkey flew out of my arms. I heard a thunk and then something hit the floor. Cringing, I turned around to see a middle aged woman lying on the ground out cold. I stood there in shock. I had knocked out someone's mother. With a turkey. Holy crap, I was going to hell.

The store manager called security, and pretty soon, I was sitting in a back room being guarded until police arrived. What else could go wrong? I just wanted that damn turkey. Thank God it wasn't a frozen turkey, I thought with a frown.

The police arrived, and I explained my side of the story. They didn't seem too forgiving, though. They yanked me around and put me in cuffs. They were being kind of rough, and I didn't think this was the way it was supposed to go, but I wasn't that well informed on the law. I did however, have an in with a certain police officer.

"Please, call Sean. He's my friend."

"Yeah? What's his last name?"

One of the officers looked at me like he really would release me if I could just answer the question. Damn it. Why hadn't I ever thought to ask his last name?

"He's Officer Sean....Damn it. I don't know his last name, but his best friend is my boyfriend, Jack Huntley."

Officer number two stepped forward. "Hey, aren't you the lady that assaulted a robber with a poster?"

I rolled my eyes. It seemed like everyone in town had heard that story. "Yes, that was me."

"Yeah, we're definitely taking this one in. History of assault and all. First a poster. Now a turkey. At least she keeps it interesting." They dragged me off to the police car and shoved me into the back seat. The cuffs were digging into my wrists from how tight they cuffed me.

"Excuse me. Could you please loosen the cuffs a little? They're digging into my wrists."

"Oh, the princess wants us to loosen the cuffs. Why don't you go back there and take care of that, Stanley. Then, go get her a cup of coffee to warm her up."

When they laughed at me, I glared back at them. I wanted so badly to say something, but I was smart enough to keep my mouth shut and wait for my phone call. I sat in holding at the police station for four hours before I was allowed to make a phone call. I called Jack and told him he needed to come down to the police station right away and bring Sean with. He was down there twenty minutes later, and I could hear him yelling in the main area of the police station. I was still cuffed from earlier and I really had to pee. The door slammed open and I yelped in surprise, all while hoping my bladder would hold. Sean came storming into the room with anger all over his face.

"I'm so sorry, Sean. I swear I didn't mean to hurt anyone. It was an accident. I was just trying to get a turkey for tomorrow."

I was rambling and I knew it, but frankly, at this point I was lucky

I wasn't on the ground crying my eyes out. I had always been a trouble magnet, but never anything that involved the police. Now I had been involved with the police twice in less than six months. Sean walked over to me and knelt in front of me.

"Hey, Harper. It's okay. I'm not mad at you. I'm pissed because they didn't follow procedure. You should have had your phone call hours ago." Then he seemed to notice that my arms were still behind my back. He exploded. "What the fuck?"

He pulled out a key and quickly took the cuffs off my wrists. I sighed as the blood started flowing more smoothly through my hands. Sean held my hands and started massaging them. He stopped for a minute and was staring at the cuts that were on my wrists from where the cuffs were digging in. He was taking deep breaths in and out, trying to control his temper. His jaw was clenched so tight, I was sure he would break a tooth.

"Let's clean you up before Jack sees this and we have a murder on our hands."

"Um, Sean? Can I use the bathroom quickly?"

"Sure, sweetheart. Door is right across from here."

I quickly made my way to the bathroom and sighed in relief when I was done. When I came back into the room, there was a man waiting there for me. He had a medical bag and was pulling out items.

"Ms. Abbot, let me take a look at your wrists. Come sit down." I walked over to the table and took a seat. "I'm James. I'm a medic, and a friend of Sean's. He asked me to come take a look at you."

I smiled at him. "Thank you so much. I really appreciate it." He cleaned up the scrapes around my wrists and put some ointment on them and wrapped some bandages around them. "Try to keep them on for a few hours, but then by tomorrow, take them off so the air can help dry it up."

I turned to Sean as James left the room. "So, what's going to happen to me now?"

"Well, you, my dear, are free to go home. Jack is waiting for you in the lobby. Come on, I'll walk you out."

We started to leave when I remembered the lady from the store.

"Wait, what about that lady I knocked out with the turkey? Is she okay?"

"Yes, she's fine. She wasn't really out, more stunned. The mother wanted you charged with assault with a deadly weapon, but when the woman came to her senses, she asked us to drop the charges. Said it was an accident, and she didn't want to ruin anyone's Thanksgiving."

"Wow. That was really sweet."

Sean put a hand on my back and walked me out to the lobby. Jack had been pacing around, but when he saw me, he ran up to me and wrapped me in his arms. I had never been so relieved in my life. This had been a horrible day and I wanted to go home. When he saw the bandages around my wrists, he froze.

"What the fuck, Sean? You told me you would take care of her. Why does she have fucking bandages on her wrists?"

"Tweedle-dee and Tweedle-dum decided to wrap the cuffs on extra tight. They're currently getting an ass-chewing from the boss."

Jack nodded and then brought his attention back to me. "How are you, pretty girl?"

"I'm tired. Can we go home now?"

"Yeah, let's go home."

We had made it all the way out to the truck before I broke down in tears. I wasn't normally a crier, but this day was horribly humiliating. I was cuffed and dragged downtown. They had thrown me in a cell and forgotten about me. I had wanted Jack so badly, and he didn't even know I was in trouble. The part that upset me the most was that I didn't get what I needed for the feast tomorrow. I had planned everything perfectly, and now we didn't have everything we needed. My first Thanksgiving with Jack would be ruined. Jack pulled me into his arms and I felt his body vibrating in anger.

"Babe, I know that was scary, but it's over now. Let's go home and I'll draw a hot bath for you. Okay?"

"I'm not crying because of that, you idiot. I didn't get my shopping done, and that was the last fresh turkey. Now I have no turkey to cook for Thanksgiving, and half the ingredients I need for the other dishes are missing. Nobody is going to have anything to eat tomorrow. What are we gonna feed them?"

"I'll take care of it, babe. Let's just go home and I'll figure it out."

As he drove us home, the sway of the truck lulled me to sleep. I felt him lift me from the truck, but I was too tired to care. I hadn't realized how much of a toll this would take on my body. One minute I was in the air, and the next, I was wrapped in the comfort of my bed, where I slept for another three hours. It was almost five o'clock at night when I woke. I got up from bed, feeling much better, and made my way down the hall. I heard voices talking and recognized one of them as Sean. I entered the living room and saw Sean and another officer standing there.

"Uh.... What's going on? Am I in trouble again?" Sean smiled.

"No, darlin'. We brought you a little present." He hefted a bag up and pulled out a turkey. "We thought we'd return your deadly weapon to you."

I would have been excited, but after all that happened, I just couldn't find it in me to be happy. Still I put on a small smile for them.

"Thanks, guys. That's really great. I guess Thanksgiving won't be a total bust after all."

I took the turkey from Sean, ignoring the concerned look on his face, and went to stick it in the fridge. Then I went back to my room and crawled back into bed. I woke up in the middle of the night to feel Jack wrap himself around me.

"Baby, you can't let today get you down. We're still gonna have a great Thanksgiving."

"I just wanted it to be perfect. I've never had a perfect Thanksgiving. Mom never cooked, so we always ended up going to someone else's house. Dad tried to make it really special for me, but Mom always fought with him over something. She was always picking at him. They would end up arguing and we'd head home right after dinner. Kind of sucked all the fun out of Thanksgiving." I paused thinking about what my perfect day would look like. "I just always imagined cooking in the kitchen with family and sitting down to a nice, big meal, laughing at funny stories. Maybe next year." I fell asleep to Jack rubbing my arms lightly. It had been a crappy day, but lying here with Jack made it all better.

CHAPTER 14

JACK

I LAID in bed staring at the ceiling. I had no idea this day meant so much to her. I knew she was excited, but I didn't realize how badly she wanted all this. I wasn't going to let her down. After she fell asleep, I slid out of bed and headed downstairs to the kitchen. I had work to do.

Harper's shopping list was in her purse, so I called the one woman that could help, my mom. She had heard about the incident today and was very upset on Harper's behalf. I went through the list of things we still needed. Mom had a few of the items, and we both started calling people looking for the rest of the ingredients. After an hour, Mom called and said she had secured all the items from her list and would be over at six the next morning to get started. More at peace with tomorrow, I went to bed with every intention of making tomorrow perfect for Harper.

The alarm blared at 5:30, and even though staying in bed sounded wonderful, I was excited to get the day started. Harper didn't wake up with the alarm, so I shook her like a kid on Christmas morning.

"Harper, come on. It's time to get up."

She groaned and mumbled something about letting her sleep longer. I shook her again, but she swatted at me like a fly.

"I've got a surprise for you," I said in a sing-song voice. She rolled over and stuffed her face into the pillow. This would take some finesse. I moved her hair away from her neck, kissing the smooth skin on her neck, across to her earlobe. When she still didn't move, I nipped her ear, earning a small moan. I continued kissing a bath down her back until I was at the base of her spine. Rolling her over, I placed wet kisses on her stomach, trailing down to the juncture between her thighs. As soon as my lips met her wet pussy, she was moaning and writhing on the bed. I licked and sucked until her legs were shaking and her knees were squeezing my head. Her legs dropped down to the bed, and I placed another kiss on her belly, then crawled up her body and gave her a hard kiss.

Looking into her eyes, I knew I would never meet another woman like her. She was everything to me and her smile made my day better. I saw the same thing in her eyes. I placed a slow, sweet kiss on her lips.

"I love you, Harper."

She smiled brightly at me. "I love you too, Jack."

It was the first time either of us had said it. I had every intention of pleasuring her and then yanking her out of bed when I started this, but now I had to have her. I stood and shucked my pants, then climbed back over her and nestled between her legs. She wrapped her legs around my waist as I slowly slid inside her. I thrust in and out until it drove us both mad. Harper was begging and pleading with me to make her come again. My mouth moved to her nipple, sucking it into my mouth just enough to drive her crazy. I could feel Harper tightening around me, urging me to move faster. As I came, I slowed my thrusts to a lazy pace and stopped, still seated inside her. I was panting hard and laid my forehead against hers while I caught my breath. I could feel her heartbeat slow to a normal pace as I pressed soft kisses against her lips.

"Let's get up. We need to shower and get ready to have the best Thanksgiving ever." Her smile dimmed slightly.

"Jack, that's sweet, but remember, we don't have all the stuff we need."

I smacked her ass as I stood. "Don't worry, babe. I got us covered."

I winked and walked toward the bathroom. We showered quickly and dressed for the day. It was six-thirty, so I knew Mom was in the kitchen already. What I didn't expect was my entire kitchen to be filled with people. Mom was at the counter handing out directions to Anna for chopping.

"Luke and Sean, you run over to the Walmart and pick up the last few items on the list. That should take you no more than three hours. That's an hour and fifteen minutes there, a half hour to shop, and an hour and fifteen back. I need those ingredients fast. I'm timing you, so move, move, move," she said clapping her hands at them. They glanced at the clock to calculate the time, then headed for the door. She was like a drill sergeant. She turned and faced Sebastian and Cole.

"You two, go get the decorations out of the attic and put them up around the house and decorate outside. I'll be coming out periodically to check on you, so you'd better do it right the first time." Then she turned to Ryan and Logan.

"Ryan and Logan, get the leaves for the kitchen table out of the closet. Put them in, and then go help the boys hang decorations outside. You'll probably have to do the decorating on the house so those numskulls don't take off a finger. Lord knows construction isn't their area." As she finished, the guys all stared at her wide-eyed. "Well don't just stand there. Let's go! Chop. Chop!" They took off in various directions to complete the tasks given.

"So, Mom. What can I do to help out?"

"You can go get Harper and bring her out to get this food made. Just make sure she's taken care of today and that will be enough." She held out her cheek for me to kiss, which I did. I set off toward the bedroom to get Harper and ran into her in the bedroom doorway. "What's all the yelling? Is someone here?"

"Baby, everyone is here. They came to help out. We've all been assigned tasks by Ma and she's requesting your help in the kitchen. Harper flung her arms around my neck and gave me a good, long hug.

"Thank you so much, babe. I love you."

"I love you, too. Now let's go get started before Ma sends out a search party."

Ma, Harper, and Anna spent the morning preparing for dinner, which would be at three o'clock. With all three of them working on it, all the prep was done in no time. Ma had made the pies the night before, so they had the rest of the morning to relax. Harper and Ma made a huge breakfast for everyone, while Anna excused herself to the living room. She said she wasn't feeling well, possibly coming down with the flu. They shooed her out of the kitchen, and when breakfast was done, we all sat down to a buffet style breakfast. When everything was cleaned up, the guys brought out the beer and sat down to enjoy pre-game shows.

I watched my mom laughing with Harper in the kitchen about something. I wanted to make her that happy all the time. If she wanted a big, splashy Christmas, that's what I would give her. I realized in that moment that I would do anything for Harper. She was definitely the woman I wanted to settle down with, but our relationship was pretty new. I wanted to give us time to be just us before bringing up marriage.

The longer I stared at her, the more I could imagine our lives together. I could build up the business for a few more years, really save up some money, and then I could take Harper on the trips that I had always dreamed of as a kid. I wanted to travel to Italy and Spain. I wanted to see the Greek Islands, maybe take a cruise around the world. Every year would be a new adventure for us.

As much as I loved working at the garage, I couldn't see that being my life, day in and day out monotony. I wanted adventure, and Harper was definitely the woman that I wanted to have that with. I just had to take it a step at a time, so I didn't scare her off with my grand plans.

Ma and Harper laid out munchies for everyone, then came to watch the game with us. We drank beer and yelled at the TV, generally lazing around the house for the afternoon. The girls got up to finish dinner in the middle of the game, and we all grumbled when they called us to the table. When we saw all the food, we shut up and sat down for the feast.

Harper raised her wine glass in a toast. "I want to thank all of you for being here with Jack and me to celebrate today. I wanted everything to be perfect, and yesterday, it didn't look like that was going to happen."

Sean interrupted, "Only woman I know to be charged with assaulting someone with a turkey." Harper glared at him. "What? Too soon?" That got a few chuckles from the table.

"Anyway, aside from the unfortunate turkey incident, this has been the best Thanksgiving I've ever had, so thank you for being here."

I stood and kissed Harper on the cheek, then turned toward the table.

"Actually, Harper has some pretty exciting news to share with everyone. Her last book has been doing pretty well, so next week will be her last week at O'Malley's and she'll be writing full time." A round of applause erupted at the table and everyone shouted out their congrats to a very red Harper.

When the applause died down, Luke stood. "Well, since this is the time for announcements, you all know that Anna and I were hoping for a spring wedding, but it looks like that's not going to happen." Everyone's faces showed shock. "Anna is expecting, so we're eloping to Vegas on New Year's Eve!"

"Expecting what?" Logan asked with a face of pure confusion.

Ryan smacked him on the back of the head as he stood. "A baby, you idiot." Then he reached over to shake Luke's hand. Harper had already made her way over to Anna and they were hugging.

I wondered if Harper wanted kids. I didn't have anything against them, but I didn't really want one of my own. But as I stared at her, she looked so excited. Could it be that she was just really excited for her friend? Harper was young. What were the chances that she wanted kids? I hadn't thought to bring it up before. We were always on rocky ground, trying to find our footing, so I hadn't really thought much of how the future would play out.

It didn't really matter though, right? What woman wanted kids at her age? Harper liked to have fun, so I doubted that changing dirty diapers and being saddled with kids was something she wanted. Besides, she was a writer, and she could do that from anywhere. It would be perfect.

We all sat down and started to dish out the food. There was turkey, gravy, a crock pot stuffing, sweet potatoes, mashed potatoes, corn bread, garlic green beans, orange-cranberry relish, crescent rolls, apple pie, and pumpkin pie. Everything was delicious, and there were no leftovers with this group of guys. We made a chain, clearing the table, rinsing, and loading the dishwasher. After everything was cleaned up, we all went outside to play touch football.

We broke up into teams, the same ones as in paintball. I knew that Harper didn't know too much about football, so I threw the first couple of passes to Cole or Sean. Harper tried to block, but she was no match for any of the guys. The dog was even doing a better job playing than she was.

"Throw me the ball, Jack." Harper came up to me panting. Frankly, I wasn't sure she was going to be able to stand much longer. She was wheezing, and I was seriously considering telling her to go sit down before she fell down, but Harper was stubborn.

"Are you sure? You kinda look like you need a break. Do you want to sit down?"

"Yes, I'm sure. I want to try."

"Baby, there's no shame in sitting this one out." I lowered my voice so Cole and Sean wouldn't hear.

"I said I'm fine. I can do this." She huffed over toward the sideline and got in position.

The ball was snapped and she sprinted down the field. She turned to catch the ball, but I could see it was a lot closer than she thought. She put up her arms to catch the football, but wasn't fast enough. The ball hit her on the outside of her eye and she dropped like a sack of potatoes. She lay on the ground in an unmoving heap.

Shit. I ran over to her and knelt down beside her. Guilt washed over me as I looked at her face. I should have made her go sit on the sidelines for a while. She was tired and wasn't ready to play with the guys. We were rowdy and played rough.

"Ow," she said as she lifted her hand to her face.

"Baby, are you okay?" I was hovering over her face, moving her hand to inspect the injury. "I am so fucking sorry. I didn't mean to throw it so hard."

"Maybe next time you should do a gentle underhand toss."

Logan, always the smart ass just had to open his mouth and be a jackass. I shot him a death glare.

"Fuck off, shit head." I turned back to Harper. "Harper, how do you feel?"

"It's not bad. Just feels like I got hit with a water balloon." I reared back in disbelief.

"Seriously?"

"No, not seriously, you moron! I got hit in the face with a football. How do you think it feels?"

Okay, I should have seen that coming. Harper was notorious for lashing out when she was injured, uncomfortable, or pissed off. Mom was rushing over with a bag of peas with a worried look on her face.

"Here, Harper. Let's get you up and over to the lounger. You can put this on your face before it swells to the size of Texas."

I followed her over to the lounger, sure that at any second she would fall over. I went inside and grabbed a fleece blanket off the back of the couch and made my way outside.

"Here, pretty girl. I got you a blanket to keep you warm." I laid the blanket over her and crouched down next to her. Moving her hair out of her face, I inspected the bruise that was forming. She had a pretty sizable lump around her eye, and it would be black tomorrow.

"He's gonna need a new nickname for her. *Pretty girl* ain't gonna work with a third eye sticking out the side of her head."

I walked up to Logan and punched him in the jaw.

"Shut the fuck up, man." I was seething with anger. My friends could be real douchebags at times. I turned at the sound of Harper's laughter.

"Jack, lay off. He was just joking. Calm down." She had a big grin on her face for all of two seconds before she grimaced in pain and put the bag of peas back on her head. "I'm a big girl, and I'm fine. Just go play with the guys. I'm gonna hang here with Betty Crocker and preggers."

Maybe she had hit her head harder than she thought. Since when did she use pet names for people?

Ma didn't seem to care. She beamed at the nickname and Anna blushed at being called preggers. Women. I didn't understand them. We went back out onto the field and played for another hour. Fortunately, no one else got hurt the rest of the game. I walked back over to where the girls were sitting and found an empty bottle of wine and a second that was almost gone. Harper obviously wasn't feeling any pain. She was laughing so hard, she fell out of the lounger. I walked over and picked her up, setting her back on the lounger.

"Baby, how much have you had to drink? Anna can't drink, so you and Ma finished off these bottles in an hour?"

Her cheeks were rosy from the cold and she had a silly grin on her face. She tilted her drink back and took a large swallow.

"When in Rome." Anna rolled her eyes and Ma was laughing just as hard. Her glass was almost gone, and since I had only seen her drink a handful of times in my life, I assumed the alcohol hit her pretty hard. She was wasted. There was no way she was driving home tonight. She could have the guest room.

"Ma, you can stay with us tonight. You aren't driving home."

Harper turned to me in confusion. "Are you sleeping on the couch? Because there is no way all three of us will fit in that bed."

She was slurring slightly, and I had this feeling that she had actually drunk most of the wine herself.

I sighed, "Harper, we have a guest room with an extra bed. She can sleep there."

"Thank God. For a minute there, I was worried about you." She picked up the bottle of wine and poured another glass. I plucked it out of her hands before she could drink anymore. She would have a terrible night if she kept drinking.

"I think that's enough wine for the night. Maybe we should get you inside."

Harper put her hands on her hips. "I worked hard for that wine. I had to food all the cook for you and do all the preparing stuff. And don't you forget, I beat a woman with a turkey and got arrested so that you could eat turkey for Thanksgiving. I *earned* this wine." She stomped her foot as she said it. I really couldn't argue with that, so I gave her back her glass. The guys were all chuckling behind me. Anna stood up from her spot with a tired smile on her face.

"I'm exhausted. I need to go home and go to bed." Luke walked over to her and put an arm around her shoulder. "Do you need anything from us before we go?"

"No, thanks, Anna. We're good." I gave her a hug and shook Luke's hand. Then I said goodbye to the other guys and guided Mom and Harper inside. I plopped Harper down on the couch and took Mom to the guest room, making sure she had everything she needed. Then I went back for Harper. She was passed out on the couch with one leg on the floor and an arm flung over her head. I carried her into the room and pulled her clothes off. For a moment, I considered getting her in pajamas, but her arms were going everywhere and it just seemed like too much work for me. She could sleep naked.

The next morning, I got up and put on coffee. Lots of strong coffee. We would need it to get through this day, and I was talking about myself and Harper. A hungover Harper would be interesting to deal with. Mom was up first, looking only slightly worse for wear. She was in an overall good mood, and said that she was going to start a good, homemade breakfast for Harper to start the day right. Ma was halfway through cooking when she looked behind me with eyes bulging. She schooled her features quickly.

"Uh, dear, perhaps you would be more comfortable with a few more pieces of clothes on."

I turned around and saw Harper standing in only a pair of panties. Shit. Harper didn't even realize she was naked until she rubbed the sleep from her eyes and looked down. She grabbed the blanket off the back of the couch in haste, bumping into the low-sitting table to her other side and falling ass-backwards over the table. She landed with an oomph. Her legs were straight up in the air.

I had tried to grab her, but I didn't reach her until she was already on the ground. I knelt down beside her.

"Is this going to be our thing now? You on the ground and me kneeling over you?"

Harper groaned, "I am never drinking again. Why am I naked, and why didn't you tell me your mom stayed the night! God, she saw me naked!"

"Dear, I still can. You haven't really covered up anything," Ma said with a chuckle. "Don't worry. We've all been there. I used to have my fair share of alcohol too, ya know. This one time, I had drunk too much at a New Year's Eve party, and Jack's father took me into the bathroom at his parents' house. We were-"

"Ma! I'm begging you not to finish that thought."

"Can you please help me up so I can get dressed?" I held the blanket up in front of her as she untangled herself from the table. Then, I wrapped the blanket around her body and walked her back to the bedroom. Harper stayed in the bedroom until Mom left and then ignored me the rest of the day.

CHAPTER 15

HARPER

AS CHRISTMAS APPROACHED, I found myself feeling happier and happier every day. Jack seemed to have forgotten about what he said about only putting up a tree. We had been walking through some shops downtown, and I had seen some beautiful wreaths hanging in the shop window. Jack looked at me and said something that shocked me.

"Why don't we go in and take a look at them? Maybe we'll find one for the front door."

After I broke myself out of my shocked state, we walked into the shop to look at the beautiful wreaths on display. There were so many to look at, and I found it hard to focus on one. There was a green one with a winter frosting covering most of it. Holly berries were strategically placed around it with pine cones near the bottom. There was a shimmery red ribbon woven around the wreath with a few small snowmen to bring the whole decoration together. It was beautiful. I saw some others that I loved also, but that was the one I kept coming back to. Jack walked up behind me and wrapped an arm around my waist.

"Is this the one you want?" I tilted my head and considered again.

"I think so. It's between this one and the one over there." I pointed across the aisle to another equally impressive wreath.

"Let's get both. We can put one on the door to the garage."

"Are you sure that's not too much?"

"Nah. I think we need to add a few more decorations."

We paid for the wreaths and went down the street to a cute little craft store. This one had nutcrackers, wooden snowmen, Santas, nativity scenes, and other Christmas decorations. Jack suggested we stop in and my eyes bulged out of my head. Who was this man and what had gotten into him? We left that store with so many bags that we had to go right back to the car to unload. Jack asked me if I wanted a real tree or a fake tree, and I thought a fake one would be best. I wanted to enjoy it for as long as possible and I didn't want to deal with all the needles. He took me to Walmart to look for a tree because none of the shops in town had anything that was big enough, according to his standards.

"Jack, are you sure you want to do all of this today? We have plenty of time to get this all done."

"We might as well do it today. That way you can decorate when you need to take breaks from writing."

When we arrived at Walmart, let's just say I was not impressed with the selection. I wanted a really tall, full tree that was a beautiful, dark green, and really thick. I didn't see that, and apparently Jack wasn't impressed either. He practically dragged me out of the store muttering about shit trees and that we were going to order online. We unloaded the bags when we got home and Jack pulled up a website online to look at trees.

"Here, pick out a tree and order it."

He handed me his bank card, which equally baffled me. Watching him walk away, I decided I wouldn't look a gift horse in the mouth. I started scrolling through the pages, looking for something perfect. There were a ton, so I thought maybe I should narrow it down by price.

"Okay. Should we get a white tree or a green tree?"

"Well, of course we need a green tree, but you should get a white tree also for your new room."

"Um, that's a lot of money to spend. We really only need one tree. Besides, I don't even have any ornaments to add to the tree, and the room isn't finished yet."

"Really? You don't have any ornaments from when you were a kid?"

"We didn't do that in my family."

I turned back to the computer and started searching through the trees. I thought Jack would walk away, but he stayed behind me, looking through a magazine. It was obvious he was trying not to pay attention, but every once in a while, he would tell me a tree wasn't tall enough or full enough. Then, the color was wrong and the needles were wrong. Next thing I knew, he was sitting next to me, shoving me aside to put in his specifications in the filter section.

"We need a big tree," he said, his brows furrowed as he scanned the trees. "See, all of these are crap." He adjusted the filters and pulled up a new page. "See, this is what I'm talking about. Look how big that is."

I nodded and then looked in the living room, wondering how it was going to fit. I briefly considered placing my hand on his forehead to make sure he was feeling okay. Maybe he was really sick and he didn't want to tell me. Maybe he was dying and he wanted to make this last Christmas really good before the final death blow came.

"Alright," he said, rubbing his hands together. "Now that we have that picked out, we should get a white tree for your room. I'm thinking we should decorate it with blue ornaments. Ooh!" I jumped at the excited shout. "Or we could make it an all red tree. What do you think?"

"I think you've lost your mind."

"What are you talking about?"

"Are you dying?"

He frowned. "Why would you think that?"

"Because you hate Christmas."

"I don't hate Christmas."

"You practically tore my throat out when I told you I wanted to decorate for Christmas. Now you've got bags of decorations in the other room and you've ordered a tree."

"And I'm not done yet."

"Do you know how ridiculous that is? The other room isn't even finished. It would be silly and wasteful to buy a tree for there."

He waved me off and continued searching. "What do you think about this one?"

"I think it looks white...like death. Is that the feeling you're going for? You want a tree that reminds you of how you're going to look dead?"

"Has anyone ever told you you're obsessed with death?"

Huffing, I crossed my arms over my chest and watched as he ordered another tree and paid the bill. I shook my head at the ridiculous amount of money he had just spent.

"Alright," he stood, clapping his hands together once. "I have to go to the garage to take care of a few things. I shouldn't be too long." He pressed a kiss to my lips and turned to go, but then turned back, pointing at me. "You know, you should unpack some of these bags, make it look really Christmasy in here."

I started to protest, but he was already out the door. I went over to the bags and started to unload everything. After all the tags were off, I tried to decide where I wanted everything. It was hard without having the trees up yet. I put everything off to the side and decided to write for a few hours. I was completely immersed in writing my book when Jack walked in.

"Pack your bags. We're taking a little trip."

He walked off towards the bedroom without another word. I furrowed my brows at his brusque statement and quickly saved my book. I rushed down the hall to figure out what was going on.

"What do you mean *we're taking a trip*? Where are we going?"

Jack walked out of the closet and threw two bags on the bed. "Pack enough for a few days. We're taking a road trip. Pack warm clothes."

I stood stunned for a minute, but he turned and gave me a look that said not to argue with him. I quickly packed and we were on the road fifteen minutes later. We dropped the dog off at Luke and Anna's house on the way out of town.

"Where are we going?"

"It's a surprise."

We sat in silence for a while, but when I couldn't take it anymore, I turned to Jack and stared. Sensing my gaze, he glanced over at me.

"What?"

"I don't understand. What's this all this about? All the sudden you want to do all this Christmas decorating. Why?"

"It's not that I don't like Christmas, it's just that my dad was killed right before Christmas, and it kind of sucked all the fun out of the holiday. We still celebrate, but it's always difficult." He shrugged. "I don't know. I see how excited you get and I just want to make it special for you."

Good Lord. This man was so sweet. I was definitely in the Christmas spirit now. Since his thoughts had changed, I now felt more at ease to decorate and get excited for the holiday season.

"Thank you, Jack."

I smiled at him and then turned on the radio. Jack took out his phone and hooked it up to the jack in the truck. Christmas music filled the air and I felt warmth spread through my body as I sang along with the music. After a while, I dozed off in the passenger seat. When Jack shook me awake, I looked up to see a cute little German village. It was fully decked out in Christmas decorations. There were Christmas lights on the streets, the lamp posts were decorated with garland, and there were Merry Christmas signs hung across the street made from garland and lights. It was the most beautiful place I had ever seen. It had even snowed recently, giving it a Christmas wonderland feel.

"Where are we?"

"Frankenmuth, Michigan."

"This place is amazing! What are we doing here?"

"That surprise is for tomorrow. For now, we're checking into our hotel and taking a walk around the town."

We parked next to a German style hotel called *The Drury Inn*. Jack grabbed our bags and we headed inside. He checked us in, and we took the elevator to our second-story room that overlooked the streets below. It was beautiful. We got settled in our room, then went downstairs to take a walk around town. We strolled down near a lake and sat on a bench to enjoy the scenery. Snow started to fall, and Jack pulled me in close to keep me warm. We sat there enjoying the view for a half hour before we got up and explored the town a little more. As we walked, Jack told me about the history of the town and pointed out things he thought I would like.

We made our way back to the Inn and got ready for bed. Neither of us were up for much tonight. We'd had a long drive and wanted to go to sleep. The next morning, we slept until eight o'clock and then went downstairs for breakfast. I was eager to find out what this trip was about, and started pestering him as soon as I woke up. He didn't give an inch. We got in the truck and drove a short distance down the road where I saw Christmas lawn decorations all around a parking lot. Then I saw the sign, *Bronner's Christmas Wonderland,* and practically screamed with joy. I still didn't know what this place was, but I was really excited. As we walked through the doors, my jaw about dropped to the floor. There were so many Christmas ornaments and decorations.

I started dragging Jack around by the hand. "Jack, look at this one! How cute is this! Oh my gosh, have you ever seen anything like this?"

It went on and on as we made our way through the store. By the time I was done shopping, I had an ornament for each of the guys that depicted their profession, an ornament for Anna and Jack with a snowman and snowwoman that said they were expecting, and one for

Agnes that was about baking. I had also picked out a Christmas pickle that you hid in the tree. Whoever found it on Christmas morning got to open the first present. That wouldn't matter much now, but if we ever got married and someday had kids...

I shook my head, trying not to think too hard about the future. I was getting way ahead of myself. Jack and I had moved pretty fast with our relationship, but it was less than a month ago that we told each other those three little words. I didn't want to start wishing and hoping for things that may not happen. I had learned growing up with my parents that nothing lasted. I really didn't want to think about Jack and I not making it, so I shoved those thoughts down and focused on what was in front of me.

After picking out a whole basket of special ornaments, I wandered over to another station where you could place special orders and have ornaments personalized. I placed quite a hefty order of those also. Jack had picked something out also, but he wouldn't let me see. We brought our ornaments to the counter and paid, then headed back out to the truck. We stopped by the Bavarian Inn for lunch and made reservations for Frankenmuth Brewery for dinner. We went back to the hotel to relax after our morning of shopping.

A nap sounded heavenly after all that shopping and Jack had to return phone calls, so I laid down for a while. Jack had left one of the guys at the garage in charge, but he left on such short notice that he wanted to check in. After I woke up from my nap, we spent the afternoon in bed watching movies. At five-thirty, after I took a shower and cleaned up, we made our way to the brewery. We had a great dinner and then headed back to the hotel. We would be leaving early in the morning, but that didn't stop Jack from making love to me for a good part of the night. I was floating on cloud nine. It had been a perfect trip.

It was a week later and things were back to normal. I was at home, writing in the living room when Jack called.

"Hey, can you go check on my mother?"

"Why? Is everything okay?"

He sighed. "Yeah, I think so, but she seemed a little off. I just want to be sure she's okay, and I'm slammed at work."

"Of course. I'll go right now."

"Thanks, I really appreciate it."

I hung up and grabbed my coat, whistling to the dog. "Hey, Hooch. You want to go for a ride with Mommy?"

I rubbed his neck and brushed my nose against his, eliciting a small yip from him.

"Do you want to go in the car?"

He barked and spun around, eager to leave the house. Of course, it wasn't that easy. I had to wait for him to go to the bathroom first. I finally carted him into the back of the car and headed toward Jack's mom's house. Pulling in the drive, I got out, letting Hooch run ahead of me. Luckily, Agnes had no problems with the dog being in the house, because he pushed past me before I could stop him. He raced through the house, rushing in to find her.

"Oh, dear," she laughed as he jumped up on her.

"Hooch, no!"

He immediately sat back on his haunches and waited to be told what to do. His tongue was hanging out of his mouth as he stared up at Agnes.

"Is everything okay?" I asked, wondering why Jack was worried.

"With me? Oh, everything's fine. I moved something too heavy earlier, and it tweaked my back, but it feels fine now."

"You're sure?"

"Of course," she said brightly.

"Because Jack seemed to think that something was wrong."

"Oh, you know how men worry, especially about their mothers."

I did know that, and Jack was especially protective, so I trusted him when he said something was off. But over the course of the next few hours, I studied Agnes carefully and didn't see anything unusual going on with her. Her back didn't seem to be bothering her at all, and when I tried to do things for her, she just waved me off. I loved Agnes, and I really wanted to make sure she was okay, but she seemed perfectly normal to me. Maybe Jack was just overreacting. After our visit, I drove home with my thoughts glued to the plot of my book.

Hooch, once again, ran ahead of me and bolted through the door as soon as I opened it. I was just about to shrug off my coat when I heard his voice behind me.

"Stop." Jack stepped out from behind the door and wrapped his arms around me. His lips caressed my cheek and I smiled at the gesture. His hand came up to cover my eyes as he whispered in my ear, "No peeking." He guided me through the house, making sure I didn't hit any furniture along the way.

"Jack, what is going on?"

"You'll see, pretty girl."

"Is this really necessary?"

"Of course it is. Have you ever known me to do something that wasn't necessary?"

"Um...well, I think calling me a slut in front of the whole bar was a little unnecessary."

"Still holding a grudge over that one, I see."

I huffed in irritation, but realized that we were back by the addition. I hadn't been in there yet because the decorators hadn't been in to finish it, something Jack had insisted on.

"Are you ready, baby?"

I nodded and Jack removed his hand. The room was completely done. It had windows along all three walls that were trimmed in white. The walls were painted a medium blue and the floor was a plush tan carpet. There was a heavy wood desk by one window, and my laptop sat on top. He must have ordered furniture, because there was a living room set in the middle of the room, big enough for me to get together with some friends and hang out. Off in the far corner of the room was a reading nook with a lamp next to it. There was a small table next to the chair that would hold a book and a cup of coffee. I turned to face Jack, but a fireplace on the wall caught my eye. How did I not notice that? It would be perfect for cold days, but the best thing about the whole room was the white Christmas tree in the corner between the fireplace and the desk. It had lights, but hadn't been decorated yet.

"Babe, how did you get all this done?"

"I had the decorator come over when we went to Michigan. Then she came over this morning when you were at Ma's and put in the finishing touches. Go ahead and walk around. This space is yours."

With a huge smile on my face, I sat in each chair, at the desk, looked at the fire, and imagined how I was going to decorate the tree.

"This is the best present ever. I can't believe what a great job they did with everything. This is my favorite room."

"Well, I hope there's still one other room you prefer over this," Jack said with a wicked grin.

"Yes, you're right. I think I prefer the kitchen."

Jack slapped my ass. "You're such a smartass."

I kissed him and he pulled me in to deepen the kiss. I could feel him hardening against my belly and reached down to stroke him through his jeans. He let out a growl and pulled me toward the bedroom. In a flash, I was thrown through the air, landing on the bed, with a hot, sexy body climbing over me. He was kissing me like it was the last time he would see me. I wound my arms around his neck and slid them down to his shoulders. I felt all his taut muscles as they rippled with his movements. I pushed him back and started slowly unbuttoning my blouse. I sat up and slowly shrugged the blouse down my shoulders and let it slide down my arms. I stood up and popped the button on my jeans. I watched the fire burn in his eyes as I shimmied my jeans to the floor and stepped out. I was standing in just my bra and panties as his gaze traveled the length of my body. I could feel the moisture building between my legs as I walked forward to stand between Jack's legs. I pulled his shirt up over his head and stepped back when he tried to take off my bra.

"Nuh uh. We're doing things my way tonight."

I pulled him to a standing position and rid him of his boxers and jeans, then knelt down so I was eye level with his cock. I leaned forward and slowly licked him from base to tip and swirled my tongue around the swell of his cock. As I guided him into my mouth, I relaxed my throat and took him all the way in. He fisted my hair and started to move, but I pulled back and gave him a stern look. He released my hair and moaned as I continued to swallow his cock. I knew he didn't have much more patience, so I stood up and released the back of my bra and let it fall down my arms to the floor. My fingers hooked in the sides of my panties and slid them down my legs.

"Go stand at the end of the bed," I said as I crawled over to the head of the bed.

I sat with my back against the headboard and raised my knees up. I spread my legs and reached down to touch my pussy.

"You're going to watch me touch myself."

I started to stroke my pussy with one hand while my other hand massaged my breasts. I moaned as I watched him reach down and slowly stroke his cock. My speed increased as I watched him stroke a little faster, my breathing becoming erratic.

"Stroke that pussy, pretty girl. God, you are so fucking sexy."

I began panting and slid a finger inside as I watched his eyes turn molten. He groaned and threw his head back as he pumped his cock. He lowered his head back to meet my gaze and stared me down as he beat his cock. I could feel my orgasm building and couldn't hold back as I called his name. He came seconds later in his hand, breathing hard and saying my name. My chest was heaving as he walked over to me and held out his hand.

"Lick it."

A thrill ran through me as I reached forward and swiped my

tongue over his hand and watched his eyes darken. I licked until his hand was clean, then sucked his thumb into my mouth and ran my tongue around it. He picked up my hand and sucked the juices off my fingers and then licked his lips. I glanced down and saw that he was at half mast again. I looked up at him through my lashes and gave him a sexy smirk. It was almost a challenge.

Jack picked me up and threw me back against the headboard. "Now it's my turn. Stay."

His eyes bored into me and I could see the lust in his eyes as he turned and walked into the closet. He returned a moment later with a tie and wrapped it around one of my wrists and then drew it through the slat in the headboard, then tied it to the other wrist. His hands caressed my breast, and he cupped it in his hand as his thumb brushed my nipple. My head fell back in pleasure when he took his now hard cock and slapped it against my pussy. A moan fell from my throat when he put the very tip into my pussy, but then stopped and pulled out. He did this several times, torturing me with every stroke. Then he slammed into me with such force that my head slammed into the headboard.

"Oh God, Jack. More."

He fucked me hard and I loved it, needing more from him. He ran his hands along my breasts down to my clit and rubbed his thumb in circles. Then he pulled out, and I whimpered at the loss. He flipped me over and pulled my knees up. Then he went to the headboard and slid the tie down the slat to the mattress. I was yanked back against his cock, and I couldn't move with my arms being stretched as they were. He slammed into me from behind, and I felt so full, I thought I would explode. His hand worked my clit and I was over the edge in a matter of seconds. His fingers replaced his cock, and he pumped his fingers in my dripping pussy.

"God, you're so wet. Perfect. Just how I need you."

Then he moved his slickened fingers to my ass and pushed one finger inside. I squirmed at the burn as he pulled his fingers out and did it again.

"Push out."

I did as he said and could feel the burn ease up. He did it again and again, adding another finger after a few times. Then he pulled out his fingers and thrust his cock into my pussy a few more times before I felt him again at my back entrance.

"Time for hole number three."

Then he started to push in, but I wasn't prepared for his thickness. This was nothing like having his fingers there.

"Push out, baby. I won't hurt you."

I wanted so badly to believe what he said, so I did as he asked, even though it still burned. He stopped and waited for me to let him know I was ready. When he eased in further, I wasn't sure I liked it, but I didn't stop him as he started to move. I felt extremely full, but the lines of pain and pleasure were still blurred. I was about to tell him to stop when he leaned over and kissed my shoulder.

"Trust me, baby."

Then he wrapped his arm around me and started playing with my nipples. He was pulling and pinching them, and I could feel myself getting wetter. He started moving, thrusting again, and this time started to rub his thumb against my clit. I could feel an orgasm building as he started to pound into me. It actually started to feel good, and I started to push back into him.

"Fuck yeah, baby. Give me more. Fuck my cock."

Knowing that he liked it so much spurred me on, and I slammed my ass back onto him again and again as he strummed my clit. His balls slapped my pussy and pushed me over the edge. I was screaming and moaning his name.

"God, Jack. Yes, harder."

He grabbed me by the hips and slammed into me a few more times, his skin slapping against mine. He fucked me so hard, I wasn't sure I would be able to sit in the morning. As he pinched my nipples, I came again on the waves of the last orgasm. He thrust into me twice more before he stilled deep inside me. He slowly pulled out and then collapsed on the bed next to me.

"I can't move my legs out of this position. I'm gonna need some help."

He laughed and got up to move my legs straight. Then he untied my wrists and carried me into the bathroom. He started to run a bath for me, filling it with bath salts, then gave me a kiss and left. I went to the bathroom, then got in the tub and soaked, feeling deliciously sore.

CHAPTER 16

JACK

HARPER AND I agreed that since we spent so much on the addition, we would just exchange small presents Christmas morning. I had been trying to come up with a great idea for her, but I was really struggling. I wanted something to symbolize our time together, but Harper really wasn't the type to wear jewelry.

"Why don't you just get her a puppy?" Logan suggested.

I stared at him blankly. "Because we already have a dog."

He nodded slightly. "Right, I forgot. Well, maybe you could get her a cat."

I sighed, rubbing my hand over my face. "Maybe you should stop giving ideas."

"Just think to yourself," Sean said. "If you were a girl, what would you want for Christmas?"

"Car parts."

"I said, *if you were a girl*," he said, tossing his cards at me.

It was poker night, and since Anna wasn't feeling well, Harper went to stay with her while Luke came over here.

"Well, I'm not a girl, so how the hell should I know?"

"Get her a new car," Cole suggested. "You know she needs one."

"That's not exactly a small present, and even if I wanted to get her one, that would just piss her off."

"How about a washing machine," Ryan said. "I hear all the time from clients that the women want these new, fancy washing machines. You could totally get her a new washer and dryer."

I stared at him, thinking about tossing my drink in his face. "Let me get this straight, you think that for our first Christmas together, I should get the woman I love a washing machine."

"And a dryer," he said, pointing his cards at me. "They come as a set, you know. You'll end up in the dog house if you only get her one."

"You'll end up in the dog house if you get her a washer for Christmas," Sean pointed out. "Do you know how many domestic disturbances I've dealt with, all surrounding men getting their wives gifts that are useful instead of meaningful?"

"Hey," Ryan said, like he was offended. "A washing machine *is* meaningful. It says *I want to make life easy on you*. It says *I want you to have the best*. It says—"

"It says that you want her to wash your clothes," Sebastian piped up, still staring at his cards. "I'm guessing laundry is not what should be on her mind on Christmas morning. Not if you want her to stick around."

"Then what would you suggest?" Ryan asked, glaring at him.

Sebastian set down his cards and folded his hands on the table. "First, I would suggest getting her something pretty."

"Harper doesn't wear jewelry."

"Get her something for her hair. Like a tiara or something."

"A tiara," I said, shaking my head slightly.

"Hell, I don't know, but a tiara would be a hell of a lot better than a washing machine."

"Okay, first of all, where the hell would she ever wear a tiara? The Mechanic's Ball?"

"Do they have one of those?" Logan asked.

"No! I was joking." Tossing down my cards, I sighed heavily. "I don't have time to figure this out, and I can't figure it out with ideas like washing machines and tiaras."

Logan opened his mouth, but I held up my hand to stop him. "And I'm not getting another fucking animal."

He snapped his mouth shut and hung his head. "I wouldn't mind getting a cat," he grumbled. "Just tell me that you couldn't see her curled up and reading a book with a cat in her lap."

"With my luck, the cat would attack her and scratch her to hell. The last thing I need is something that could potentially maim her."

Sebastian snorted. "You do remember that she beat a woman with a turkey and bashed a thief in with a poster, right?"

"Guys, come on. I need serious ideas here."

"Well, what does she like?" Logan asked.

I shrugged. "Books and stuff."

"Wow, you're a plethora of information," Sean said, his eyes wide. "You should look into becoming a detective."

"I was talking more sexually. Maybe you could get her a good vibrator, ooh, or some lingerie."

"I'm going to pretend that you didn't suggest I get my woman a vibrator for Christmas. *Here, honey. For your pleasure.*"

"And not just hers," Logan nodded. "It's pleasurable for you too."

I looked at him with disgust. "I'm not letting her use a vibrator on me. You're sick!"

"I meant on her, asshole. Haven't you ever played around in the bedroom? Or are you too boring for that?"

"Trust me, I don't need a vibrator for the bedroom. We have plenty of fun in that department."

"If you think you don't need improvement, things are going to get stale," Sean grunted. "Just saying, there's always room for improvement."

I sighed heavily, rubbing at my eyes. "This is not helpful at all. I need something that will really get her excited."

Logan opened his mouth, but I glared at him.

"I don't need a vibrator. I need...I need something that will make her melt."

"Get her a frying pan," Ryan laughed. When no one else laughed, he shrugged. "Fine, pretend like that was a bad joke."

"It was," Sebastian said.

Cole was being awfully quiet, so I turned to him. "What would you get a woman you loved?"

He shrugged. "I have no clue. It should be meaningful, something that shows her how much you love her. Something that tells her that you pay attention to her."

"Something that symbolizes our time together," I said, nodding at his suggestion.

"Sure, something like that," he shrugged. "Not that I would know, but it sounds good."

My eyes glimmered as I realized what I was going to get her. It would be perfect.

"Aw, crap. He's going all mushy on us," Logan sighed. "Boys, we no longer have tough-as-nails Jack. No, now we have love-struck, pansy-ass Jack."

"Shut up, fucker. I want this to be special."

He held up his hands. "I'm just saying, I'm not going to be there Christmas morning. I don't need to see that."

"No one invited you," I said, tossing my cards at him. I grinned to myself. This was going to be really good.

Every year, about a week before Christmas, my mom and I got together to make ravioli for Christmas Eve dinner. We made them from scratch and then used the leftover dough to make fatties. Fatties were dough rolled into a pencil shape that you fried in olive oil until golden brown, then heavily salted. Harper came with me and learned how to make the ravioli, singing Christmas songs as we worked.

"So, Jack, I thought your family was English and Scottish? Where does ravioli come in?" Harper asked as she sipped some wine.

"Dad's side of the family is English and Scottish, but Ma's side is Italian."

"Really? That is so cool. No wonder you have some mad baking skills."

Ma rolled out some more dough and started to put the filling in evenly spaced balls. "My mother came over from Italy and married my father in an arranged marriage. I know they loved each other, but I don't think it was that way at first. He was twenty-two years older than her. Anyway, she was always cooking Italian food growing up, and I really wanted to learn. I have a bunch of old recipes that I wrote down. You know you can't rely on my memory for too much longer, and these have to be passed on to someone else who will use them to cook for their family." She glanced at me, but spoke to Harper. "Maybe someday I'll pass them on to you?"

I rolled my eyes. The Italian matchmaker in her was coming out. Ma wouldn't be happy until she had a house full of kids running around. I hadn't told her that I didn't want kids. It would probably kill her.

"I would love to make some of these meals with you. We could have a big dinner once a week and make a new meal every time. It would be so much fun," Harper said excitedly.

We finished making the ravioli and rolled out the dough for the fatties and fried them up.

"Jack, sweetie, why don't you go put on the movie." Mom was getting the plates out and pulling out another bottle of wine.

"What movie are we going to watch?"

Harper started filling her plate with fatties. She took a bite and moaned as the flavor hit her tongue. I loaded up a plate for myself. I usually ate about two plates of these because they were so good. Traditionally, we only ate them once a year, so you had to load up when they were made.

"We always watch *It's a Wonderful Life* after we finish the ravioli." Harper squealed and made her way to the living room. I put on the movie and we all sat down to watch it and eat our fatties. Each of us got up several times to get seconds, thirds, or fourths. I relaxed into the couch with Harper leaning against my side. She was wrapped in my arms as we enjoyed the movie, but my mind started to wander to our earlier conversation and how Ma had pointedly looked at me when offering to pass the recipes on to Harper. Obviously, that was her way of saying that she expected me to propose, but I was way ahead of her. I had been thinking about it for a few weeks now, but I didn't want to do it at Christmas. It was so cliché. I wanted it to be out of nowhere, when she least expected it. Besides, Christmas was her favorite holiday, and I didn't want to share this moment with anything else.

The next day, Harper called me at work. "Hey, babe, um…it looks like we might have a house guest for Christmas." She huffed out a laugh and I could tell she was nervous.

"Okay, and who would that be?"

"My dad. He's flying in from England for Christmas. I haven't seen him in almost a year."

"Alright, pretty girl. We'll make sure the room is ready for him and we'll have a family Christmas with Ma and your dad."

"Really? You're not upset?"

"Why would I be upset?"

I didn't think I came across as a jackass. Harper should know me better by now. I would never take away her time with her dad. She didn't see him that often, and Christmas was meant to be spent with family.

"Well, it's just that, he won't be leaving until after Christmas so, ya know, it kinda puts a damper on sex."

She was using sex as an excuse to feel me out. I wouldn't stop having sex with her because family was visiting. Besides, we lived together and shared a room. We were consenting adults and frankly, it didn't matter what anyone else thought.

"Baby, do you really think I'm not gonna have sex with you because your dad is here? We'll be quiet, and if he doesn't like it, he can stuff it. You're mine, and I won't go around pretending we're abstaining for him. You'll just have to learn to control yourself for a few days." She laughed on the other end, seeming relieved at my attitude.

Her dad arrived the next day and Harper picked him up at the airport. I left early from work to go to the store to pick up stuff for dinner. I wouldn't say I was trying to impress him, but I did want her dad to feel welcome in our home. There was also a very important conversation that I needed to have with her dad at some point during this visit, so I wanted to have him on my good side.

Harper had texted me that they were on their way back from the airport, so I went to take a shower. When they walked through the door, Harper had her arm linked through her dad's and was laughing at something he was saying. She was all lit up, and a small pang hit my chest that I wouldn't be sharing this holiday with my own father. However, this made her happy and that was all that mattered to me right now.

"Dad, this is Jack. Jack, this is my dad, Mark."

I stepped forward to shake his hand. He had a strong grip and the vibes I was getting from him said that he was trying to intimidate me. He wanted me to know that he wouldn't allow anything other than the best for his daughter.

"It's a pleasure to meet you, sir."

"What exactly are your intentions with my daughter, son?"

Okay, so let's get right to it.

"I love your daughter very much, sir."

"Yeah, yeah. That's nice," he waved his hand in front of his face, "but what are you gonna do about it? Is she going to be living here, out of wedlock, for the rest of her life, or are you going to man up and ask her to marry you?"

"Dad!" Harper looked mortified. Her face was bright red and she was wringing her hands. She didn't need to be here for this.

"Harper, why don't you go to the kitchen and get the steaks prepared for dinner. Your dad and I need to have a talk."

I crossed my arms in front of my chest and stood with my legs spread. I wasn't backing down from this guy, and I wouldn't be taking his shit. I was good for Harper, and it wouldn't take him long to see that. Harper huffed and went into the kitchen.

"How about I show you around the house." I turned and walked away, not waiting for a response. A few seconds later, I heard Mark's footsteps behind me.

"This is your daughter's new room. We had it designed specifically for her so she had a place to write or relax. It was just finished recently. She spends a lot of time out here."

Mark looked around the room, seemingly impressed. He caught sight of the tree and walked over to it. It was decorated with ornaments that she bought when we went to Michigan, but I had also taken her back to Walmart to get some ornaments in bulk to fill in the tree. We would build her ornament collection over time, and soon the tree would be filled with memories we made together.

"It appears you're taking care of my girl. This room is something else. I have to say, I'm impressed." He turned and looked at me with an intensity that reminded me of a tiger before he pounced. "I still need to know that she isn't just some piece of ass to you, that you'll be there for the long haul."

She does have a nice ass that I thoroughly enjoy.

"Christ, son. I don't need to hear that shit about my daughter."

"Shit, sorry sir. Just comes out sometimes. Look, you need to stop talking about this stuff around Harper. I have every intention of proposing to her, but I wasn't going to do it for a few more months. If you keep talking about it, it's going to get awkward between us and ruin what I have planned."

"Good to know son, but let me tell you something. My baby deserves the world. She deserves a man that cherishes her, a big family, kids, friends, all of it. If you can't provide her with all of that, walk away. She didn't have all that growing up, and I won't have her missing out on it for the rest of her life. We understand each other?"

"Yes, sir."

Mark nodded and walked away. I hadn't really considered kids being a deal breaker with Harper, but Mark was right. I needed to be sure that I could give Harper everything she desired, but for now I needed to get through this visit with her dad. I went back into the kitchen where Mark and Harper were discussing how her writing was going.

"So, this next one is a romantic comedy," she grinned. "There's this hilarious scene about a guy that's super overprotective, and his girlfriend gets robbed at her apartment." This sounded familiar. "And she beats the robber with a rolled-up poster, giving him all these papercuts."

Mark squinted. "And this is a comedy?"

She rolled her eyes. "You'll just have to read it."

Mark laughed, rubbing the back of his neck. "No offense, honey, but I don't want to read anything with sex scenes that you've written. God knows where the inspiration comes from."

"Well, everything I write now is inspired by Jack. He gives me so much material," she said, winking at me.

"Hey, I don't screw up that much."

"No, you're absolutely perfect." She turned back to her dad. "In fact, it was Jack that convinced me to stop waitressing and write full-time."

"Really?" he said, raising an eyebrow at me.

"Well, I knew it was what she really wanted. She was just too worried about finances. But now that she's writing full-time, she's making her own way. I'm very proud of her."

Harper beamed at me, obviously needing to hear that. I reminded myself to keep telling her every day, just so she was certain she was on the right path.

Mark shook his head. "That's just what every father wants to hear, that his little girl is taken care of, and encouraged to pursue her dreams. *All* of her dreams."

Harper frowned, but I smiled, trying to ease her worries. I knew exactly what he was talking about though. I couldn't stop thinking about it through dinner, becoming distracted to the point that I missed a lot of the conversation. I had every intention of proposing to her in a few months, but now I was doubting myself. What if Harper really wanted kids and that was a deal breaker for her? Would I be able to give her that? I liked kids, but I had other things I wanted to do in life. I wanted a wife to travel the world with. Kids had never been in my plans.

When we went to bed that night, I shuffled through my routine of getting ready for bed, and Harper had to ask me three times to turn off the light before I heard. When I got into bed, I stared at the ceiling for a while, thinking Harper had gone to sleep.

"Babe, what's wrong? You've been quiet all night. Did my dad say something?"

"Huh? Oh, no. Everything's fine. I've just been thinking about something for the garage, and I can't get my mind off it."

Well, it was sort of true. I had been considering expanding the garage to take on custom builds. It would be a huge expansion that would mean building a second garage and hiring more employees. I had the money to do it, and there was a market in the area for it. I just had to bite the bullet.

"Do you want to talk about it?"

"I was thinking of expanding the garage to do custom builds. It could be very profitable for us. It would mean a lot of extra hours for a while, but once it's up and running and profitable, we could go traveling every year and see the world. It's something I've always wanted to do."

"If expanding is what you want to do, then you should go for it."

We were talking about the future, so now seemed like as good a time as any to talk to her about it. I just wasn't sure I wanted the answer.

"Harper, do you…" I took a deep breath. Once this was out there, I couldn't take it back. "Do you want kids someday?"

Harper sat up and looked at me. "Yes, I want kids. I didn't have a big family growing up. I can't imagine not having a house full of kids to love."

"But, wouldn't it be enough, just the two of us?"

Her face fell when she understood what I was saying. She shifted to face me, chewing her lip.

"Jack, it's not about whether you're enough or not. I want to carry a baby, feel it kick, hold it in my arms. I want that feeling of being the most important thing in the world to a child."

My stomach sank. This was not going to go how I wanted.

"You're the most important thing in the world to me. I've always had this dream of taking trips once the business is more solid. There are so many places I want to go, and I'd like to do that with you. We could have a great life together, exploring and experiencing the world together. That's a great life, too." I was practically pleading with her to see it my way.

"You're right. It is a great life." Harper glanced away and when she turned her eyes back to me, they were shimmering. "It's just not the life I want. I'm sorry, Jack. That's what I want out of life."

We stared at each other in sadness for a few minutes. Both of us realized what the other was saying. Neither wanted to give up their dreams for the other.

"Come here." I pulled Harper down to me and the silence was deafening with all the things that needed to be said.

"We don't need to think about this right now. We have a few days before Christmas, and I plan to enjoy every minute with you. The rest we can figure out later."

I knew it was an empty promise. How could we figure it out later when neither wanted to budge? I was going to have to do some soul searching over the next few days and decide if I could give her what she needed, but deep down, I already knew the answer. Having kids was just not in the cards for me. I wasn't interested in that kind of life.

I wanted adventure. I wanted to travel. I didn't want to be held down by obligations. With kids, that would all change. Sure, we would still be able to travel, but traveling with kids came with restrictions. Not to mention that eventually they would be in school. There would be no leaving at the drop of a hat like I had done when we went to Frankenmuth. And then there would be sports, and someone would have to drop them off and pick them up, watch the games, cheer them on...

Not to mention that with kids, we would also have to think about added health insurance, braces, college...There were just so many responsibilities that came with having kids. I wasn't sure I was up for that. It would completely change my life. And if I had to give up what I wanted for Harper, I would eventually start to resent her. I would always see pictures of all the places I was missing out on. I would be just like George in *It's A Wonderful Life,* only I had the feeling that I wouldn't come around to his way of thinking.

I was finally able to fall asleep around one in the morning. I got up early and went to work, still having two days before Christmas Eve. I needed to finish up everything I could before then so all the guys could enjoy the holidays with their families. Luckily, Harper already knew this and didn't mind at all. She explained it to her father so he didn't feel like I was trying to get away from him. I came home around nine that night, and the two of them were having a nightcap. I went to the kitchen to eat and then went to get cleaned up. Luckily, her dad had turned in for the night, so I didn't have to go put on a happy face. I was beat after my long day at work and my lack of sleep the night before, so I headed to bed and was up by four the next morning.

At lunch, Harper stopped by to drop off some food. "Hey, babe. I brought you some lunch."

That was one of the things I loved about Harper. When she wasn't busy or if she needed a break, she would bring me lunch. All the guys were jealous of my homemade lunches and every once in a while, she brought in enough for everyone. I walked over to her and gave her a kiss, then brought my food to the office.

"Thanks, baby. I'm starved." I sat down and started eating. When I looked up, I saw a strange look on Harper's face and she was fidgeting with her purse.

"Is everything okay, Jack? You seem a little distant."

"Everything's fine, pretty girl. I just have to finish stuff up so the guys can take off for Christmas. I don't want to have to come in to work tomorrow."

She gave me a smile and walked over, plopping down in my lap. I gave her a hard kiss to reassure her that everything was fine.

"I get it. I just wanted to be sure."

"It's all good, pretty girl. Just getting shit done."

She left and I went back to work. I got home after eleven, but all the work was done and I could take the rest of Christmas off.

I slept in the next morning until nine and decided today was going to be a great day. I followed the smell of coffee to the kitchen and saw Harper had just finished making breakfast. I walked over to her and gave her a big hug and kiss.

"Merry Christmas Eve, baby."

"Merry Christmas."

She was glowing this morning. I was determined to give her the best Christmas ever. We all ate breakfast together and I talked a little about my plans for the shop with her dad. He seemed impressed by my aspirations. By noon, we were ready to head over to Ma's house for our Christmas Eve feast. We snacked on finger foods all afternoon and around five, we sat down to dinner. We had ravioli, salad, and homemade bread. Everything was delicious.

After dinner, we opened presents. Harper's father gave us plane tickets to come visit him in England. Harper had special ornaments made for her father and Ma. Ma gave her the best gift of all. She had a recipe book made for her with all the family recipes inside. Harper was so excited, she ran over and practically barreled over Ma with a hug. After opening presents, we all played Mexican Train until late in the evening.

Mark had a nine o'clock flight the next morning. It was the only one he could get since he booked at the last minute. We drove him to the airport, and as I shook his hand at the drop off, Mark leaned in and reminded me in a low voice to remember what we had talked about.

Harper and I went to the kitchen and made some hot cocoa when we got home. Then we headed into the living room where the presents were under the tree. Harper had gotten me an ornament of a car. On the bottom it said Jack 2016. I smiled and hung it on the tree. She handed me another present in the shape of a book. It was her newest book that hadn't been released yet. I opened it up and read the dedication.

For Jack. You are my inspiration and the reason I have been able to chase my passion. I will always be grateful for all you have given me.

"Thanks, baby."

I leaned over and kissed her on the mouth. She was one of the most thoughtful people I knew. I wasn't much for presents. I could buy most anything I wanted, and she had done something to let me know how much she appreciated me.

I pulled out my presents to Harper from under the tree. Harper opened the first present and saw a car ornament for when her car broke down. Next, was a door for the door we broke down the first time we had sex. I gave her an ornament that said *First Christmas In Our New Home*. There was a turkey, for her getting arrested because of hitting the woman with a turkey. I also gave her a football because of her getting hit in the face on Thanksgiving.

The last ornament I gave her was two penguins holding each other. Above the penguins was a banner that said *First Christmas Together*. Below, our names were printed. Harper gave me a kiss and I felt her tears on my face.

"I just wanted to fill your tree with special ornaments," I said.

"Thank you, Jack."

She looked away and wiped her tears. I knew she wasn't crying because of the gifts, but what they meant. They were a memory for her. They were supposed to be on our tree every year, and we would hang them when we decorated together. Now, they would be a reminder of what we had. We both knew this would be our last Christmas together. She really wanted kids, and that wasn't what I wanted. I tried to wrap my brain around it, but I couldn't make himself want to be a dad.

"Jack, I want you to know that I love you so much, and I wish I could give you what you want, but it's just not who I am."

I brushed a strand of hair back from her tear-stained face, tucking it behind her ear. I would always remember that day I showed her the new addition, beautiful and so full of life, ambitious, and eager to take the life she wanted.

"I know, baby. I love you too. We had a good run, and I'm gonna miss the shit out of you. I wish I could give you what you need."

My emotions were getting the better of me. I did my best to steel myself and leaned forward to kiss her, but she pulled away from me.

"I think I need to go check into a hotel room. Staying will just make this harder. I don't think I can stay knowing I don't get to stay forever."

I looked down and stared at the carpet. I couldn't look into her sad, beautiful eyes right now because it would be my undoing. She was everything to me, but she was leaving, and I knew I couldn't stop her. My throat felt thick, but I swallowed it down so she wouldn't see how much I was hurting.

"If that's what you need."

A kiss was pressed to my cheek before I heard her leaving the room. I sat on the floor trying to figure out how things had gone so wrong. One minute we were decorating for Christmas and celebrating with family, and the next, she was walking out of my life. I was going to ask her to marry me. We were supposed to be planning a wedding in a few months. If only I hadn't brought it up the other night, we would still be going about our lives without a care in the world. If I had waited though, it would have been harder on both of us. I heard her walk into the room a while later.

"I got a reservation at the hotel in town." I nodded. "Goodbye, Jack."

She walked out the door and I stayed sitting on the floor staring at the ground. When her car started and pulled away, I stood, grabbed the coffee table and flung it over with a roar.

"Fuck!" I walked over to the wall and punched it several times. Blood dripped down my hand, but I didn't feel a thing besides the tightening of my chest. I needed something to numb the pain, because I was pretty sure my heart had just been ripped out of my chest. I headed to the liquor cabinet. Scotch would be my friend tonight.

CHAPTER 17

HARPER

I PULLED into the hotel downtown, unloaded my luggage, and checked in on autopilot. I didn't say anything more than I had to or look anyone in the eye. If I did, I would break down, and I didn't want to cause a scene. I wanted to get to my room and break down in private. When I opened the door, I walked to the bed and sat down numbly on the bed. I must have stared at the floor for a good hour. I was filled with indecision. I wanted so badly to run out the door and go back to Jack, but we wanted different things. That wouldn't help either of us in the end.

Not knowing what else to do, I went into the bathroom and filled the old-fashioned claw foot tub with hot water and bubbles, stripped my clothes, and climbed in. I soaked, drawing the warmth into my body, now that I felt chilled to the bone. I was numb, completely unsure of what to do now. All I had was this bath to warm me now that his arms were gone. I stared at the opposite wall, thinking of my life with Jack over the past six months. I had been so happy. *We* had been so happy. There wasn't a single memory before him that ever left me feeling so content. I had a family and friends with him. His friends had become my friends. Would that all go away now? Agnes had become a mother to me. I hadn't spoken to my own mother in months, and I doubted I would again for a long while. Now I had no one, aside from Anna and Luke.

When the bath turned cold, and I could no longer stand to stare at the white wall, I pulled the plug and watched the water circle the drain. It was just like my life, vanishing into a black hole. One minute, I had everything, and the next, it was gone.

I dried myself off and climbed into bed. I stared at the wall for a while, but sleep finally took hold of me and pulled me under. When I woke, I was disoriented and couldn't figure out where I was. Then it hit me like a semi truck. I was alone again. I would never kiss Jack again or feel his warmth at night. I wouldn't hear him make fun of me or see his beautiful smile. I would have to stay away from all our regular hangouts to avoid running into him and his friends. His friends. Not only was I losing Jack, but I was losing the friendships that I had built during my relationship with him. I could still hang out with Anna, but Luke had become good friends with the guys, and I couldn't interfere with that, even though Luke and I were childhood friends.

I cried for a few hours before falling asleep again. The whole morning wasted away until I was awoken by pounding at the door. I hurried out of bed, my heart pounding in excitement. It had to be Jack. When I looked through the peephole, disappointment ripped through me. It wasn't Jack. It was Anna.

I opened the door and took one look at Anna's sad face, then burst into tears. Anna came in and held me, rubbing my back as she guided me back to the bed. I told Anna everything that happened between us over the past few days.

"How did you know I was here?"

"Jack called. He said you broke up, and asked me to come check on you. He sounded pretty rough. He didn't explain, so I had no idea what happened."

The tears wouldn't stop now that the floodgates had opened. I laid my head in my best friend's lap, but it wasn't the comfort I needed. I wished that I had Jack, but if I couldn't have him, I wanted Agnes. She was like a mother to me, but that wouldn't be fair to Jack. I couldn't cry on her shoulder when I knew Jack would need her just as much.

"I miss him so much. I can't believe it's over. I wanted so badly to stay, but I forced myself to go. I don't think I would have been able to if I had stayed any longer. I would have convinced myself that I could live without kids, and then I would have been miserable or always hoping he would change his mind. I know it's better this way, but it sucks."

She sighed, running her fingers through my messy hair. "Maybe it's better this way. I know you loved him, but sometimes people come into our lives for a reason. Jack helped push you into writing full-time. Maybe that was his purpose all along."

"Do you really think so?" I whispered.

"No," she said after a moment. "I think you and Jack were meant to be together, but if you think you did the right thing, then trust your instincts."

I laid in bed with Anna for a while, and then Anna insisted on ordering room service and watching movies. I had no desire to do that, but she was trying to help, so I let her. I wanted to sink down into the bed and close my eyes. I didn't want to face the world, but I knew Anna wouldn't leave until she was satisfied I would be okay. When the movie was over, I insisted that Anna leave so that I could get some sleep.

I slept like a rock all night and well into the next day. I found that getting up to go to the bathroom was a difficult task. It was strange how I could sleep all night, but still feel like I had been up for three days. I climbed back into bed and slept a while longer. When I woke up, it was seven o'clock at night. I had basically slept for twenty-four hours.

Still exhausted, I rubbed at my eyes and glanced around the room. I couldn't live here forever. I needed to start looking for a new place. I needed to find a new way in life. I had done it before, and this time was no different. Sure, I was leaving the man I loved behind, but it was just like with everything else, when things were down, you found a way out. I didn't have to live the perfect life. Right now, I just needed to fake it until I was myself again, and that included getting my ass out of bed and moving on with life.

Since I had lived with Jack for about five months, I had some money set aside and would have no problem getting something to rent. The problem was, I didn't have any furniture, kitchen items, or even a bed. We had sold all my stuff when I moved in with Jack. I was kicking myself now, wishing I had listened to my gut when it told me not to move in with him. I wouldn't trade that time for anything, but now I was stuck, and I knew all along this would be a possibility. I ordered some food from room service and started searching listings for furnished rentals. I came across a cute, little house that was in my price range. It would be lonely to live by myself again. I had woken up next to Jack and gone to bed with him every night for five months. The silence would be deafening.

I scheduled an appointment online to view the property tomorrow. My food arrived and I pretended to eat it. I had moved the food around my plate enough that it appeared I had eaten. I pushed the tray to the side of the bed and laid back down. Turning on the tv, I scoffed at the selections available. Everything was a romantic comedy, news, or murder mysteries. What I needed was...well I wasn't sure what I needed. Nothing seemed to be appropriate for my mood, so I switched the television off, took my tray to the door, and climbed back into bed.

The next morning, I decided to get up and take a shower. I really smelled, and I was sure my sheets did too. The appointment with the realtor was in an hour, so I dressed and went downstairs for breakfast. I made sure to remove the Do Not Disturb sign as I left. If that room didn't get cleaned today, I wasn't sure it would be sanitary to stay another night.

I went to see the house the next, which wasn't very big, but it had an open floor plan downstairs. The front opened to the living room and the kitchen was behind that with a kitchen nook off to the right. To the left, as you walked in, was a staircase. Next to that were a set of french doors that opened into a small office. Past the french doors was the downstairs bathroom and a small hallway that led to the back door. I took the stairs up and saw a short hallway. To the left, at the top of the stairs, was a small bedroom. There was another bedroom directly across from the stairs, and a bathroom at the end of the hall. There was a linen closet to the right of the staircase. It was nothing special, but it would do.

I walked through the house one more time, looking at everything, trying to see myself living there. The bedrooms were small, but cozy. I had a quilt that my grandmother had made that would go on top of my bed. The other bedroom could be used for storage since I didn't need a second bedroom and didn't really know anyone that would come stay with me besides my dad, and he had just been here. I walked back downstairs to the most important room. The office. It was an older house, so everything was trimmed in dark wood. It was beautiful, but I had spent a couple of weeks using my office at Jack's. It was the total opposite and great for writing. This was a sad office.

I met with the realtor and decided I would take it. I handed over my first and last month's rent checks, plus security deposit, and headed back to the hotel. The woman told me I could move in at any time and had given me a key. I got back to my room and flopped down on the bed. Usually, getting something new was exciting. This depressed me more than I already was. I curled up in a ball, still in my coat and shoes, and went to sleep.

Some time later, I woke to my phone ringing. I looked at the screen to see it was Jack calling. I tried to answer the phone, but I wasn't fast enough. I was just about to call him back when the voicemail sounded. Better to check the voicemail first. When I heard his voice, I almost broke down in tears.

. . .

"Hey, baby. I mean Harper. It's..uh.. It's Jack. I was just calling because your shit is here, and I don't know what you need. I packed it up already, so it's ready whenever you need it. Anna says you're staying at the hotel downtown, but I doubt they'll let me drop it there. Just call me back and let me know when and where, and I'll get it where it needs to go....Bye, Harper."

That's it? Seriously? He had already packed my stuff and had it ready to drop off? I had never felt so expendable in all my life. I dialed Anna, knowing I was about to explode.

"Hello?"

"He packed my shit already! He packed it! Just like that. All done."

I paced the room as I talked to her. I needed to punch something to let out my aggression.

"I'll be right there, Harper. Just hang on." She hung up without another word. I paced around the room fuming until Anna finally arrived.

"Listen to the message." I thrust the phone at Anna and stared at her while she listened. When Anna was done, she handed the phone back. She had a confused look on her face. Her brows were furrowed and she chewed on her bottom lip.

"It doesn't make sense. He's a wreck. This just doesn't make any sense."

"I don't understand. How does someone just move on like that? He packed up my stuff like he would move it out and life would go on."

The tears started to come before I had a chance to rein in my emotions, and I hated myself for that. I had never been a crier.

"I can barely get out of bed. I haven't been eating. I only showered once in the past few days, and that was because I could smell myself. How did he just erase me like that?" I slid to the floor and cried as Anna held me.

"Maybe he thought if he moved your stuff out it wouldn't hurt so much. Men do silly things like that. All I know is that he's a wreck, Harper. Luke went over there the other day while I was here. He said Jack looked horrible. There was a broken coffee table and holes in the wall. That doesn't sound like someone who is handling it well to me."

My crying slowed and I wiped my nose on my sleeve. "Maybe you're right. I need to let him know where to take my stuff. I don't need to spend any more money at this hotel."

"Where are you going?"

I totally forgot to let Anna know. "I'm renting a furnished house. I don't have any of my stuff from before, so I had to find something that already had everything...If I give you the information, will you make arrangements with Jack about having my stuff brought over? I don't think I'm ready yet."

"Sure, honey."

I checked out the next morning, but when I went to pay the bill, the manager said the bill had already been settled. Apparently, Jack had come by and told them to charge everything to his card. That man was so sweet. How did I think for one minute that he was over me already? I headed over to the new house and stood in the doorway feeling depressed. It was a nice house, but I couldn't get over how much my life had changed in a year.

I took my bags upstairs and started to unpack my clothes. Then, I got in my car and headed to the grocery store. I was very selective in what I bought. I was making better money now, but I was also taking care of all the bills. What if my next book didn't do as well? No, I needed to stay on a tight budget for now.

I was in the meat department buying some chicken when I saw a frozen turkey in the next case over. At first, a few tears fell, but then I was all out sobbing in the middle of the store. A woman came over to see if I was okay.

"Dear, are you alright? Can I do something for you?"

"Can you make the man I love want to have children with me? Because if you can't do that, there is nothing anyone can do!"

"I'm so sorry, honey." The woman looked at me with sad eyes. I stared at that turkey, hating it for all the memories it brought back, but when I saw a woman reach into the case to grab it, I flipped out.

"Don't you dare touch that turkey! It's mine!" I reached forward and grabbed the turkey and put it in my cart. The lady scurried away, looking at me like I was nuts. And I was nuts. I was in the grocery store sobbing over a turkey. The old lady that was trying to comfort me was looking at me with wary eyes.

"Is there a problem here?"

I turned around to see the same store manager from the Thanksgiving incident standing in front of me. My eyes slid shut, and I knew I was in trouble. That didn't stop my temper from getting the better of me though.

"Oh, that's just perfect. Of course it's you! My day just keeps getting better and better. Do you know that I just lost my boyfriend? After all I went through with that last turkey, and in the end it didn't matter. Nothing mattered, except the one thing that did matter, and then it all fell apart. And here we are, again, back to the turkey!"

I threw my hands in the air and looked up at the ceiling like I was praying for a miracle. I was standing in sweatpants, a ratty t-shirt, and an open wool trench coat. My hair was thrown in a messy ponytail, and I was pretty sure I hadn't brushed my teeth yet today. I was a mess and I was acting like a total basket case.

"Ma'am, I'm gonna have to ask you to leave the store."

I sighed in defeat. "Sure, just let me finish my shopping, and I'll be out of your hair."

"No, ma'am. I'm afraid you're going to have to leave right now. You're causing a disturbance. Again."

"Listen, mister, I'm sure you're just doing your job, but have a heart. I lost my boyfriend, had to find a new home, and have no groceries in the house. Just let me finish my shopping, and I'll be gone."

Tears pricked my eyes as I felt a meltdown coming on. I was going to lose it at any second, or maybe I already had, and that's why I was being asked to leave. I knew my face was swollen from crying, and my eyes were bloodshot. It was my second freak out in a grocery store, over a turkey, in a little over a month. I was going to have to find a new place to shop.

I heard the manager calling for security, so I decided to be proactive. I pulled out my phone and called Sean. I had programmed his number in my phone after the last incident. He answered on the first ring.

"Hey, honey. How ya doing?"

His voice was sweet and sad. He had obviously heard about Jack and I. This was a little awkward, but I couldn't allow that to get in the way right now.

"Um, Sean, I need your help. I'm kind of in trouble."

"Where are you?"

"The grocery store."

"Again? Jesus, Harper. Find a new spot to have a melt down. I'll be right there," he said with a sigh.

In the meantime, security had walked over and started to escort me to the back room that I was so well acquainted with. Then I heard Sean.

"Excuse me, sir." The guard turned and Sean raised his badge. "You are the manager, correct?" he said to the guy on the other side of me.

"Yes, I am."

"Can I have a moment of your time please?" The manager nodded his head.

"I understand Ms. Abbot has gotten herself into a little trouble again. What was it this time? A chicken?" He was trying to lighten the mood, but it fell flat when the manager answered.

"No, it was a turkey again." I lowered my head so Sean couldn't see my face.

"Seriously, Harper? Another turkey? You didn't hit anyone with it, did you?" I started crying. This was all too much, and I wasn't sure

I could take going to jail for the night on top of it. Sean's face softened and he turned back to the manager.

"Look, I'm sure we can come to some kind of understanding here, Mr. Smith."

"I don't think so. She has caused two disturbances in my store in less than two months. I can't have that going on here. I have a business to run."

"Look, what if she promises to not come back in the store for two months?"

"Banned for life."

Sean's eyes went wide. "Six months," he countered.

"Life," the manager said.

"Life. And you don't file any charges?"

The manager agreed and Sean walked me out of the store to my car. "Harper, please don't come back here. I don't know if I can get him to drop the charges if there's another encounter. I'm sorry, but you're gonna have to go grocery shopping somewhere else."

I gave a watery smile to Sean. He really was a great man to come to my rescue. I had caused trouble enough for him. "Thank you so much for your help. I'm not myself, and I kinda lost it in there. I promise not to be any more trouble."

I reached up and gave him a hug, knowing that it was probably the last time I would see him. I got in my car and headed to my lonely house. Who needed to eat, right?

CHAPTER 18

JACK

I WAS LYING on my back, barely conscious on my couch. My arm was hanging over the edge, clutching a whiskey bottle. There wasn't much left, most was in my stomach, but some had spilled on the floor. I was floating in and out of consciousness when I heard a banging on the door. I was trying really hard to get up, but I just couldn't get there. I rolled over and fell flat on my face on the floor. My arms hadn't even made a move to catch me.

My face was smashed against the carpet right in a puddle of whiskey, and I had a strong desire to start lapping at the carpet. I would take the alcohol any way I could. I didn't want to feel a thing. I heard the pounding again, but my body wouldn't cooperate. I floated off in my dream world where Harper was still here, and I was still happy. Then I really was floating, well, sort of. I was being hauled up by my armpits and dragged over to the kitchen table. My head fell against the table with a thud.

"Ow," was all I could think to say, though I didn't really register the pain. Then I was drowning. A bucket of water had been poured over my head and it was freaking cold. I jumped from my chair and the whole room spun. I stumbled around for a second before catching myself on the counter. I looked up to see Sean and Ryan in my house.

"What the fuck, man? I don't come over and swim in your house."

"You were passed out with your face in the carpet. If we had gotten here any later, you wouldn't have been breathing. You've got to pull it together, or do we need to take turns staying with you to make sure you don't fall head first in the toilet?"

I staggered back over to the table and took a seat. If I wanted to get drunk, I would. Neither of them knew what this was like. My life had been ripped apart in a matter of days, and I just wanted to forget for a while.

"Shit, my head is fucked up right now. I need some coffee."

Ryan walked over to the coffee pot and got to work. Sean pulled out some bacon and eggs and started making some breakfast. I must have fallen asleep because one minute I was staring at the table and the next, a plate of food appeared in front of me. I devoured the food and started to feel better. Then I drank the coffee, feeling the liquid scald my throat on the way down. My senses were starting to come back to me.

"You need to go sleep this off, man. Let's get you to bed, and we'll talk when you aren't drunk. Here, take some ibuprofen." Ryan handed me the pills and a glass of water. They helped me down the hall to my room and made sure I wasn't going to smother myself while sleeping.

I woke up to the sun shining through the window and decided it was time to get up and face the day. A shower sounded good right about now. I smelled like a distillery, and it was making me a little nauseous. After I dressed, I walked into the living room, noting that the entire house was clean. The hole in my wall was patched, but I would have to repaint. The remnants of the coffee table were gone, and the stain from the whiskey had been cleaned up. The garbage that had built up from my drunken stupor over the past few days was absent. The kitchen was clean too.

I had packed up all of Harper's stuff the day after she left, hoping it would ease the ache in my chest. Instead, I felt worse and decided the only way to get rid of the pain was to drink it away. I had been drunk or passed out for going on four days now. At least I thought it had been four days.

I walked over to the coffee pot and poured myself a cup. When I turned around, Sean, Ryan, and Sebastian were all sitting at the table staring at me.

"Please, make yourselves at home." I sat down with the rest of them and looked at their faces. They looked pissed. Sebastian was the first to talk.

"Do you know how much it pisses me off to get a call at six a.m. that Sean and Ryan found you passed out with your face in the floor? You know, that's how I found my old man, and it's not something I ever want to experience again."

I ran a hand over my face as the guilt crept in. I knew Sebastian's father was a drunk, and he had been the one to find him dead. When you're so low, though, it's hard to remember that kind of stuff. All you can think about is erasing the pain.

"I'm sorry, man. It got out of hand. It won't happen again." Sebastian watched me for a minute, then nodded his head.

"Harper almost got arrested again," Sean said.

I glared at him and leaned forward. "What do you mean she almost got arrested. What the fuck happened? Is she okay? And why am I just hearing about this now?" I was practically shouting at Sean.

"First of all, I called you yesterday, but you didn't answer your phone. I called you about twenty times. I called again this morning and had to break in when you didn't answer the door. Second, she's fine. I handled the situation and nothing is going to come of it. She was in the grocery store and apparently had a meltdown when she saw a frozen turkey. She caused a scene and the manager was going to press charges, but I talked him out of it. She's banned from the store for life, though."

I barked out a laugh. I pressed the heels of my hands to my eyes and rubbed. "Figures. Leave it to that girl to get in trouble twice over a turkey." I smiled a big smile. "I remember the first time I met her, I knew she was gonna be trouble. Remember when she beat the shit out of the robber? Man, my girl is a piece of work." *My girl.* A sharp ache jabbed me in the chest and my smile dimmed as I realized she was no longer my girl. The whole table fell silent, not knowing what to say.

"You've got to get it together, man. We understand this is hitting you pretty hard, but we can't find you passed out on the floor. You haven't checked in at the garage since before Christmas. Your business is going to go under if you don't take care of shit.

"I know, it's just...I was going to propose to her in a couple of months. Then her dad showed up and made me promise to give her everything or walk away. He said she deserved a big family with lots of kids." I took another drink of coffee. "I don't want kids and she does. Neither of us was willing to bend, so here we are. We opened our presents Christmas morning, and then she told me she loved me, but she couldn't stay because it was too painful. She just left." I shook my head, still not able to believe that she had walked out on me. We both knew it was coming, but I thought I had more time. "I knew she would leave eventually, but damn...I wasn't expecting it to happen like that."

"Are you sure you two can't work it out? She's miserable. I saw her yesterday and she looked like shit. And I mean that in the nicest possible way," Sean quickly added so he didn't piss me off.

"If I could, I would give her kids, but I don't want them. That wouldn't be fair to her. I would start to resent her for forcing me into parenthood, and she would be miserable because I would be an asshole. I can't ask her to give up kids for me. The way she talked about being a mother, she was meant to do that. I won't stand in the way."

"What do you need from us?"

I turned to look at Sebastian. "Don't let me fall down a hole I can't crawl out of. I need you guys to make sure I pick my ass up and get back to work." All three nodded and I knew I could rely on them to keep me going.

I got Harper's new address from Luke and decided the best thing to do would be to take Harper her stuff and say a proper goodbye. I loaded up the boxes in my truck and headed over to her house. I was happy to see that she lived in a good neighborhood. I pulled in and walked the path to her front door. I knocked twice and then chastised myself for being such an idiot. This was a terrible idea. Harper opened the door, and my heart instantly filled at the sight of her beautiful face.

"Hey, pretty girl. How are you?" I croaked out. Harper smiled back at me. She looked thinner and the light in her eyes was gone, but she was just as beautiful as she'd always been.

"I've been better. How about you?"

It was like she was waiting for my answer, as if my response would make or break her. I decided to go with the truth. I didn't want her thinking that I was okay with what happened between us.

"Honestly, I've been pretty shitty. The guys had to drag me off the floor yesterday. Sean told me you had a little bit of trouble at the grocery store the other day. You always were pretty feisty." Harper turned red, but then started laughing. I needed to hear her laugh so bad. It lightened my heart and broke me all at the same time. But I clung to the lighthearted bit, hoping it would help me like things might be alright.

"Yeah, I think I lost my mind for a minute. I didn't assault anyone this time, so I guess that's an improvement."

We laughed, but then it got quiet. There wasn't really anything left to say between us, but I didn't want to drop her stuff and leave either. I didn't want to leave her. I wanted to hold on to her for as long as I could, even though it would hurt.

"Well, I brought your stuff by. Anna told me that you had a new place, and I wanted to see it, make sure you're safe. The neighborhood is good, but I would like Sebastian to come and install a security system for you." She started to protest, but I held up a hand to stop her. "I'll pay for it. I know I can't have you, pretty girl, but I still need to know you're safe." She nodded and thanked me.

"I brought Hooch by for a visit. Do you want to keep him or should I take him home?" He was for her, to keep her safe, and I really hoped she would keep him.

"I would love to have him, if that's okay with you. I have to check with the landlord, but I'm sure it's okay."

"Sure. I bought him for you, and I would feel better if he was here with you. I brought his stuff with me, just in case."

We hauled in the boxes, and Harper showed me around the house. Hooch played in the backyard for a little bit and then found a spot by the couch to lay down. She took me upstairs to see the layout and stopped in her room. The air thickened, and I wanted so badly to kiss her. She was staring at the bed, and I came to a decision.

I walked up behind Harper and wrapped my arms around her. I held her for a minute, and we both relaxed in the comfort of each other's arms. I slowly kissed her neck, memorizing the taste of her skin. This would be the last time I would ever hold her, taste her...the last time she would be mine. She turned in my arms, staring into my eyes. Slipping her fingers between mine, she looked up at me for permission before pulling me over to the bed. When she sat down on the edge of the bed, I leaned in, pushing her down with my body.

My lips trailed along her skin, tasting every inch of her. I felt her body tremble beneath mine, and I instinctively knew that this was killing her as much as it was healing her. We needed this closure though. If I had known the last time I kissed her would be my last, I would have made it last longer. I would have kissed her and never let go. I would have made love to her for hours, not stopping until sunlight lit the morning sky.

But it had ended, and this was all I had left of her, just these few stolen hours, and then we would go our separate ways again. I would have to learn to function without her, and she would be out there on her own, maybe falling for some other guy that would give her everything I couldn't. And if that's the way it was going to happen, if I had to sit by and watch the woman I loved fall for another man, I was going to make damn sure that she remembered me.

Resting my head against hers, I slowly kissed her, slipping my tongue inside her mouth as my hands caressed the body I loved. I cupped her breast in my hand, burning the feel of her into my brain. Every dip and curve to her body would always belong to me, if only in memory. My throat thickened with emotion and my hands shook. This was torture.

Like she could sense that, she sat up and slowly drew her shirt up over her head, taking control for me. My eyes were glued to her as she dragged her shirt over her head. She was so fucking gorgeous. I stood and slid off my pants and pulled her to a standing position. Kneeling down, I pulled down her pants, kissing her hip, across her belly as my hands slid down her legs.

Yanking the pants away from her feet, I gripped her hips and slowly kissed from her belly button down to her pussy. I could feel her arousal through her panties and slowly pulled them down, then pushed her legs apart so I could see her. My tongue shot out and licked her core. When she moaned, I continued to lick her pussy and nibble her clit. I could feel her legs shaking and had to hold her up as she came. She started to collapse, but I caught her and laid her on the bed.

I settled between her legs, my chest vibrating as I felt my cock touch her core. As I pushed inside her, time seemed to slow. Every breath she took, every time her eyes slid closed, it was all locked in my head. I would replay it over and over again, never truly letting her go. I knew I couldn't. Staring into her eyes, I slowly made love to her, resting my forehead against hers as my cock slid in and out of her. I felt her tears slip down her cheeks, but I couldn't look at it. I would break.

She wrapped her legs around me and urged me deeper and harder. When she lifted her hips, I grabbed one leg, pulling it to me as I changed the angle. I thrust deep and slow, dragging it out as my heart hammered in my chest. Sweat slipped from my body, coating hers. Her eyes were filled with ecstasy and she was moaning my name. My breath caught when my brain caught on that this would be the last time I heard her call out my name. I came hard inside her, resting my body against hers, panting hard.

I swallowed hard, shifting to the side so my weight wasn't resting on top of her. I stared at her and she stared back, neither of us speaking. I brushed her wavy hair from her face, cupping her cheek as my heart broke. I felt a tear slip from my eye, and didn't move when her thumb came up and brushed it away.

I held her until she fell asleep. "I will always love you, pretty girl." I kissed her one last time on the lips, my tears coating her soft lips. I watched her sleep, barely able to hold back as I stared at her. I wanted to stay and hold her forever, but it would be easier if I left now. I stayed for another half hour, but when a half hour turned into an hour, I knew I had to tear myself away now. Getting dressed, I looked back at her one last time, knowing I was leaving the love of my life behind.

Walking down the stairs, Hooch sat up, his eyes trained on me as I swiped at my face. He got up, but I gave him the signal to sit. Getting down on my knees, I rubbed his neck and then gave him a hug.

"You take care of her, okay? Don't let her do anything..." I huffed out a laugh, because the list was so long. "Just take care of her."

Standing, I walked to the door, my heart breaking when I heard Hooch whine. It was like he knew what was happening. I shut the door and took a few deep breaths before walking to my truck.

I sat in my truck for a good fifteen minutes, telling myself that I had to leave. It felt so wrong to, but it would be torture for both of us to drag this out. I talked myself into going back inside five times, but each time backed out before I opened the truck door. I finally started the engine and headed home.

I walked through the door to my house, immediately seeing her room at the back of the house, and then looked at the bottle of whiskey on the counter. I wanted it so bad, but if I lost it now, I might never recover. I had made a promise to Sebastian and I would keep it.

I got lost in work, knowing that the only way to move on from the woman I loved was to distract myself. I spent New Year's Eve doing research for the addition to my business, and laid out a plan. I made a list of possible employees to interview and a list of supplies I would need for the new garage. Next, I called Ryan and set up a meeting with him and Logan to go over construction plans. I needed to get this off the ground and move on with life. Burying myself in work was the solution that didn't result in my life going up in flames.

Two days later, I started the interviewing process for mechanics and guys experienced doing custom builds. I found some great guys and had it narrowed down. There was still one more guy I needed to interview. This guy had the most experience with custom built motorcycles. It was an area I had considered would be especially profitable.

I decided to rent a space on the other side of town until my new building was up. I had hired five new guys, and together, we found all the equipment needed to set up a makeshift shop. Weeks passed with me dividing my time between my original shop and the makeshift shop. One of the guys had been working on finding cars and he had a few for us to look at. A few needed to be rebuilt, and I didn't want a single opportunity to pass me by, so we purchased what we could and got to work. Things were moving along right on schedule and we would be moving into the new building in a few weeks if we didn't have any delays.

I spent sixteen hours a day between the two shops and was completely exhausted every night. I came home, took a shower, and laid in bed thinking of Harper. It was the only time I allowed myself to think about her. Mostly because I couldn't erase her from my bed.

Her scent was no longer there, but I could still see her lying next to me, looking so peaceful as she slept. When sleep wouldn't come, I would go for a long run. There were nights I wasn't able to because of the weather and those were the worst nights. If I didn't totally exhaust myself, I couldn't fall asleep. So that became my new routine. Work, run, sleep.

CHAPTER 19

HARPER

I HAD WOKEN to an empty bed. Jack had left me. I knew this was goodbye, but it still hurt. When I left him Christmas morning, I had never stopped to consider that we had already had our last kiss, last hug, made love for the last time, even a last look. It was just all gone. When I opened the door and saw him standing there, I refused to let myself hope it meant something more. And then, when he told me he had my things, my heart sank in my chest.

What happened between us in bed was so much deeper than anything we'd had before. Knowing it would be the last time between us almost broke me, but here I was, still alive, just severely depressed. I couldn't bring myself to leave the comfort of my bed. It still smelled like him, and even though I knew I should throw the sheets in the wash and immediately erase his scent, I couldn't do it.

I laid in bed the rest of the day, staring at the ceiling and dozing off and on. I thought of the first day I met him, how I was so sure that this was all one, big cosmic joke. I could never really get a guy like that, yet I did. I just couldn't keep him. Part of me wished that I had something from him that would remind me of our time together. I had our ornaments now, but those would only go up at Christmas, unless I decided to put up my tree year round. Even in my depressed state, I knew that would be taking things too far.

I decided I was going to give myself this one day to grieve. I got up to let Hooch out a few times, but he seemed to sense my somber mood and didn't try to get me to play. Instead, he came to bed with me, laying his head on my stomach. He always knew when I needed him, and tonight more than ever. It was New Year's Eve. I would be starting tomorrow, the new year, with no Jack, no man that loved me and wanted to kiss me and bring in the new year with me. There was nothing to celebrate, except for maybe the fact that I had survived this long without him. Tomorrow, I would start fresh. I would make this new year a good one, leaving behind my troubles and kicking destiny's ass, or whoever it was that decided to play this fucked up game with me.

The next morning, I was up at six o'clock and ready to start my day. I took a shower and got in some yoga pants and a long sleeved tee. I got some coffee started and began unloading the boxes from yesterday. Some, I took right up to the second bedroom and set them aside for later. There were Christmas decorations in others. I wasn't going to touch those. I would end up a crying mess on the floor. I took those to the second bedroom and shoved them in the closet. I needed to shut them away for a long time.

Around nine o'clock, I sat down and made some breakfast. I had driven to the next town over yesterday morning, before Jack arrived, to go grocery shopping. It was a longer drive for me, but I didn't have a choice. I wouldn't ask Anna to help because she was pregnant, and that was just too much to ask. I had gotten myself into this, and I didn't have anyone else to ask anyway. Jack had gotten all the friends in the break-up, and I was once again alone, but I wouldn't let that get me down. I had been alone for a long time before Jack came along. I would be fine.

I took a break from unpacking around noon and made myself a sandwich. I took it into my office and started to set up my desk. It wasn't as cozy as I would like, but I did my best to make it comfortable. After that was done, I sat down and stared at the blank page on my laptop. What was I going to write about? All my inspiration was gone. I couldn't write romance, not the fluffy stuff anyway. I had too much sadness and anger racing through me.

I just started typing and before I knew it, six hours had passed. The story I started was nothing like I had written in the past. It wasn't a flowery love story. It was dark and sad, and I kind of wondered if it would even sell. I didn't know how my editor would like it, but it was my book and this was all I was feeling. I decided to take a break from writing and went to watch some television. I cozied up under a fleece blanket with Hooch on the couch and settled in. I ended up falling asleep there, snuggling up with my dog. At least he still loved me.

The next day, I got up and started right away. Coffee in hand, I sat down at my computer and started typing. The words flowed through my fingers and I worked all day, only stopping to refill coffee, go to the bathroom, and go for walks with Hooch. By mid-afternoon, my stomach was growling and I was going cross-eyed from staring at the computer screen. I got up to make a sandwich and watch some television when my phone rang. Good Lord, it was my mother. Just the person I needed to speak to. It was better to get the call over with so that I didn't have to speak to her for another few months.

"Hi, Mom."

"Harper. I sent out invitations for a dinner party in a few weeks. I expect you to attend."

No, *hi, how are you, daughter?* or *honey, how is your book coming?* Nope. Not my mother. Right down to business.

"It's really a party for me to show off my new family, but I suppose it would be best if you were there also. Are you still seeing that young man? Will he be attending also?"

I rolled my eyes. Of course she was only wanting me there to keep up appearances. I was a nuisance to her. I didn't fit in her perfect, little mold, so I was essentially useless. We hadn't really gotten along when I was growing up, but Mom had become more and more snooty as time went on. There weren't any traces left of the woman I grew up with. My mother apparently didn't consider me part of the family anymore. There was no way I was attending this party.

"No, Mom, we aren't together anymore, and I'm afraid I won't be able to attend."

"Really, Harper. I just don't understand why you can't seem to hold on to a man. You need to just give him what he wants. You need someone to take care of you. Lord knows you won't ever make any money driveling on in those silly books of yours. You know you're not getting any younger, and the longer you wait, the harder it will be for you to find a reasonable prospect."

Ouch. That hurt. *Need someone to take care of me, silly books, won't make money, not getting any younger, need a reasonable prospect...*It was like she was trying to fit as many zingers into one sentence as possible.

"Once again, I am so grateful that you have given your opinion. Whatever would I do without it?" I asked sarcastically. Although, my mother apparently didn't understand sarcasm, because she continued as if I hadn't said a word.

"Well, it's nice to see that you are finally listening. Now, what you need to do is go apologize to that young man for what you did-"

"I didn't do anything-" I started.

"That doesn't matter, dear. The moment you apologize, he'll be eating out of your palm. Men like to feel they are important, that they're always right. How do you think I got Bruce? I could ask him for a thousand dollars every day, and he would hand it over without blinking because I know how to talk to him. So you see, I will always be taken care of. And that, my dear, is the end goal."

I shook my head, wondering if she had always talked to Dad this way. How did they ever get together? Dad was loving and protective, and Mom was nothing but a gold digger.

"Mom, I'm not trying to get him back, and I'm not looking for someone to take care of me. I'm actually doing pretty well for myself.

I'm writing full time now, and I have my own house." Okay, so the house wasn't technically mine. I was renting, but my mother would never know that. "I actually have to get back to it, so look me up the next time you're in town. Bye, Mom."

I didn't wait for a reply. I hung up, grateful that I wouldn't have to hear her criticize my life choices anymore. I also noticed that she hadn't even responded when I said I wouldn't be attending her party. My guess was she was relieved that her unaccomplished daughter wouldn't be attending. After all, I was a failure compared to her new, rich family. All the sudden, I had an overwhelming desire to prove her wrong. I got up and started writing again. There was no time like the present to prove I had what it took to become a bestseller.

With nothing to do but work on my book, I didn't bother to shower all that much, or even bother to look presentable. Right now, I was snuggled up in fleece pajama pants and a long-sleeved t-shirt while I typed on my computer, cross-legged on my couch. Some days, I was really motivated. I got out of bed and showered, I dressed for the day, and busted my ass working. Other days, days like today, I was wearing the same pajamas I had worn for the past two days. I had some kind of sauce, or what I hoped was sauce, stuck to my shirt. I smelled terrible, but at least I was working.

The depressing days were hard to get through. I knew if I didn't have my writing, I would be drowning. I looked over at Hooch, who was eyeing me like a dead rodent.

"What? You lick your balls. You don't see me judging you." He let out a loud bark. "Hey, at least I bathe from time to time. Maybe not recently, but often enough that I don't have fungus growing on me."

He barked again, but this time, jumped up from the couch. The doorbell rang, and I sighed, setting my computer on the table. It was probably my Amazon order. I had recently become a Prime member, which was a very dangerous thing. I was pretty sure the delivery guy was judging me for the amount of packages he had to deliver.

I flung the door open, ready to glare at the delivery driver for his judgmental looks, but instead, I stood there with my jaw hanging to the floor. Sebastian and Cole stood before me, their eyes wide as they took in my appearance. I subconsciously ran my fingers through my messy bun, grimacing when I felt how greasy my hair was.

"Um...is this too early?" Sebastian asked.

I blinked at him, wondering what the hell he was talking about. "For what?"

"The security system? I called about it last week. Jack wanted one installed for you..."

"Right," I said quickly, like I hadn't completely lost track of time and become a hermit over the past week or weeks. I didn't even know what day it was. "Um...come in."

I stepped aside and allowed them in, grimacing when I looked at the state of my house. It was a disaster. And there was a pair of dirty panties on the arm of the couch. I walked over and quickly snatched it up, shoving it in the waistband of my pants, just so they didn't see it. I remembered taking them off the other night, thinking it was smarter to not wear underwear than to wear dirty underwear. Somewhere around here was my clean laundry, still sitting in a basket, waiting to be folded.

"Are you okay, Harper?" Cole asked, his face filled with concern.

"What?" I laughed. "Me? I'm totally fine. I just...stayed out partying last night and just woke up."

"Who were you partying with?" Sebastian asked suspiciously.

"Uh, Daniel...from...work."

"You work from home."

I narrowed my eyes at him. "From my old job."

"Are you sleeping with him?"

"I hardly think that's any of your business," I said defensively, crossing my arms over my chest, closing my eyes when I realized I wasn't wearing a bra.

"You know, it's okay to not be doing okay," Cole said. "I mean... I'm sure Jack's told you about my issues—"

"I have no issues," I said quickly. "I don't even need a security system. Things are fine around here, and I have Hooch. There's really no need for you to be here."

"Harper, you have a Cheeto in your hair."

I frowned, digging into my hair. "Again?"

"This happens often?" Sebastian asked.

"Apparently," I muttered, remembering when Anna found me after Jack and I broke up the first time. I must be the girl that walked around with Cheetos in her hair after a break-up.

"You know, Jack's not doing so great either," Cole said slowly.

I shook my head. I couldn't hear his name or talk about him. "It's none of my business how Jack is. We're not together anymore." My whole chest felt like it was caving in. I needed to get away from them before I totally broke down. "Just do whatever you need to do. I need to go upstairs and take a shower."

"Maybe brush your teeth too," Sebastian added. I glared at him, but he just shrugged. "I'm just saying..."

I stepped forward, getting in his face. "You know, I don't like you very much."

"Yes, you do. You're just pissed because I pointed out that you're hanging on by a thread. You haven't gotten arrested any more, have you?"

"For your information, I go one town over for groceries now."

He nodded. "Sean told us."

"And I don't intentionally hit people with turkeys. That only happened once. Besides, I don't even like turkey anymore, so there's no need for me to buy one. Or ham either."

"I didn't—"

"And I'll probably give up chicken too. Anything with feathers is out!"

I snapped my mouth shut, fully embarrassed at my rant. Turning on my heel, I marched up the stairs and slammed the bathroom door behind me. Staring at myself in the mirror, I was completely mortified. What the hell was wrong with me? I was snapping at him over turkeys?

It wasn't fair. I just missed Jack so much, and I was doing okay until he walked into my house. Well, I didn't feel like absolute shit until then. I wasn't functioning normally, but at least I wasn't breaking down. Tears filled my eyes as I sat down on the edge of the tub, crying into my hands. I hated this. It wasn't fair. This whole situation sucked, and now I had to see his friends?

I turned on the shower and sat in the bottom of the tub, not even bothering to take off my clothes. The shower was just to hide the sound of me crying. After the water started to turn lukewarm, I stripped my clothes off and showered for the first time in days, making sure to shave my legs and under my arms. When I stepped out, I was somewhat calmer, but my face was still splotchy and red. I had to find a way to pull my shit together. I couldn't keep falling apart every time something reminded me of Jack. I was bound to run into him or his friends again, and I needed to learn how to deal with that.

CHAPTER 20

JACK

"YOU REALLY NEED to get away from work more," Sebastian said from behind me.

I had my head buried under the hood of a car, trying to distract myself from going over to see Harper. I pushed myself harder and harder every day, telling myself that if I just kept working, eventually I would forget about her. It hadn't worked yet, but I was hopeful that one day, it would kick in.

"Just have a lot of shit to do."

"Yeah, you barely have time for your friends anymore with two businesses going."

"It's just the one," I corrected. "I'm just waiting for the building to be finished."

"Right, and you're dividing your time between here and there. I know. I've talked to Sal. He's the only one that actually answers my calls anymore."

Sighing, I stepped out from under the hood and turned to meet his stare. "What do you want me to say?"

He shrugged. "Nothing. I just came to make sure you were okay."

"I'm fine. Just busy."

"You mentioned that."

"Did you have a point coming here other than to say the same thing over and over?"

"Yeah, I did that job for you."

I nodded, ducking my head so I didn't have to look at him. "So, it's all taken care of?"

"Security is installed and the house is secure."

I nodded again. "And...what about Harper?"

"What about her?"

"Is she okay?" I asked, not sure I wanted the answer.

"Oh, you know Harper. She's...a mess, just like every other day."

"But, is she..." I swallowed hard, still unable to look up at him.

"Well, she answered the door in her pajamas, she smelled like garbage, and she had a Cheeto in her hair."

I huffed out a laugh, finally looking up at him. Was it wrong that I was glad that she wasn't doing okay? I hated the idea that I was the only one that felt this way.

"From what I can tell, she's working and everything, but she's not exactly doing great. She tried telling me some story about going out with some guy, but it was a lie."

"How could you tell?" I asked, my heart pounding faster.

"Well, you don't go out smelling the way she did. Not to mention, she's not over you, so there's no way she would go out with another guy."

"Maybe she was just hooking up. You know we've done the same thing. Why should I expect her to not sleep with other men?"

"I'm not saying you should, but while we were installing the security, she was upstairs in the bathroom, crying for a good hour. Even the sound of the shower couldn't disguise her cries."

My heart picked up, racing out of control. She was crying? I didn't want her crying. I mean, I didn't mind that she shed a few tears for me, but I didn't want her to be miserable. I wanted her to be able to move on. Not with another guy, but at least move forward like I was.

"Did you go comfort her?"

"In the shower?" he asked incredulously.

"Yeah, in the shower. You just let her cry up there by herself? What kind of asshole are you?"

"The kind of asshole that knows that you would have beat my ass if I had seen her naked," he retorted.

I was conflicted. No, I didn't want him seeing her naked, but I hated that she was so alone. I had the guys. Anna and Luke were busy in their lives, preparing for the baby. Who did Harper have?

"I need you to do something for me."

"Okay."

"I need you to go find a girlfriend."

His brows furrowed. "Why?"

"I need you to find a woman so that she can befriend Harper."

He shook his head slightly. "You want me to go find a girlfriend so that she can befriend your ex-girlfriend."

"Yeah."

"That doesn't make any sense."

"Yes, it does," I insisted. "She's all alone. She has no one to keep her company right now. She needs someone to be there for her."

"And you think she'll make friends with *my* girlfriend?"

"Fine, don't make her your girlfriend. Just make friends with a woman and set her up with Harper."

"Are you kidding me right now? So, now I'm supposed to have a fake girlfriend for you?"

"Look, she needs someone to rely on, someone to talk to. I have you guys and my mom. She doesn't have anyone right now."

"She has Anna."

I shook my head. "Luke said she's really busy with work, trying to get ready for the baby. She's not around."

He sighed. "Alright, let's say for a minute that I found a woman, and then somehow found a way to introduce her to Harper, how do you know they would hit it off? And how do you know that the minute Harper found out she was friends with me, that she wouldn't take off running in the other direction?"

"Well...just make sure that she never says anything about you."

"Jack," he said gruffly. "You have to let this go. Either you're with Harper or you're not. You can't insert yourself into her life."

"I'm not! You are."

"It's the same fucking thing. You can't just find people for her to hang out with. She has to move on in her own time, and so do you. If you keep getting involved in her life, how are either of you supposed to move on?"

I frowned. "Then why the fuck did you show up here and start talking about her?"

"Well, I was sort of thinking that you would pull your head out of your ass and go work shit out with her. Instead, you're talking about setting me up with a fake girlfriend to be her fake friend."

"Not true," I snapped. "I wanted her to be her real friend."

He rolled his eyes at me. "Do you hear how ridiculous that is? What are you going to do next? Pick out who she'll date?"

"Do you think I could do that?" I asked, trying to think of how that could work. "Maybe I could set up an online dating profile for her. Or you could run background checks on all the guys within fifty miles. Then we could weed out the ones with the least potential."

He scrubbed his hands over his face and sighed. "I don't even want to touch on the fact that you're basically stalking the woman you ended things with—"

"She walked out the door," I corrected.

"It was a mutual decision and you know it. Look, the point is, you can't keep interfering in her life. You can't choose who her friends are, and no, you can't pick out her next boyfriend. Frankly, she's not ready for that, and neither are you. I don't need to pick you up off the floor again after you pass out drunk from finding out she's moved on. And she will move on eventually. Are you sure you're ready for that?"

"No," I grumbled, "but there's nothing I can do about it. We don't want the same things."

"Then let her go."

"I know," I said frustratedly.

"No, really listen to me. Don't ask about her, don't check on the dog, don't drive past her house. Just walk away. If you don't, you'll never be able to let her go."

I knew he was right. I had nothing to say to that, so I just stared at the ground, realizing that she really was gone from my life, and there was nothing I could do about it.

CHAPTER 21

HARPER

I FINISHED my book a week later and spent another week proofreading and editing. Then, I sent it off to my editor for review. Now I had time to kill, and I would normally take some time off between books, but I had some ideas swirling about several books. I took notes on each of my book ideas and started the idea process for all of them. I had so many thoughts running through my head, I couldn't focus on one book. Every time I wrote down an idea, another appeared. I had never been so focused on work before. In fact, I realized that I hadn't spoken with anyone in two weeks. Then, I felt kind of sad that no one had thought to check in with me. Was I really so forgettable?

Shit. I wasn't forgettable, but I had forgotten my best friend. Anna had gotten married New Year's Eve, and with everything that was going on, I hadn't even thought to call or send a text. I was the worst friend ever. I called Anna, but it went to voicemail, so I sent her a text about being super busy writing and asked when would be a good time to get together. Anna replied an hour later that she would stop by the next day.

I had lunch prepared for Anna when she showed up. I was so

nervous to see her, afraid that she would be pissed at me, but when she walked up to me, she was grinning.

"Hey! It's so good to see you!"

I was immediately wrapped in a hug that almost had me bursting into tears. I held her tight, just needing something after the last few weeks. I pulled back, swiping a stray tear from my eye.

"You look so good." I grabbed her hand and examined the beautiful ring on her finger. "It's so beautiful."

"Thanks."

"How was the wedding?"

Her face lit up as she followed me inside. "It was perfect. I mean, it was Vegas, so it wasn't my dream wedding, but it was fine for us. I didn't really want to plan a wedding anyway. I'm just glad it's all over."

"Did your parents fly out with you?"

"No, neither did his. We just kept it simple. It was actually pretty nice to not have anyone there." Her eyes widened and she grabbed my hand. "Not that I didn't want you there."

I brushed her off. "Are you kidding? I would have been the most depressing guest to have at a wedding. I would have cried in the flowers and probably ripped your dress walking down the aisle."

"Why would you have done that?" she laughed.

"Well, I would have been crying so hard that I wouldn't be able to see a thing. And then I would have stepped on your train, fallen forward and grabbed onto the back of your dress, then I would have ripped the whole back off. It would have been a disaster."

She bit her lip, laughing slightly. "And why would you be walking behind me?"

I shrugged. "I have no idea, but I'm telling you, it would have been terrible."

I glanced down at the ring again, trying not to keep looking at it, but my eyes were drawn to it. I wanted to feel so happy for her, but I kept thinking about how I was supposed to have this with Jack. I listened as she kept telling me about the honeymoon, but inside, I was dying. Would it feel this way when she told me about her pregnancy? Would I feel so empty when her baby was born and I held it for the first time? God, I hoped not.

"Anna, I'm so sorry that I haven't gotten ahold of you sooner. I was so lost after what happened, and then I got wrapped up in my books. I decided New Year's Eve that I was going to start fresh, and I guess that took over. I haven't really thought of anything else the last few weeks."

"Sweetie, I saw you, remember? I know you weren't in a good place, so don't even think anything of it. All that's important is that you're able to move on and that, well, I'm married!" Anna squealed in delight and did a little happy dance. It was hard not to be happy for her when she was so excited.

I gave her a hug and jumped around with her. "I am so happy for you. So, tell me how the pregnancy is going." We walked over to the kitchen and grabbed some food while we ate.

"It's going well. I'm so hungry all the time. I swear I'm going to weigh fifty pounds more than I'm supposed to. They give you these guidelines of how much you're supposed to weigh when you're pregnant. It's crazy. If I want to eat for ten, I will. It's my pregnancy, and my baby is telling me to eat everything in sight."

With that she reached over and grabbed a second helping for her plate. Man, she could really pack it away. But where was it all going? She didn't look like she had put on any weight.

"So, how's Luke doing with all this? Has he freaked out yet, or is he the best husband ever?"

"Luke has been great. He's been smothering me with love. He kisses my belly at night and talks to the baby. I don't think the baby can hear yet, but it's absolutely adorable. I've also been getting foot massages every night, and he's been going out at all hours of the night to get me food."

Jack flitted through my head again, but I kept my smile plastered on my face. I didn't want her to think she was depressing me. This was a happy time for her. But when I tried to think of moving on, of finding someone that could give me what Jack couldn't, no man existed. No one would ever measure up to him. He had given me so much. He encouraged me in my career. He gave me confidence to go full force, when before I was stagnant. He gave me family, even if there were no kids, and I was starting to wonder why that wasn't enough.

Anna, always aware of how others were feeling, reached over and squeezed my hand. "Hey, are you okay? Did I say too much?"

"No, I'm good. I'm just adjusting still. It'll take me a while to not feel the hurt when talking about these things, but I need you to keep telling me about this stuff, because it reminds me that life goes on. Besides, you shouldn't have to hide your joy from me because you don't want to hurt my feelings. I'm a big girl. I can take it."

After that, we moved on to talking about my books and all the progress I had made. Anna stayed for another hour before needing to get back home. After a much needed pep talk, I went back to my office and got to work again. I was determined to work out my sadness, and there was no time like the present.

It was mid-March when I saw Jack again. I had decided to take a walk around the lake to clear my head. I was having trouble deciding which direction I wanted to take my book when I saw him standing off the path talking to a woman. I stopped in my tracks and started to panic. I had Hooch with me. If he saw Jack, he would race over to him. I wouldn't be able to hold him back. My heart was practically beating out of my chest, and I felt like I was going to throw up.

"Hooch, let's go," I hissed, dragging him with me. My feet propelled me backward as I tried to get as far away as possible, but I stopped when I felt a solid object behind me. I practically fell to the ground, but strong arms caught me.

"Are you okay? You look like you've seen a ghost."

I didn't have time to look at the voice responsible. I was too concerned that I was drawing attention to myself, and I couldn't run into him now. I wasn't ready. I looked back over at Jack and saw him glancing my way. I shrunk back against some trees and did my best to conceal myself amongst the branches. Yanking on Hooch's collar, I pulled him deeper into the trees with me.

"Sit," I hissed, breathing a sigh of relief when he listened to me.

"Miss, are you okay? Can I get you something?"

I glanced over and saw a handsome man staring back at me. He was tall with dirty blonde hair, and he was built like a tank. I looked back over and saw that Jack was turning to leave. If I didn't answer this man, I might draw more attention to myself, so I responded as I watched Jack leave.

"Yeah, I'm good. I just thought I saw a bear."

"A bear? I don't think there are many bears in these parts."

He still wasn't out of sight, so I continued to talk to the man, no doubt making a total fool of myself.

"Yeah, it totally could have been a bear. It was....um... big."

"Big?" The man sounded totally unconvinced with my description, so I tried to think of how else to describe a bear.

"And brown."

"Yeah," he said nodding. "Bears are usually big and brown. What else did you see that made you think it was a bear?"

I watched Jack walk away and sighed with relief, finally gathering my wits about me.

"Hmmm?" I asked him because I really couldn't remember what we were talking about.

"The bear?"

"A bear? Where?" I asked, looking all around. "Around here? Are you sure?"

Oh, crap. There had been a bear here, and I was so concerned about Jack seeing me that I didn't even pay attention to what was going on around me. Jack was right. I attracted trouble. I could have been eaten! Was it still around? I looked all around trying to see the elusive bear.

"No, you told me you saw a bear. That's what all this back and forth has been about." He gestured between the two of us. "Am I missing something here? Did you just escape the nuthouse or something?"

Nice. I was making a total ass out of myself. I stepped out from behind the trees in an attempt to escape Crazytown.

"I'm so sorry. My name is aaahhh-"

I screamed as my foot slid down the embankment, and my body quickly followed. I tried to snag a tree branch, but I was already too far away and headed into the lake. I was pulling Hooch down with me, and I quickly released his leash so I didn't drag him down with me. The man tried to reach for me, but it was as if it was all happening in fast forward. One minute he was there and the next, I was plunging through the partially frozen lake.

I was submerged for what felt like hours, but was probably fifteen seconds. My body was in so much pain and felt like knives were piercing me all over. I had never felt so cold in all my life. I felt myself being pulled upwards and dragged out onto the embankment. Two arms wrapped around me and held me close as I shook. My teeth were rattling in my head, and I felt like they were going to fall out. He hauled me up and ran to his truck. My body hurt with every step he took.

I vaguely heard him whistle to Hooch, and heard his bark as he followed us. He threw me in the passenger side, letting the dog into the back, then jumped into the driver's side. I felt like I had done this same scenario before, but I couldn't think about it now. I was freezing and needed to warm up. I spoke in broken words to the man driving the truck.

"I...live....just on the....n-next...s-street."

The man turned down the next street, and I pointed to my house with a shaky finger.

"R-right there."

He squealed into the driveway and bolted out of the truck, running around to my side. He lifted me out of the truck and started sprinting to the front door. With shaky hands, I pulled out my key and handed it to him. He quickly unlocked the door and stormed into the house.

"Which way to the bathroom?"

"Ups-upstairs."

He was already moving to the stairs by the time I finished the word. He took the stairs two at a time, and rushed into the bathroom, setting me on the edge of the tub. The water rushed behind me as I stared at the man, quickly moving to take care of me. He undressed me in record time, pulling down my pants and stripping me of my coat and shoes, leaving me in just my panties and bra. Ever-so-gently, he lifted me, setting me down in the warm water that was filling the tub. The warm water felt scalding against my frozen skin, the sensation of pin pricks almost too much to bear. I whimpered as the warmth started to work its way back into my body.

Slowly, I relaxed back against the tub, closing my eyes to think of other things. I didn't know how long I sat there before he spoke.

"You want to tell me what that was all about back there?"

I shook my head as my teeth chattered. I didn't need anymore humiliation right now. "No." After a few minutes, I decided that since I was already sitting in a tub practically naked next to this guy, he should at least know my name.

"I'm H-Harper."

He smiled a friendly smile that put me at ease. "Drew. I would say it's nice to meet you, but under the circumstances..." He didn't finish the thought and I huffed out a laugh.

"So, do you always end up in a lake while fleeing imaginary bears, or is this just bad luck for you?"

He smiled at me and I smiled back. This was the first time I had smiled since my breakup with Jack, besides with Anna. I didn't count that, because her news was joyous. This man was just able to make me smile with kindness.

"Usually I can t-take on a bear, but... I'm off my g-game a little."

We sat in silence the rest of the time I soaked. He got up and grabbed my towel off the back of the door, then helped me to stand. Wrapping the towel around me, he carried me into the bedroom, setting me on the edge of the bed. I watched in fascination as he rifled through my drawers, like he knew exactly where to find everything. He came up with sweatpants, a sweatshirt, and fuzzy, warm socks. When he turned to dress me, he realized I was still in my wet panties and bra.

"Um...how about you take off your underwear and bra. I'll get you something else to put on."

He turned and rummaged around for new underwear. I was suddenly aware of how I should be feeling shy, but I wasn't. Maybe it was because he saved me, but I didn't feel uncomfortable with him. He was being respectful of me and wasn't trying to ogle me. My arms shook as I tried to slide my panties down, but my fingers wouldn't curl properly to pull them off. Drew saw my trouble and came over to help.

"Here, let me help you. I promise not to look."

He reached behind me and unclasped my bra. His warm hands skimmed my back, making me want to lean into him and take more of his warmth. He slid my panties down my legs, his face right in front of my most intimate area, but he was a gentleman and didn't look. I couldn't have cared either way though. I was just too exhausted to care. I wanted to be warm again, and I would do anything to achieve it. He dressed me, then grabbed the quilt off my bed and wrapped it around me. Then he picked me up and carried me downstairs, setting me on the couch. I was still shaking from the residual cold, or maybe it was the memory of how cold I was. He returned a few minutes later with a cup of hot apple cider. He sat down next to me, turning me so my back was to his front, and wrapped his arms around me. I was immediately enveloped in his warmth, relishing the feeling of being taken care of. A little piece of my heart felt like it was being mended by the act of kindness. Drew was reminding me of what it was like to have someone care for me. I drank my cider and he laid his cheek against my head.

"So, are you gonna tell me what happened back there?"

I hesitated for a second, but this man had already done so much for me. He deserved some answers. "I saw my ex-boyfriend."

"Ahh, so you thought you would avoid him by jumping in the lake. Solid plan."

I started laughing. It was all so ridiculous. "I just wasn't ready to see him yet, so I decided to hide behind some trees. Then you came along, and I was sure he would see me. I was just waiting until he left to come out." I took a sip of the cider, moaning as the warmth sank into my belly. "Thank you for pulling me out."

"Anytime. Just make sure you write down a schedule for me so I know when and where to go."

Drew stayed sitting with me for a few hours. We mostly sat in comfortable silence. I dozed a little against his chest, his heartbeat lulling me to sleep. My emotions were all over the place with the day's events, and I started to wonder what I would do when he told me he was leaving. I couldn't describe it exactly, but I felt better with him here.

After sleeping on Drew's chest for a while, he picked me up and carried me back upstairs. He laid me down on the bed and left the room. My heart dropped to my stomach as he left. I just wanted him to stay the night and hold me. I knew I shouldn't, because he was a stranger, but I felt safe with him. Relief swept through me when he returned a few minutes later carrying another blanket.

"Do you mind if I stay?"

I shook my head, and he laid out the blanket on top of me, then climbed in next to me. He cradled my body from behind and wrapped me into his body. It wasn't sexual. It felt like we were comforting one another. I drifted off to sleep and slept better than I had in three months.

CHAPTER 22

HARPER

I WOKE the next morning nice and toasty warm. After my day yesterday, staying in this nice, warm cocoon sounded pretty good. I had slept through the night, which was something I hadn't been able to accomplish since Jack and I broke up. Drew shifted behind me and gave a big yawn. Unaware that I was doing it, I shifted closer and snuggled into him. He was like a big teddy bear, and I found myself sniffing the manly scent of his shirt. His arms were locked around me in a comforting way that only a man could provide.

"Good morning," he said as he looked over at me. "I haven't slept that well in years."

"It's been a few months for me."

"How about I go make us some breakfast? Maybe you should go take a shower."

"Oh my gosh, do I smell?" Suddenly very self-conscious, I started sniffing myself to find the foul odor and Drew started to laugh.

"No, I just think you're probably going to be a little stiff, and a hot shower would help to loosen you up. Go on. I'll go get breakfast started."

I sighed in relief that I hadn't sent him running downstairs due to toxic body odor. I laid in the warmth a few more minutes before dragging myself out of my cocoon and got into the shower. He was right. This felt amazing. My joints were stiff and all I wanted was to go back and snuggle in my blanket. I wasn't sure the chill would ever go away. It felt like the chill had settled deep in my bones. Although, I did wonder if part of the chill was the shock of seeing Jack yesterday. That was something I wouldn't likely recover from with a warm blanket. I got dressed and headed downstairs, my stomach growling when I smelled the bacon and eggs. Sitting down, I dug in, groaning at how good it tasted.

"So, I noticed last night that you have a security system, but it wasn't turned on. Is it broken?"

"No. My ex insisted it be installed after I moved in. I always forget to set it because I feel pretty safe here. Honestly, I don't think I've set it more than a few times."

"That doesn't sound like a normal breakup. Most guys don't make sure their ex is taken care of after they're through. What am I missing?"

I took extra time to swallow my eggs, delaying the inevitable conversation. "We didn't want to break up. We just wanted different things. I wanted kids, and he didn't. Neither of us were willing to bend, and we both knew that staying together would only hurt us both. We ended it Christmas morning. It was pretty painful, but..." What else was there to say? It was over, and no amount of me wishing for things to change would make a difference.

"So the breakup was mutual, but not wanted. Did he have a reason for having a security system installed?"

"He says I attract trouble, and he needed to know I was safe since he wouldn't be around anymore."

"I can't disagree with him there. I did meet you while you were falling into a lake."

"Hey, that's not accurate. That was at least three minutes into our conversation," I said, narrowing my eyes at him.

"Well, ya got me there," he chuckled. "So, you're the first person

I've met in this town. I was just passing through and stopped at the lake to try to find out where to go next."

"And where is it you're going?"

"Well, I haven't figured that out yet. I was kind of distracted during my musings."

"Where are you from?"

"All around. I grew up in Florida, but I've been traveling from town to town, trying to find a place to settle." He looked at the counter and cleared his throat. "Just needed a change, ya know?"

"Yeah." I nodded thoughtfully. I totally get needing a change. If it weren't for Anna, I might have decided to move on, but she was my best friend. I wasn't ready to leave the only person in the United States that cared for me. It would be too hard to move on without her. I got the feeling that he had been hurt also and had chosen to get away. I could see the pain in his eyes, and I understood what that felt like, but he didn't seem ready to talk about it, especially with a stranger.

"It feels like we might be chasing the same thing at the moment. "

I nodded. "So where are you staying? Or are you moving on?"

"That depends."

"On?"

"You. Can I leave and trust you to not fall in the lake again, or am I gonna have to stick around and watch over you?"

I knew what this man was asking. He wanted to know if he had a place in my life. I knew he felt this connection between us. It wasn't romantic, but a meeting of two souls that desperately needed a friend. I didn't want him to move, as selfish as that sounded. I liked Drew, and he brought me a comfort that I hadn't felt with anyone else yet.

"Stay."

Drew was going to find a motel to stay in until he found an apartment, but that seemed so silly to me. I trusted him, and I had a spare room that he could sleep in, so it only made sense that he stayed here. That's what I told myself. I finally convinced him to stay, and even though he fought me, he decided that I needed someone to watch over me, and it would be best for him to stay. He pointed out that I needed to work on my safety standards, since I was allowing a man I just met to move in with me, but I wasn't worried. I was generally a good judge of character, and Drew was definitely one of the best men I had ever met. Drew would never hurt me, of that I was sure.

He went out to his truck and grabbed his bags. He only had two. He said he had been renting furnished apartments, so he didn't need to buy stuff. He had everything he needed in his two bags. It made me a little sad that he had moved around so much that he hadn't collected anything more. Since the guest room wasn't set up yet, I said he could sleep in my bed again if he wanted. I really just wanted him to hold me some more. That was how it all started. Every night we slept together, and never did make up that second bed. He never once mentioned the other room, other than to ask if he could set up a weight room.

About a week after Drew moved in, Anna stopped by unannounced. Drew and I were vegging out on the couch watching a movie when there was a knock on the door. I opened it and I swear Anna's jaw hit the floor when she saw Drew sitting on the couch in his pajamas. Shock marred her face, and maybe a little bit of judgement.

"Harper, I knew you were gonna move on, but I just didn't expect you to move on so fast."

I looked at her strangely then started laughing. "Come on in, Anna. This is Drew. He's living with me now."

"What! Harper, you don't just go out and find a new man like a puppy. What were you thinking?"

"We aren't together. Drew pulled me out of a lake when I saw Jack on the trails."

She pulled back in confusion. "Sorry, start at the beginning."

Drew got up from the couch and headed into the kitchen. "I'm gonna go make some coffee and let you two catch up. Nice to meet you, Anna."

I told her the story of how Drew and I met, and then how Drew was passing through town and needed a place to stay.

"So, he's going to be living with me now."

She shook her head in disbelief. "Harper, I just can't believe this. I mean, even if you're not dating the man, you don't just move a stranger in with you. That's how you end up buried in the woods."

I quirked an eyebrow at her. "Don't you think if he wanted to kill me, he would have just let me drown?"

"Not if he gets off on killing," she hissed. "Seriously, you don't know anything about him. You just invited him into your house. He may sleep down the hall from you, but that wouldn't stop him from doing...stuff."

I winced slightly, not able to hide the reaction from her.

"Oh my God, he's already done stuff. I need to call Luke. No, I need to call Sebastian. He's trained in this. Of course, I can't tell Jack. He'll totally come over here and kick his ass. More like kill him, but either way—"

"Anna!" I cut her off, grabbing her hand. "He hasn't done anything. I promise."

"Then what was that look about?" I didn't say anything at first, and she caught on. "Oh my gosh. You're sleeping with him."

"Yes, but not like that."

"Not like what? How do you sleep with someone, but not like that?" she asked testily. "Is there another way that I'm missing?"

"We're sharing a bed, but that's it. We don't actually do anything. He's more like a brother."

"A brother? Seriously? Harper, you don't just pick up a brother on the side of the road. That relationship has to build. Of course, with you, anything is possible. I mean, look at how you met Jack."

I sighed, really wishing I didn't have to explain myself. "Look, I don't know what to tell you. There's something there...a bond between us. It's not sexual. It's just...there."

"Well, thank you for clearing that up. It all makes sense now."

"Just trust me, please. I know what I'm doing here."

She sighed heavily, pursing her lips at me, but finally relented. "Fine, but Sebastian needs to know about this. Can you imagine what would happen if you had an alarm on your house and he showed up, only to find Drew in your bed? He would shoot first and ask questions later."

I nodded. "Yeah, you're right."

"Everything okay in here?" Drew asked as he walked back into the living room with two cups of coffee. He handed one to me and one to Anna, but she waved him off.

"No, thanks. I'm not sticking around." She stood and eyed Drew warily. "If you do anything to hurt her, I will come after you with a chair, a really sturdy one. Not one of those flimsy ones that break with one whack. I'm talking about the ones that are really strong. Ask Harper, I know how to use one."

Drew looked at me slightly confused, and I nodded. "It's true. We're both highly trained with chairs and posters."

"Chairs and—do I want to know?"

"I'll tell you some other time."

He nodded. "I think I definitely need to know how a poster is deadly. You don't have any lying around, do you?" he asked, his eyes scanning the room.

"No, but I can always go get one," I said with a smirk.

Anna grabbed her purse, pulling the strap over her shoulder. "I was really just wondering if you wanted me to do your grocery shopping for you," she said as I walked her to the door.

"No, I just go to the next town over. Besides, you don't need to be doing my shopping while you're growing a little bean sprout."

Drew raised an eyebrow at me. "Why would she need to do your grocery shopping for you?" Anna smirked and gave a flick of her wrist as she laughed all the way to her car. I shut the door and turned to face him.

"I'm waiting." Drew stood with his hands in his pajama pockets staring at me.

"Okay, so when I was dating Jack, we were doing a big Thanksgiving feast together. I was doing the shopping and had an...altercation with an old lady, and another woman ended up being hit with the turkey."

I peered up at Drew with a sheepish look on my face. He just stared at me with a dumbfounded expression before a huge belly laugh escaped him. I rolled my eyes at his reaction. Everyone thought it was funny. I had become the laughing stock of the town, the lady that wielded a deadly turkey when someone pissed me off.

"Laugh all you want, but that's not even the worst part. I was arrested for assault with a turkey and was thrown in jail for several hours."

Drew did laugh all he wanted. In fact, he seemed to think it was downright hilarious what I went through. After a minute, I couldn't help myself and joined in the laughing. When I had calmed down enough, I told him the rest.

"After Jack and I broke up, I was doing some grocery shopping and I saw a turkey in the case. I started sobbing, and I threw a fit when another woman tried to grab it. The manager that was there the first time, was there the second time also. He wanted me arrested, but I called a police officer that's a friend of Jack's. He was able to keep him from pressing charges, but I'm banned from the store for life."

I burst out laughing again, but Drew just smiled.

"I know it's not funny, but it's either laugh or cry, and I really don't want to cry anymore."

Drew pulled me into a hug. "It'll get easier. Maybe not for a while, but you'll see. One day you'll wake up and it won't seem so bad anymore. The pressure will be gone from your chest, and you'll feel like you can live again."

"Is that what it's like for you?" I murmured into his chest.

"No, but it's gotten easier being here with you."

After a few days, I went back to my writing. I was almost finished with my next book and just had to decide how I wanted my character to die. Memories swirled in my head of things I had threatened Jack with when I was upset. Of course, I would never perform any of those heinous threats, but who said my characters couldn't? An evil grin pulled at my lips and I started plotting. I was pretty sure I was entering the anger stage of grief, because I seemed to enjoy death and torture scenes a little more than I should. I finished that book a few days later and started writing another book while that one was being edited. I just couldn't stop typing. This next book was kind of insane and I knew it. All my anger was pouring out on the pages. I was sure when my editor read this, she would have a talk with me about the erratic nature of my writing style. Each book, as a whole, was fine, but could I keep my readers interested when each book was so different? The good news was that I had gone to self-publishing, so even if my normal fan base didn't like it, I didn't have to answer to a publisher. As it turned out, my editor loved it.

Drew had been living with me for a little over a month and things were very good between us. We were still sharing a bed at night, though it never went any further than us holding one another. In a way, Drew had become my new best friend. It wasn't that Anna was missing from my life, but she had a new baby on the way, and I didn't want my bad mood to put a damper on things. We still got together, but mainly to talk about having a baby shower and how to decorate the nursery. I helped Anna do research on baby safety, and we figured out all the ways she would need to baby-proof her house. It was still early, but better safe than sorry.

Drew and I were sitting around on a Saturday night watching a movie when I felt Drew staring at me.

"What?"

"I think we need to get out of the house. We've both been sitting around here moping for too long. Go get your best cowgirl outfit on, and let's go line dancing."

"I don't know. It's kind of late. I'm gonna be going to bed soon."

"Harper, it's six o'clock. Get your butt upstairs and get dressed. We leave in a half hour."

Drew could be commanding just like Jack. I had always hated when Jack got too alpha with me, but after we broke up, I found that was one of the things I missed most. He did it because he cared, and wanted to take charge and make sure I was okay, not because he wanted to rule me.

I jumped up and ran upstairs. A half hour didn't give me much time to get ready. I decided to wash my hair really quick and towel dry it. Then, I got out my favorite jeans, a blue plaid collared shirt, and my favorite cowboy boots. I came downstairs, ready to go out and have some fun. I had never hung out with Drew outside the house, so this should be fun.

We drove to the country club and my spirits lifted immediately. We ordered some drinks and sat on the stools at the bar. After a few drinks and us poking fun at other dancers, we got out on the dance floor and started shakin' it. Some dances were line dances, but some, Drew wrapped me in his arms and we slow danced. Drew surprised me when he pulled me in for a two step. He was quite good and was spinning me around the dance floor with great ease. I was laughing, and for the first time in a long time, I felt like myself. Drew was slowly healing me and I hoped I could do the same for him.

The next day, Drew told me that he was going to need to find work if he was going to stick around. I felt panic swell in my chest at the thought of him leaving.

"What are you looking for?"

"I don't know. Maybe something in construction. I used to do quite a bit of that, and I'm pretty good with a hammer."

"Well, I know the owners of the construction company in the area. I could put in a good word for you, if you want."

"How do you know them?" He seemed suspicious.

"Well, they're friends of Jack's actually, but they're really nice. I think you'd like them."

"I'm not so sure that's a good idea. What if we became friends? That would put you in an awkward position."

"Well, they no doubt already know about you from Anna, so I'm sure they're all gonna look into you anyway, if Sean hasn't by now. If I introduce you, and explain about you and I, they're gonna see it as helping out a friend and not the enemy."

"And what exactly would you tell them?"

"Just that you're a friend of mine and that you're looking for work."

"But you said they would have heard about me from Anna. They're gonna know that we're living together. I'm sure they're not gonna like that."

"I'm just going to explain to them that you're my friend, and I need you. You don't realize what you're doing for me, Drew. You're helping me heal, and I don't know where I would be right now without you. Besides, if I don't talk to them, they probably won't hire you out of loyalty to Jack."

He thought about it for a minute, and then agreed that I could talk to them. It was better if I talked to them and cleared the air first. I worked up the nerve to make the phone call, then dialed Ryan at the office. I hadn't spoken to him since Christmas, so it was difficult to just pick up the phone and call.

"Jackson Walker Construction. How may I help you?" a woman answered.

"Hi, this is Harper Abbot. I'm a friend of Ryan's, and I was wondering if I could speak with him?"

"Hold one minute, please." A minute later, the line picked up and Ryan was speaking to me. It took me a few seconds to shake off the daze I was in at speaking to Jack's friend.

"Hey, Harper. How ya doing?"

"Uh, I'm good, Ryan. I'm calling because I have a favor to ask."

"This isn't about Jack, is it?"

"No, it's about a friend of mine." The line was silent for a minute and I thought I lost the connection. "Hello?"

"Yeah, I'm still here." He blew out a breath. "Is this about the guy you're shacking up with? Cuz, I'm not too sure I can be a part of that. Jack's my friend, Harper. It wouldn't be right."

"Ryan, look, I understand that this could be uncomfortable, but I'm not asking you to accept my relationship with Drew, but I am asking you to listen."

"Look, why don't we meet at The Pub. We'll get a drink and talk. Say, half an hour?"

"Okay, I'll see you there."

I walked upstairs to the second bedroom that Drew had converted into a weight room. He was lifting weights when I walked in.

"Hey, you got a minute?" He put down his weights and looked up at me warily.

"Sure, what's up, buttercup?"

I smiled at his new nickname for me. "So, here's the thing. Ryan wants to meet me to discuss the situation, and I want you to come with me."

"Are you sure that's a good idea?" He blew out a huge breath. "This is gonna look bad."

"I know, but I want them to meet you and give you a chance. When they see us together, they'll understand. It'll be a lot easier this way.

"Okay. Whatever you think is best."

Drew took a shower and we met downstairs fifteen minutes later, then left for The Pub. When we walked in, I saw Ryan and Logan sitting at a table in the back corner. They had smiles on their faces until they saw Drew walk in behind me. Their faces turned lethal.

"Shit. This is gonna be fun. Okay, let's go get the interrogation out of the way."

We walked over to the table and Ryan and Logan both stood to give me a hug. They sat back down, barely acknowledging Drew.

Sheesh. I knew this would be tough, but they were being downright rude.

"Guys, this is Drew. Drew, this is Logan and Ryan." I gestured between them. Drew held out his hand, and after a moment, Ryan and Logan shook his hand.

"Nice to meet you," was murmured amongst them, but it was anything but friendly from anyone but Drew.

"So, as I'm sure you've heard, Drew is living with me. We aren't in a relationship. He's a friend, and he's been really great the last month."

"Yeah, I'm sure he's been helping you out," Logan muttered.

"Don't be an ass, Logan. Drew and I aren't sleeping together. Well, I mean, we aren't having sex, and we have never kissed. There is nothing romantic going on between us."

"You're sharing a bed with him? Look, I know you may think this guy has the best intentions, but Harper, he's still a guy. It won't take long before these sleepovers turn to a little light petting, and then he's crawling into your pants at night." Ryan was pissed and obviously thought I didn't have a brain.

"It's not like that, man. Harper and I will never be anything more than friends." He looked at me for a moment, but something flickered in his eyes and he quickly looked down at the table. After a moment, his face had cleared and he looked up at Ryan and Logan. "I don't want to go into details, but I needed to leave and start over. Everything in my life had turned to shit, and I wasn't dealing well. Then, I met Harper and we just clicked. We both needed each other. We're just trying to get through the day."

They both stared at me, waiting for some confirmation of this or something. I knew they didn't get it, but leaving Jack was the hardest thing I had ever done. Drew made that easier. I needed them to understand that, because I couldn't lose him too.

"Guys, I need Drew. The past few months have been so hard without Jack. He helps me get through the day without feeling like total crap. We all know why Jack and I didn't work out, but that doesn't mean my heart isn't completely broken. I'm not asking you to be best friends. I'm not even asking you to give him a job. I'm just asking that if you interview him, you be fair to him."

"Alright, Harper," Ryan said quietly. "We can do that." Then he looked over at Drew. "Why don't you stop by tomorrow morning and we'll see what you can do. Eight o'clock."

"Thanks. I appreciate it." He reached across the table and shook both their hands. Ryan and Logan got up and left.

"Those guys really care about you."

"I'm sure they do, but when Jack and I split, I only had Anna. They've always been more Jack's friends than mine. I would have never met them if it weren't for Jack."

"Well, you have me now too." He put his arm around my shoulder and pulled me to his side. I finally felt a little bit of relief. He was staying and I would be okay.

CHAPTER 23

JACK

IT HAD BEEN months since we'd all gotten together for poker night. I had been so busy building my business that I barely had time to even talk to anyone else. Things were moving along great at work, and with all the headaches of starting up a new business, I didn't really have time to think of Harper. I hadn't asked anyone about her, taking Sebastian's advice, but I knew that would change tonight. I needed to know how she was doing.

The guys all came by around seven, and we set up the table and ordered food. We were in the middle of a hand when I took the leap. I was going for smooth and indifferent, but instead I blurted out, "So has anyone seen Harper lately?" I stared at my cards, hoping the guys wouldn't see the eagerness on my face for any scrap of news. When no one said anything, I looked up to uncomfortable faces.

"What? Did something happen that I don't know about?"

Luke was the first to speak up. "Anna says she's doing alright. She's been writing a lot, and the books seem to be selling well."

That didn't tell me anything about how Harper was. They were all avoiding me and the question.

"What aren't you telling me?"

Luke started to stutter out a response, obviously not wanting to be the one to say. "Well, you see...well, the thing is." He stopped and rubbed the back of his neck uncomfortably.

"What *is* the thing, Luke?"

"She's living with someone now." That slammed into me like a sledgehammer. Spots danced in front of my eyes at the thought of her moving on to someone new. I swallowed down the bile that was threatening to spill free.

"He came into town a little over a month ago, and he's been living with her ever since." Ryan was the one to lay that little tidbit on me.

"Well, shit. That didn't take her long," I sneered.

"It's not like that, asshole. They aren't messin' around. The guy just...he's just there for her, man. She needed someone and he was there. She saw you at the lake one day and was trying to hide from you. She slipped and fell in, and he saved her," Logan said.

Logan was normally the asshole of the bunch, so I knew I had to back off when Logan snapped. Shit. She fell in a lake. That girl was trouble. I was worried about someone breaking into her house in the middle of the night, not her catching hypothermia from lake diving. Then it hit me. All my friends knew for a month and hadn't said a word. I was dreaming of Harper every night and she had someone new in her life. It didn't matter if they were just friends. She was with another guy.

"So, what? You guys all knew about this and didn't have the balls to tell me?" Everyone was silent for a moment. Cole, always the one to speak his mind, was the first to speak.

"We just found out. Well, most of us just found out. Besides, what did you want us to say? You didn't want her anymore. You threw her away. What good would it do to tell you?"

I stood so fast my chair fell backward. That was complete bullshit. I didn't throw her away. I loved her more than anything, and we both decided not to stay together.

"Of course I wanted her," I shouted. "I love her so fucking much that it kills me every day to be away from her. I don't sleep more than a few hours every night because she isn't next to me. I didn't throw her away. We wanted different things, and it wouldn't have worked. I wanted it to, but I couldn't ask her to give up something she wanted just to be with me."

Cole got in my face. "We know you love her, but apparently not enough. When you love someone, you give that person everything. If you aren't willing to do that, then you never deserved her. Because that woman, she was good to you. She was sweet and caring. She never asked you for anything. You had to practically twist her arm to get her to accept anything from you. So, yeah, you did throw her away. There isn't one of us here that wouldn't have given his right arm for the love of a good woman like that."

And there it was. When I assumed I was doing the right thing by letting her go, my friends all thought I was being a shit bag. Not one of them had my back, and I really needed it.

I took a breath, and spoke a little more calmly. "So, who is this guy? Have you checked him out, Sean? Is he a good guy?"

"Yeah, his story checks out. He's a good guy."

"We met with them last week," Ryan said. "He started working for us Monday. He needed a job and the two of them met with us. She didn't want to cause problems with all of us, so she asked us to hear her out. He's a good guy and one hell of a worker. You have nothing to worry about with this guy. You'd probably like him."

I huffed out a laugh. "I guess this is what I should have expected. I didn't really think about her moving on without me. It sucks."

"They aren't together," Luke said.

"No, but it's not me that's there for her. Someone else is the one that gets to see her every day. I just..." I scrubbed a hand down my face and stood to get a beer. I popped the top and downed the beer, then went outside and stared at the night sky. If I thought I understood before that she was really gone, this just reinforced that feeling ten-fold. I had been working so hard to not think about her that I totally missed the fact that she would eventually move on with life, because that's when it became real.

I felt a hand on my shoulder, and that show of support almost sent me over the edge. Moisture built in my eyes, and I blinked it back to keep from breaking down. That horrible pain I felt the night she left was back. I rubbed my chest hoping to make it go away, but it didn't. Something had to change or I would go crazy. I couldn't keep living with this pain, but I didn't know how to make it go away either.

"Just so you know, she's not doing any better than you are. She's hurting just the same, and this guy is just holding her together. He makes the day easier for her, but that doesn't mean she's living."

I nodded, but couldn't think of anything to say. Ryan went back inside and I stayed outside staring at the sky. Maybe eventually I would figure out what to do.

A few weeks later, I was at The Pub with the guys having a beer. We were shooting pool when a stick thin blonde woman with huge boobs walked over to me. She had two beers in her hand and held one out to me. I didn't take it, but took a drink of my own beer.

"Hi. Do you need me to hold your stick for you?"

I spit my beer all over her. She did not just say that, did she?

She batted her caked on lashes at me and pressed her shiny, red lips together. When I looked at her, all I saw were the differences between her and Harper. Harper never wore that much makeup, and she never looked so fake.

"Aww, you got beer all over my chest. I think you should lick it up. No point in wasting good beer." She thrust her chest out at me and ran her tongue over her lips. I gagged a little, because this woman obviously thought she was sexy, but she reminded me of a blow up doll.

"Um, I'm good. Why don't you just head on back to the ladies room and get yourself cleaned up." She ran a manicured finger down my chest and then brazenly grabbed my cock. I didn't feel a thing. I couldn't get it up for her if she was the last person on earth.

"Why don't you come with me and I'll take care of this for you." She was rubbing me and trying to make me hard, but it wasn't happening. "It's not really that small, is it? Or do I just need to try another approach?"

"Darlin', he only stands at attention for the real deal. I'm afraid your fake tits aren't gonna do a thing for him. Now, please remove your hand from my cock and go find someone else to fuck."

I made a move to turn around, but she made a last ditch effort and grabbed my arm. She flung herself at me and wrapped her arms around my neck, her lips pressing to my mouth. I was stunned for a second, but then shoved her away from me and wiped the nasty lipstick from my mouth. When I looked up, Harper was standing in the doorway with tears in her eyes and a pained expression on her face. Anger swept over me that this woman had inadvertently caused Harper to think I would move on to a slut. I moved toward her, but Sean caught my arm.

"Let her go, man. Drew's got her." I shot Sean a withering glare at the mention of Drew. "Just let her calm down, and then you can explain what happened."

I sulked in the corner, drinking the rest of the night. I decided that the next day I would go to her house and apologize for what she saw and explain the situation. Sebastian gave me a ride home, since I was now thoroughly tanked. As I stood in the doorway of a house that used to be so full of life, all I felt was loneliness. This house no longer brought me peace because Harper wasn't in it. I imagined us at Christmas opening our presents, but then the memories of her leaving invaded my mind. I didn't know if I could keep coming back here. I was either going to have to sell the place or find a way to make peace with Harper's memory.

The next day, I stopped by Harper's and walked to the front door. I was nervous as hell to see her again. Would she be happy to see me? Would she need me to hold her as bad as I needed it? There was no time like the present to find out, so I knocked. But what I wasn't expecting was for Drew to answer the door in only a towel.

Anger filled my insides as he stood there with a cocky grin on his face. I had waited too long and now she had moved on.

"Where's Harper?" I grumbled through clenched teeth.

"She can't come to the door right now. She's....occupied at the moment."

Before I had a chance to think better of it, my fist was flying through the air. I landed a few good punches to his face before he got the upper hand. He maneuvered himself so that he caught my wrist and torqued my arm up behind my back. This guy fought amazingly well for being dressed only in a towel.

"I let you get a few shots in, but that's enough of that shit." He released me and shoved me toward the door. "Harper isn't here right now."

"If she's not here, then why did you make me think you two were just upstairs fucking?" I spat back at Drew.

"Call it revenge for last night. She was heartbroken."

"I didn't do anything. That slut came up to me and just grabbed me."

Drew just shook his head. "Dude, you don't get it. She didn't think that you were doing anything with her. She was heartbroken because she saw you. Now she's gone."

"Gone where?" Panic clawed at my throat. I didn't know how to fix things with her, but I couldn't let her go either.

"She went to visit her dad in England. She didn't say when she was coming home."

"Fuck. I need to see her. Where did she go in England?"

"Calm down. You need to let her go right now and be alone. She needs this, so don't take it away from her."

I started to pace the living room. "How do I know if I'm ready to give her what she wants? I feel like I just keep thinking I can, but I always go back to thinking that letting her go was best. Shit, and if I fuck it up again, she'll never take me back." I stopped and looked at Drew. "What do I do?"

"How the fuck should I know? I'm not your therapist. If you need to lay your head down on a pillow and talk it out, look in the yellow pages. But I will tell you this, if you aren't one hundred percent certain that you can give her everything, then you keep your mouth shut."

I wanted to yell at him, but instead I just glared. I couldn't be mad at the man that was helping Harper, even if I really wanted to take a paintball gun and shoot him in the balls a few times. It might make me feel slightly better.

I stormed into Ryan's office, ignoring the fact that he was on a phone call. "I need Drew's number."

He frowned at me. "I'm gonna have to call you back."

"I need Drew's number."

"You said that already."

"So, give it to me."

His frown deepened. "I'm sorry, did I miss the part where I was supposed to hand out employee information to you?"

Frustrated, I clenched my fists. "Look, I just really need his number. I need to know when Harper's coming back."

"Why?"

"What do you mean, why? So I know when she'll be home."

"Yeah, I got that part, but what are you hoping to accomplish?"

My jaw clenched in anger. What was I hoping to accomplish? I wanted Harper more than life itself. Being away from her these past months had been absolutely terrible. I just wanted her back, however I could get her.

"Have you changed your mind about kids?" he asked.

"I...I don't know, but I know I need her."

He shook his head. "That's not good enough, man. You can't just walk back into her life if you're not sure."

I pulled out a chair and sat down. "What the hell do you expect me to do? Am I supposed to suddenly change my mind about kids? Decide that I want them when I'm not sure if I do?"

"Do you really want to do that to her? Are you prepared to walk back into her life and then break her heart all over again? Because that's what you're going to do if you're not sure. That's not fair to her."

Hell, I knew that. I was a bastard for even considering going back to her. I had seen the look on her face at the bar. She was devastated, exactly how I felt every single day. If we were both miserable, wasn't it better if we were together?

"You need to ask yourself, do you really not want kids? Or do you just have these grand plans and kids would be in the way?"

I looked up at him and really thought about it again. "I've never wanted them. I have this idea of how my life is gonna be—"

"Yeah? How's that working out for you? You've started up another branch to your business, and you think you're gonna just take off and go on vacation?"

"I don't know..."

"Man, look at all you're throwing away. You have the love of your life right in front of you. You're miserable without her. Hell, you were talking about selling your house, the same one that you built onto for Harper just months ago. You put your heart and soul into making that place perfect for her. You haven't celebrated Christmas in five years, but you put that all aside to make it perfect for her. Are you really sure that kids is your breaking point?"

"If I had kids, that would mean giving up all my travel plans."

"Do you really think that parents don't go on vacation?"

"With their kids. That's not what I want. Besides, it's not just about vacation. You make me sound so immature. What the hell would I do with a kid?"

He stared me down, shaking his head slightly. "You would take care of it, have someone else to love. You'd have a little Harper running around. Can't you see it? A little girl with dirty blonde hair, running around and scraping her knees in a pink dress?"

"Blue," I corrected. "Harper rarely wears pink."

He grinned at me. "So, blue. And she'd come running up to you, arms outstretched, screaming for her daddy. Are you telling me that doesn't sound like the best fucking dream of your life?" He shook his head slightly. "And you think traveling around and seeing all these exotic places could ever take the place of having the woman you love and a family that's all yours? Man, you're looking at the wrong dream. You could go to all those places, see everything in the world, but your heart would always be back here with Harper. Even when she moves on, finds another man to take your place, you're still going to think about her and all you've missed out on."

I sat back in the chair, feeling like I had just been hit by a truck. He was right. Maybe I wasn't completely sure about kids, but the picture he laid out sounded a hell of a lot better than going around the world on a cruise ship by myself. The truth was, kids or no kids, I needed Harper in my life. She was the air I breathed, and if I didn't get her back, none of those other dreams would mean a damn thing.

I looked at Ryan, determination in my eyes. "I need Drew's number. I've got to get Harper back."

Three weeks passed without Harper. I called Drew every day, looking for any scrap of information I could. Every day was the same. He hadn't heard from her, and he had no idea when she was coming home. I needed to wait. I had done a lot of thinking since my conversation with Ryan, and I had come to the conclusion that if kids were what she wanted, I would give them to her. They might not be that bad. I would suck it up and be the man she needed, and I would never hold it against her, because without her, there was no point to any of it. I may not make the best dad, but I would give it my all. Besides, I had good examples from my parents. I would just have to learn from what they taught me.

Luke and Anna had their kid a few days ago. It was a little girl, and I couldn't believe that Harper had missed it. I really expected her to be back for that. More than anything, I just wanted her home for myself. I was over at Luke and Anna's, helping to build the back deck. Anna had wanted it so that she could sit out on the back porch with the baby in the summer. It had gotten pushed to the back burner, so all the guys went over to get as much done as possible today. By the pace we were going, most of it should be completed today.

I was nailing down a board when I heard her voice. My hammer stopped mid-air, and I slowly looked up to see her beautiful face. Time stopped moving. All I saw was her. Except for the hammer that came smashing down on my thumb. Had I been paying attention, I would have known that my finger was not a nail.

Swearing, I stood and stuck the tip of my thumb in my mouth to try to lessen the pain. I could see Harper inside with Anna, cooing over the new baby. She looked absolutely radiant. Traveling had really agreed with her. Screw the deck. I needed to talk to her. I walked inside, but she totally ignored me.

"Hey, pretty girl. How are you?" She didn't look up at me. She just stared at the baby and smiled.

"Hi, Jack. I'm good." She picked up Lila and started walking around the house, talking to her. "You are so pretty. Yes you are. You are the prettiest little girl I have ever seen, little Lila Rose. Auntie Harper is going to spoil you and give you little kisses all the time. Yes, I will."

She was walking with the baby and bouncing her gently. She was a natural. Why had I never seen it before? She looked absolutely beautiful holding a baby. All those excuses I made were just that, excuses. It would be different with Harper. I stood there staring for about five minutes when I finally came back to my senses and remembered what my end goal was.

I was just about to ask her to talk for a minute when she said, "I have to go. I have a date tonight, but I'll come over and tell you about it tomorrow."

She gave Anna a kiss on the cheek and left the house. I stood there dumbfounded when Luke came up behind me. "Yep, she's back, and totally different. You've got your work cut out for you. Anna said that she has a whole slew of dates lined up. I can't imagine why she would do that. Can you?" He gave me a slap on the back and walked away.

A date, huh? So, she was trying to push me out of her thoughts, and she thought going on a date would do that. Well, two could play that game, and I would win. I spent the next twenty minutes trying to pry the details out of Anna. Then I asked Logan if he knew anyone I could take out at the last minute. Logan just smirked at me and gave me a number. I called and asked the woman to go to dinner with me, and told her I would pick her up at six o'clock. Game on.

CHAPTER 24

HARPER

I RECEIVED a text on my way home from the airport from a guy I met on the plane home from England. The encounter was brief, but he seemed nice enough, and he was a doctor. He asked for my number, and I had given it.

I had done a lot of thinking in England and decided that if I was ever going to get over Jack, I was going to have to move on. Having a one night stand wasn't exactly appealing to me, but I had to try something to get past this ache that constantly followed me around. We had been broken up for months, and still, seeing him in that bar nearly tore me apart. There was no way I could handle another relationship right now, so what better way to move on? Plus, I was in a foreign country and I would never have to see said person again.

William was very sweet and pretty good in bed, but I had ended up crying after sex and freaked the poor man out. He had dressed in record time and was gone before I even had time to apologize. So that didn't go so well, but the rest of the trip was a great refresher for me. I came back with a new game plan: Act like Jack didn't affect me anymore. I would have to see him at some point. We lived in the same town, shared friends, and with Anna having the baby, I was bound to see him sooner rather than later. I had to steel myself against him. It was a really solid plan and well thought out. Right.

Anyway, Dr. Dan had texted me when I was driving home and asked me to dinner. I agreed, even though I wasn't in the mood. I almost changed my mind and told him I was too tired, but then I walked through the door and who was there? Jack. I tried out my new plan of basically ignoring my feelings for him, and thought I did a pretty good job. Things were going well, but I really couldn't stay and have him stare at me. When I said that I had a date, I didn't miss the shocked look on his face. Score one for me.

So here I was, on my way to a restaurant to have dinner with a man I really had no interest in. At least I was getting a hot meal out of it. I walked into the restaurant and told the hostess what name the reservation was under, and followed the hostess to my seat. Dan stood and grabbed me by the arms, then laid a harsh kiss on my mouth. Instantly, I disliked this guy. I pulled back right away and tried to compose my frazzled nerves.

"Um. I don't think we're there quite yet."

"I'm sorry, Harper. I was just so excited to see you that I got a little carried away." It was sweet, and a little weird that he was so excited. I shrugged it off as nerves.

"It's alright, Dan. Let's just-"

"Dr." Dan interrupted me, and I looked at him in confusion.

"Excuse me?"

"You called me Dan, but I prefer to be called Dr. Dan."

"Um, but we aren't in a medical office." He moved his head from side to side as if he was considering something.

"I know, but it's my title, so just..."

I cleared my throat, then ran my tongue over my teeth, as if to clean off the disgust of saying Dr. Dan in a private setting.

"Anyway, *Dr. Dan,* should we see what's good here tonight?"

I opened the menu and wondered if I should even stay for dinner.

This was really weird. Okay, so he liked to be called Dr. Dan. Maybe it just made him feel better about himself.

"I hear that oysters are a great appetizer. Apparently, they are quite the aphrodisiac."

He was looking at me with creepy bedroom eyes, and I felt a shiver snake up my spine. The look of disgust on my face was evident, but he didn't seem to notice.

"I don't eat fish. I think I'll order the chicken. So, tell me, Dr. Dan, what kind of medicine do you practice?"

He perked up and set down his menu. "I'm a podiatrist."

"Oh, a foot doctor."

"Not just a foot doctor. We work with so much more than feet. Your ankles and your lower legs are also included. Many people don't realize that feet are the most important part of your body. Why, if you don't have good structure at the bottom of your body, your upper half can't function properly."

Well, your body isn't going to function at all if I cut your heart out.

"Pardon me? I didn't catch that because you were mumbling."

Shit. Apparently I didn't just say my thoughts out loud in front of Jack. It also extended to idiots. Speaking of Jack...my gaze caught sight of him. He was here, sitting across the dining room with a leggy blonde woman. And she was running her foot up his leg! Jealousy rippled through me, and I gripped the water glass harder than I should have. It didn't really appear that he was having a hard time with our breakup anymore. In fact, he looked like he was quite enjoying his time with Long Legs Linda, or whatever the hell her name was. Either way, he wasn't exactly pushing her away.

Dr. Dan started snapping his fingers in front of my face, and I had a hard time tearing my eyes away from my sexy ex. Sure, I may have been on the verge of walking over to him and snapping his neck, or cutting off his balls, but that didn't mean that I didn't find him attractive.

Again, with the thoughts of murder?

"Sorry, I was just saying that I always thought the heart was the most important part of the body."

"Oh, goodness, no!" And so it went, on and on until the waitress arrived to take our orders. I kept glancing at Jack, and the man across from me kept boring me with all the marvelous things about podiatry.

CHAPTER 25

JACK

I WALKED INTO THE RESTAURANT, my face falling when I saw Harper across the room on her date. I had to keep in mind that she was trying to push me away. She didn't really want this. I had to keep telling myself that, or I would go insane. The hostess stopped in front of a table where a blonde bimbo sat. Normally, I wouldn't be so judgmental, but she literally looked like a bimbo. Sighing, I sat down across from her. Leave it to Logan to set me up with someone totally unbelievable as a potential date.

"Hi, I'm Jack."

I extended my hand to her and she placed the tips of her fingers in my hand and did something that resembled a shake. Then she giggled. Fucking giggled. It was worse when she spoke though, because it came out all nasally with a Queens accent.

"Candi with an I. You know, at the end of the name. The beginning starts with a C. C-A-N-D-I. Candi," she said as she giggled. Then she tossed her hair over her shoulder. "That's me," and she giggled again.

Oh, Lord, please save me now. This was such a bad idea. I didn't think I could take five more minutes of this, let alone a whole dinner.

But as my gaze drifted back to Harper, I made the executive decision that I was not going to leave. I needed to see this through. I grinned, thinking I was making an executive decision for one person. Could you really make an executive decision for yourself? Didn't an executive decision require more than one person to be involved?

Shaking the thoughts from my head, I turned back to my date. "So, what sounds good for dinner tonight?"

"Well, normally I don't choose my dinner based on the noise it makes, but that is definitely an interesting way to choose."

I glanced up from my menu, my brows furrowing in confusion. *Say what? What was she talking about?*

"Let's see, now, a pig makes a snorting sound, and that's just annoying, so let's skip that. Let's see. Hmmm. What else is there?"

I was staring at her with wide eyes and an open mouth. I must have looked like an idiot, but then again, she sounded like an idiot. She had to be messing with me. Maybe this was a prank from Logan. Maybe he was just fucking with me. That had to be it. He told this woman to act this way, just so he could make my night even more miserable than it already was. There was no way she was serious.

"Well, I suppose cows don't sound too bad. We could have steak or hamburgers. Ooh, what about pork chops!"

"That's a pig." I continued to stare at this fascinating woman in front of me, and not in a good way. More like a, *This woman could kill me with her stupidity* kind of way.

She made a face and waved her hand in front of her face. "Let's skip it then. Ooh. We could have chicken. Now, is there a difference between a chicken and a rooster when you eat it? Because I don't really like to be woken up by roosters in the morning, so that sound is definitely out for tonight."

I took out my phone and hit record. If I was going to suffer through this, I was going to make sure the guys heard it. That way, when I beat the shit out of Logan, they would understand why.

"Do fish make any noise? I guess we wouldn't be able to hear it since they're underwater. Maybe that's the way to go tonight. They make the least amount of sound, so I choose fish as my sound for tonight!" She snapped her menu closed and looked at me triumphantly.

The waiter stopped by to take our drink orders, and I ordered us wine. I really wanted something stronger, but even I knew that getting hammered on a date was bad form. Still, I was going to need alcohol to get through the night.

"So, Jack. Tell me what you do."

"I'm a mechanic."

"No way! You work on robots? That is so cool. Ya know, my brother loved robots when we were little, and he's like twice as smart as me."

So still pretty stupid, I thought.

"We all knew that he was going places. Ya know, he was always a deep thinker. He could sit down with a calculator and just come up with all the answers to the math problems. He just knew what he was doing, ya know? Anyway, he got involved with drugs and now he's on the streets somewhere."

"That's...interesting." I wasn't sure what was a safe topic to talk about. It appeared she didn't really have any clue what she was talking about.

"So, what do you do?"

She sat up straight and beamed at me. "Well, you are never gonna believe this, but I do nails. Ya know, like I paint them. In a salon. See?"

She held up her nails for me to see and wiggled them in front of my face. I hated it when women got all done up, and she had the longest, ugliest nails I had ever seen. I didn't mind if women put some paint on their nails, but these were all sparkly and shit. She looked so proud, and I didn't want to be rude, so I nodded politely and cleared my throat. I had no idea what to say to that.

I started to scratch the stubble of my jaw, trying to come up with something to say. I glanced around the room, my eyes immediately drawn to Harper and the douchebag she was sitting with. Luckily, she looked absolutely disgusted by him. I wished I could hear what was being said. My date was saying something, but I was too busy trying to figure out what was going on at Harper's table to listen. Finally, I gave up and brought my attention back to Candi with an *i*.

"So anyway, I crawled under the table and gave him a blow job, and that's how I met Logan."

I had just taken a sip of wine and now I was choking on it. That shit head set me up with a girl who gave blow jobs under tables. I was going to kick his ass.

The waiter stopped by to take our orders, and I didn't think to order for her. Big mistake.

"Hi, Mr. Waiter. I'm Candi with an *i*, and this is my friend, Jack. We're gonna order food based on the sounds they make. Isn't that fun?" And then she giggled, again. I glanced at the waiter, almost laughing at the look on his face. He looked like he had stepped into some bad fantasy novel. I shook my head slightly to let him know to just let it go. I hoped he didn't ask any questions, and luckily, Candi continued before he had a chance.

"So, since I'm not in the mood for anything that makes noises, I'm gonna order fish." She smiled at the waiter, and he stared expectantly at her. When she didn't get it, he explained.

"Miss, I need to know what kind of fish you would like to order."

I tried to interject, but she was too fast. "You mean like color or mood? Ooh. How exciting! I think a colorful fish would be so much fun, but I don't really want a fun fish, like his mood, because I don't want him jumping around my plate."

"The fish will be dead when it's served," the waiter deadpanned.

"Wait, then why are we ordering by sound?" She cocked her head to the side and furrowed her brow. I took in a long, deep breath and blew it out while rubbing a hand over my eyes. Seriously, I was going to kill her or myself before the night was over. Anything to escape this hell.

"Just get us the fastest dish you have." Then I signaled with two fingers for the waiter to lean down. When he was close enough, I whispered to him, "I will give you a hundred dollars if you can make sure we are out of this restaurant in less than an hour." The waiter nodded and hurried off to the kitchen.

"Why did you order something fast? Do they serve exotic animals here, like cheetahs and antelope? Ooh, I'm so excited to see what he brings." She clapped her hands and bounced in her seat. "Ya know, while we wait, I could crawl under the table like I did for Logan."

I felt her bare foot slide up my leg, and then she was playing with my crotch. I shifted suddenly to avoid her foot being anywhere near my dick and nearly pulled the tablecloth off the table. That food better arrive fast.

CHAPTER 26

HARPER

I LOOKED over and saw the contents of Jack's table almost go flying, for the third time tonight. He looked like he was playing keep away with his date. It made me chuckle, and Dr. Dan stopped eating to look at me.

"Did I miss something?"

"Sorry, no. I was just thinking of something funny."

"You know, you can tell a lot about a person by their feet. Just as you would keep a horse's feet shooed and maintain those shoes to keep the horse healthy, we also must care for our feet diligently. See, a person's feet provide the life blood for their whole body. For instance," he reached down and grabbed my foot and slipped my shoe off. I hurried to pry my foot away, but he held on tight. I was more concerned now with keeping my skirt in place so I didn't flash the whole restaurant. I glanced over and saw Jack laughing at my predicament. Dr. Dan was still talking, but I didn't have a clue what he was saying. There were people staring at us and I was completely mortified. Then, he lifted my foot to his nose, sniffed it, and started to lick my toes. Totally repulsed, I squealed, and yanked my foot as hard as I could out of his grasp. Screw modesty, I had to get away from this sicko.

"Gross! What are you doing?"

I knew that my voice was loud, but I didn't care. This guy was creepy and I couldn't stay with him to finish dinner. Who licked a person's toes at the dinner table? Or anywhere? It's just weird.

"Dan, I appreciate-"

"Dr. Dan," he interjected.

"Whatever. This has been fun, but not that fun. I'm pretty sure that having someone call you Dr. Dan in a private setting is just to stroke your own ego. Grabbing someone's foot at the dinner table is inappropriate, and I'm pretty sure I could file a sexual harassment charge against you for licking my foot in a restaurant!"

The whole restaurant was quiet except for Jack, who I could hear snickering at his table. I stood up and stormed out of the restaurant with one shoe on. I could have turned back for the other one, but it would totally ruin my exit if I went back. I was almost to my car when I heard Jack call my name.

"Harper, wait!"

I turned around and saw Jack running toward me, shoe in hand. He stopped in front of me and we just stared at each other a moment. Then, we both started laughing.

"Here's your shoe. I take it your date didn't go well?" I took the shoe and put it back on.

"What gave you that clue? My skirt being hiked up for all the restaurant to see my lady bits, or him licking my feet at the table?"

"Well, my date was quite the failure also. Logan set me up with Candi with an *i*. She thought we were ordering our food based on the sounds the animals make. She also tried to molest me with her foot at dinner."

"Ah, another foot person. Perhaps we should set up Dr. Dan and Candi with an *i*."

"I did," he grinned. "I introduced them before I left." We stood in silence for a moment, neither knowing where to go from here.

"Harper, I wanted-"

"I need to-"

We both started to speak at the same time.

"Go ahead," Jack said.

"I need to be honest with you. I'm not really ready to see you yet. I went to England to try to clear my head, but I'm not quite there yet. I tried for nonchalant earlier, and I don't think I really pulled it off. I just need some time to get my head on straight."

CHAPTER 27

JACK

JUST LIKE THAT, my hope died. I was hoping to tell her that I had changed my mind. That I was thinking maybe I could have a family, but if she wasn't in the right frame of mind, she would just end up getting pissed at me. Besides, I needed to be one hundred percent ready, not almost there. I would give her time, but I would also try to find ways to chip away at her in the meantime. I pulled myself together, hoping she didn't catch the disappointment on my face.

"Yeah, I totally get it." I swallowed down the words and motioned for her to go ahead. "Let me walk you to your car."

"Thanks."

We walked in uncomfortable silence, so I decided to lighten the mood and bring it back to her date.

"So where did you meet that guy anyway?"

"I met him at the airport when we were getting off the plane. It was a very quick meeting, otherwise I'm sure I would have seen how odd Dr. Dan really was."

We got to her car, but she didn't get in right away. She fiddled with her keys, which I took as a good sign. Anyone that had seen the movie *Hitch* knew that meant that she wanted a kiss. At least, I was banking on his wisdom on the subject, even if he was a fictional character. Brushing my hand slowly up her arm, I stopped, resting my hand on her bicep. I took a step forward, brushing my lips lightly against her cheek. I could feel the pull to her still, and I didn't miss the way she dragged in a ragged breath. My heart hammered in my chest. I just wanted to pull her into my arms and tell her I loved her.

Just do it. Just tell her. Don't waste another minute without her. What's the worst that could happen? At least she would know that you still want her, even if she's not ready to hear it. Go for it. It's now or never. Just—

She stepped back, her cheeks flushing as she ducked her head. "Goodbye, Jack."

She spun quickly and got in her car, avoiding looking back at me. I stood there, staring at her car as she put it in reverse and backed out of her spot. I briefly considered jumping in front of her car and confessing my undying love to her, but the moment had passed.

Sighing, I ran my fingers through my hair as I slowly made my way across the parking lot. Kicking at the pebbles on the ground, I berated myself for not taking the chance when I had it. I needed her back. But before I could plan my next step, I needed to take care of something.

I headed over to Logan's house, not surprised at all when he opened the door with a knowing grin on his face. There was nothing more I wanted than to knock that look off his face, and that's exactly what I did. My fist connected with his cheek and he fell backward, not expecting me to hit him.

"Seriously, asshole?" I growled, standing over him. "Candi with an *i*? She tried to molest me with her foot during dinner. I ditched dinner halfway through."

Shooting me a glare, he stood and rubbed at his cheek. "That was payback."

"For what?"

"We were supposed to hang out at a bar a couple months ago, but you ditched me because you were all weepy over Harper. Candi wouldn't shut up. I had to have her crawl under the table to suck me off just to shut her mouth."

I just stared at him for a minute. "She thought we were ordering off the menu based on the sounds animals make. Then, she thought the food was coming to the table alive." I shook my head and widened my eyes in disbelief. If I hadn't been there, I would never have believed it. "That was the worst date ever."

He huffed out a laugh. "Man, what I wouldn't give to have seen that."

"Well, you might not have been there, but I recorded the whole thing."

"Seriously?"

"Well, I had to have proof so the guys would understand when I kicked your ass."

"Hey, you got one punch in, and that's all I'm giving you."

"Like you could take me."

I narrowed my eyes at him, and he backed up. "Don't push me right now. I still have that date on my mind. Not to mention, I didn't get Harper back."

His face fell. "I'm sorry, man."

I shrugged. "I just need a better plan."

"You want a beer?" he asked, like that would cheer me up.

"Sure, why not."

"And maybe play that recording?" he grinned.

"After I had to go through it, it's only right you should have to listen to it."

We sat down and listened to the recording, but I stopped it when I realized that I had recorded my uncomfortable conversation with Harper. Logan, always trying to lighten the mood, joked about Candi, completely ignoring the part about Harper. By the time I went home, I was in a considerably better mood. Now I just had to put a plan together for getting Harper back.

CHAPTER 28

HARPER

I WAS SO happy that Drew was waiting up for me when I got home from dinner. The date from hell was bad enough, but seeing Jack was just as bad. And when his lips pressed against my cheek, I thought I would fall into his arms and beg him to take me back. I definitely wasn't strong enough to be around him yet. That little one night stand had done nothing to help me get over the one man I could never have.

As soon as I walked through the door, Drew's eyes locked on mine and he instantly knew it hadn't gone well. He stood and walked over to me, wrapping me up in his arms. I held onto him, not wanting to let go. I gripped him tighter, feeling like I was about to cry.

"When does it end?"

He sighed against my hair and rubbed my back. "It doesn't," he whispered. "I wish I could make it all go away for you."

I sighed, pulling back to wipe the tears from my eyes. "Maybe dating isn't the right thing for you, especially if you come home crying."

I huffed out a laugh. The date was terrible, but I'm not crying because of that. Jack was there."

He nodded, ducking his head, like he knew.

"You knew that he would be there?"

He nodded. "He wanted to see you. He grilled Anna about your date."

I stared at him in shock. "Why?"

"Because he still loves you."

"But—"

He sighed and shoved his hands in his pockets. "I can tell the guy loves you. Maybe this isn't the way it ends."

I thought about what he said, wishing it could be true, but how? We wanted different things out of life. Honestly, though, my thoughts were drifting more and more toward chucking kids out the window and running back to him. Not literally chucking kids out the window. That would be dangerous and just silly. I laughed to myself and Drew looked at me funny.

"What?"

"Nothing, I was just thinking of throwing kids out of windows."

"Do that often, do you?"

I smiled slightly at him.

"So, how'd the date go?"

"Absolutely horrible." I told him all about my date and about running into Jack. Drew was trying his hardest not to laugh at my situation.

"Sorry, but it's pretty funny. That's just your luck, huh? Having a bad date and running into Jack all in the same night."

"Yeah, it was kind of strange. The date was terrible, but I guess the fact that I didn't run crying from the restaurant is progress."

Drew interlocked his fingers with mine. "You know, maybe you need to think about whether or not this is really over between the two of you. It seems to me that both of you are having second thoughts."

"But how do I decide that? I mean, what if I say I want to give it another shot, and then we still come to the same conclusion? Isn't it better to walk away now than risk breaking my heart all over again?"

He stared straight ahead, not looking my way. "If I could do it all again, I would in an instant. That kind of love comes around just once. If you have it, I would run with it, no matter the consequences."

CHAPTER 29

HARPER

I SPENT the next Saturday at Anna's house. I wanted to give the new mommy a break and spend some time with my goddaughter. Luke was running errands with Sebastian, so it was just the girls.

"So, did going on a date help you any?"

"Not really. I mean, wow, I had it good with Jack. This guy was a nut job. I guess I just have to lower my standards now. What are the odds that I would get another guy as good as Jack?"

"Well, you're going to have to keep dating if you want to move on. Have you thought about maybe just having a one night stand? Maybe if you get that part over with, it'll help you move on."

I blushed furiously, because I hadn't yet told Anna of my one night stand in England. It was a sad experience and I was embarrassed. "Um, I kind of already did that."

Anna stared at me in shock. "When did this happen, and why didn't you tell me?"

"It happened in England. I didn't want to say anything because it was horrible."

"The sex was bad?"

"No, the sex was good, really good, but I started crying afterward and the guy took off. I was so embarrassed. I cried after sex!"

"Well, the good news is that you never have to see him again, so there's really nothing to be embarrassed about."

"Sure, except I'm someone's story. I'm in a story right now, floating around all of England for people to laugh at."

"Does this guy know your last name?"

"Uh, we met at a bar, and I don't know that I even gave my first name."

"See? It's not a problem then. It's not like there's a chance you'll ever run into one another again, so it's all good."

"I have to say, something changed afterward. It's like I finally accepted that I needed to move on and let Jack go. I'm not over him, but I don't feel so sad anymore." I got up and walked over to Anna. "I need some baby love. Let me hold the little peanut." I started walking with Lila and bouncing her playfully.

"I wouldn't bounce her too hard. She's been-"

Anna never got to finish her sentence, because Lila chose that moment to spit up on my back. Spit up wouldn't really be an accurate description. It was more like a volcanic eruption. Then I felt the vomit slide down under my pants and soak my underwear.

"Eww. Gross! It's going into my pants! It's gonna leak down my butt crack!" I started bouncing around trying to change the direction of the flow and keep it from going where it was going. Anna was no help. She was doubled over laughing at me. I pulled Lila away from my chest to hand her to Anna when she threw up again, this time down my front.

"Oh my, God! What is wrong with this kid?" The smell was starting to get to me. I practically threw Lila at Anna and ran to the bathroom. I heard Anna's footsteps follow me down the hall as I struggled to open the toilet lid. Luke had installed child proof locks on the toilet seat and I couldn't get the lid open. I turned and hurled into the bathtub.

"How can you stand that smell? Maybe I'm not cut out to be a mom, if I can't handle a little vomit."

I sank back against the side of the tub and breathed deeply to calm my belly. But breathing deeply wasn't a good idea because I got another whiff of the vomit on my shirt and threw up over the side of the tub again. I really needed to take a shower, but changing my shirt would do until I could get home.

"Come on. I'll get you something else to wear." She turned to walk out of the bathroom when Lila let out the loudest sound either of us had ever heard, and brown stuff started to leak through her onesie. "I'd better change her first."

"Uh, I think you need to rinse her off. It's starting to drip down her leg."

Anna squealed as warm liquid started to cover her hand. "Aah! Gross. Eww, eww, eww. Get it off of me!"

I looked in the tub, but it was too gross to clean a baby in.

"Quick, let's go to the kitchen sink and clean her off there."

We raced into the kitchen and started stripping Lila's onesie off. There was a bag of flour on the counter, so I quickly tossed it on top of the fridge so it would be out of the way. We pulled the onesie over Lila's head, and brown poo smeared in her hair.

"Oh my gosh. We should have just cut if off her. This is so gross. My baby has poo in her hair!" Anna exclaimed.

"Hold her in the sink and I'll get her diaper off."

Anna held her up as I started to extricate the diaper from Lila's bottom. Lila let out another loud noise as poo shot out of her butt and all over my hand. I gagged, bending over as I tried to turn away from the smell. Anna grabbed the hose attachment from the sink to spray me off, but I was freaking out over the poo on my hand, trying to shake it off and squealing. I knew it was only a little poo, but the scent was nauseating, and at the moment, I didn't want any more bodily fluids on me.

"Get it off! Get it off!" I stepped backwards and slipped on the poo covered onesie that had been discarded on the ground, and fell backward into the fridge. A big cloud of powder fell over me as the open bag of flour on top of the fridge tipped over.

Anna tried to run to me, but she realized she was still attached to the hose as it pulled the full length out of the faucet. It fell over the edge of the sink and started spraying everywhere. Water shot at me and formed a thick paste with the flour. I had my hands up trying to block the spray from hitting me in the face. Anna covered Lila to keep her from getting wet. She was screaming from being jostled, obviously unhappy.

I was sitting on the floor covered in a flour, shit, and vomit paste. This shit could seriously not be made up. I tried to get up to turn off the faucet, but fell back to the floor, as I slipped in the concoction that was covering the floor. Anna and I were both screaming, me from trying to get out of the spray, and Anna, trying to find a way out of the kitchen without dropping Lila.

"I need to get her out of here!" Anna shouted.

"Just go! I'll get the water."

She took a step and nearly slipped. "Shit! I can't. I'm going to fall!"

Lila screamed, and then Anna and I started screaming, all of us having a meltdown.

"What the fuck is going on?" Both of us stopped screaming and looked up. Luke was staring at us in disbelief. Sebastian made his way around the mess and shut off the water. The men stood back and stared at us. I looked over at Anna and we both started laughing.

"You look like a paper mache project, Harper!"

"Yeah, well you're covered in shit!"

Anna looked down at herself, and sure enough, she had shit everywhere. She must have gotten it all over herself when she grabbed Lila after the diaper was off. We burst out laughing again for another five minutes.

"How did this...How did you...I was gone for an hour! How did you do...this?" Luke asked as he waved his arm around the kitchen.

We just started laughing again. Sebastian pulled out his phone and started taking pictures. Luke sighed and shook his head, then reached for Lila.

"Okay, give me Lila, and I'll clean her up in the tub."

"Um, you can't. I kinda threw up in there," I said, trying to hold back a laugh.

"Why would you throw up in the tub? Why didn't you use the toilet?"

"I couldn't get the lid open because of the child proof locks. You do realize she's not going to attempt to get in the toilet for at least another year, right?"

Luke looked up at the ceiling. "Dear Lord, please save me from these women. Alright, Sebastian, go get a towel to wrap Lila in, I'll go clean up the tub and bathe Lila. You two start cleaning up the mess, and when I'm done, I'm putting you both in the shower and I'll finish cleaning up the kitchen."

"Hot. Can I watch?" Luke smacked Sebastian upside the head.

"Shut up, dickhead. That's my wife."

"Chill out. It was just a joke."

Sebastian left the room in search of a towel. Anna decided it would be easiest to get the majority of the mess up with towels, so Sebastian went in search of every towel he could find. We started mopping up the mess, and then we went to shower when Luke came back with a clean Lila. Luke set her down in the pack 'n play, then went to help Sebastian clean up the kitchen. After cleaning up the mess, I decided to go home and avoid any more disasters for the day.

The next day, I received a bouquet of body washes and shampoos from Jack. I was confused, but then I read his note.

I heard about the disaster at Luke and Anna's. I thought I would send over reinforcements for any future visits. Always knew you were trouble.

Jack

. . .

I covered my mouth, laughing slightly. My chest didn't hurt nearly as bad when I got this small gift from him. It was like I was healing slowly, with his help. But that wasn't the way it was supposed to work. I was supposed to be moving on without him.

Over the next few weeks, I went out on a couple of dates with guys that Anna and Luke set me up with. The first guy wasn't bad, meaning there was no toe-licking, but he wasn't a winner either. He lived with his parents in the bedroom he grew up in. It was awesome because his mom still cooked his breakfast and dinner, and packed a lunch for him. He said it gave him extra time to go after his real goals. I didn't know what those were because he talked about video games for half the dinner. I knew nothing about video games and couldn't care less. He said that he really wanted to bring me back to his place, but his mom was having a canasta game in the living room and he didn't want to disturb them with me screaming his name. I was pretty sure I threw up a little in my mouth.

The next date, I had some hope for. His name was Mark, and he was an attorney. Anna said that he took pro bono cases advocating for children in his free time. I was actually kind of nervous meeting him. I took extra time to do my makeup and put on a deep v-neck black dress. He picked me up and drove me to a restaurant a few towns over. It was a swanky restaurant and they had excellent reviews. We chatted a little on the ride over about where each other grew up and things we liked to do in our spare time. So far, we didn't have too much in common, but he definitely wasn't boring. We sat down and he ordered us a bottle of wine.

"So, Anna tells me you do some pro bono work with kids."

"Yeah, it's really just an incentive at the company."

"How so?"

"Well, I do some pro bono work and it looks better for me at bonus time."

He said it like that would make him more attractive. It didn't to me, but I decided that all people liked to earn extra money, so I let it go.

"Well, I'm sure you enjoy your work."

"I do. It's very rewarding. I make a lot of money off other people. Every time they fuck up, I can charge a little more."

Okay, chances were I had been totally wrong about this guy. He sounded like a total douchebag. His phone pinged and he spent the next five minutes texting while I sat there sipping my wine. Another winner. Maybe I could fake an emergency and slip out of the restaurant.

"Where's the waiter? You'd think with the price of this restaurant, the service would be a little better. Oh, here he comes. The dickhead is finally coming to take our order."

"Do you know what you would like to eat?" The waiter smiled at us and I instantly liked him based on his smile. He was probably early twenties and was really friendly, even with my douchebag date.

"Well, considering that we've been waiting here for ten minutes, I would say we do. I'm going to have the steak, rare. No mushrooms. No onions. I want a baked potato with all the toppings, and don't be skimpy. I want the asparagus cooked until it's just a little crunchy. If you bring me soggy asparagus, I'll send it back to the kitchen."

The waiter looked over to me for my order. I didn't really want to stay, but he drove, so I'd just eat quickly and ask to be taken home.

"I'll have-"

"She'll have a salad. Nothing with meat. Just the vegetables."

I was pissed now. Who was he to take me out to eat and order a salad for me with no meat? Was I supposed to starve?

"Actually, I'll have the steak also, with everything on it. Medium rare and whatever else is served with it."

"I'm paying for dinner, so you'll eat what I order. Trust me, you don't need the extra food."

Anger fueled me as I stood and slammed my napkin down on the table. Food or no food, I was leaving on my own. There was no reason in the world that could tempt me to stay a minute longer with this guy.

"Thank you for a horrible evening, but I think I'll find my own way home."

I shot a sympathetic look to the waiter and walked toward the lobby. I was searching for my phone when the manager came over.

"Miss, I am so sorry about your experience here this evening. Please allow me to arrange a ride home for you."

"It's quite alright. It wasn't your fault. I just seem to have lousy taste in men. I'll call for a ride, but thank you."

Dialing Drew's number, I waited for him to pick up. When he did, relief shot through me.

"Hey, it can't be good if you're calling me in the middle of a date."

"It's not. The asshole wanted me to eat a salad while he ate steak. Apparently, I didn't need any meat."

"Wow. So, you want me to pick you up?"

"Would you?"

"Of course. Text me the address."

"Thank you so much. What would I do without you?"

"Probably cry in your Cheerios every morning."

"Probably. See you soon."

I hung up and sat in the corner of the lobby waiting for him to show. Imagine my surprise when none other than Jack walked through the doors. I was slightly embarrassed at needing to be picked up from a date by my ex-boyfriend, but a larger part of me was relieved to see him. If not Drew, he was the next best thing, even though his presence brought pain also.

"Hey, pretty girl. You called for a ride?"

I felt like crying. My emotions were all over the place lately. I wasn't ashamed to admit that it was hard for the love of my life to witness my shame of yet another really horrible date, but he was gracious as ever and didn't make me feel like a loser.

"Yeah."

"Bad date, huh?" he asked, grimacing.

"You could say that."

"So, what did he do to make you leave in the middle of a date?"

Sighing, I just didn't want to hash out my bad date with him. It was so depressing. "Can we not talk about it?"

He nodded and opened the passenger door for me, holding out his hand for me as I stepped inside. But he didn't shut the door right away.

"You look really beautiful tonight."

My jaw hung open, but before I could say anything, he shut the door and walked around to his side. I half expected him to say something as we drove home, but he was silent. I had no idea what to say to him. When he pulled up to my house, he shut off the truck and stared out the windshield.

"You deserve better than these jackasses you've been dating. I hope you can see that." He paused and turned to look at me. "I still love you, and I hope-"

"Jack, please don't. I'm not ready to hear this stuff yet. I don't know what you want from me. We broke up because of our differences. Has that changed?"

"Yes."

My head snapped to look over at him and my heart was pounding loudly in my ears. I couldn't hear these things. I wasn't ready. Was he saying he wanted to get back together? What if he changed his mind? I didn't think I could take it.

"I can't say that I want to be a father. I think I'd be shit at it, but I'm willing to try for you."

I swallowed hard, staring at him intently. He was serious. I could see it all over his face. He really wanted this. But before I could go back to him, I needed him to really think about what he was saying. Now that it was out there, I needed him to think it over again. It was one thing to think it, but never say anything. You didn't have to be serious about something if it was never spoken.

"Jack, you need to really think about this, because I don't want you to have children with me just to get me back. You need to want them also."

"Baby, I've gone over six months without you, and I can't do it anymore." His voice cracked as he admitted that last part. "I don't know that I want kids, but when I think about having them with you...I just know that life without you sucks, and I don't want to do it anymore. I want to have you back in my life and not just as friends. If having children is what you want, then we'll have children. A whole house full, and I promise to love them as much as I love you."

I couldn't believe what I was hearing. Was this really happening? Jack slid across the seat. He was right in front of me, and then his lips were pressing against mine. All the heartache of the last six months just washed away with one kiss. My heart soared and my body relaxed into his. This was where I was meant to be. When he pulled back, his thumb brushed against my cheek as he grinned slightly at me.

"Just think about what I said, pretty girl."

I sat there for a minute, afraid that if I moved, he would disappear, or I would find this was all some horrible dream. I finally nodded and got out of the truck, walking numbly to the door. Jack waited until I was inside before he pulled out of the driveway. I shut the door behind me and flopped down on the couch, just staring at the floor. Drew came sauntering into the room and sat down next to me.

"So, you had a bad date, huh?"

"Jack said he wants me back and wants to have kids with me."

I still couldn't believe it and just stared at the floor.

"Say what?"

"Yeah. He said he wants me back, and he'll have kids if that's what I want. He said he doesn't want to be without me anymore."

Drew took a seat beside me and gripped my hand in his. I closed my eyes, feeling his strength soar through me. I needed him right now.

"That's great, sweetheart. That's what you wanted, right?"

"I just don't know if I can believe it. I want to, but I don't want my heart broken again."

Drew pulled me in for a hug. "Well, if it doesn't work out with him, you can always call Dr. Dan."

I laughed and smacked Drew in the chest. "I'm going to bed. I'm exhausted."

"I'll come with you."

I went upstairs and snuggled in bed. Drew took a shower, and then got in bed and pulled me close. "It'll all work out. You'll see."

"Drew, if Jack and I do get back together, are you gonna be okay?"

"Harper, I love you, and I want you to be happy. You can't take my feelings into consideration here. You have to do what's right for you. I'll still have you in my life. That's not going to change if you move back in with Jack."

Nodding, I snuggled into the covers, but my mind wouldn't shut down. I kept thinking about Jack. I wanted to see him. I wanted to get out of bed and run to him, but I forced myself to stay in bed. I had to be sure.

It was the middle of the night when I felt my stomach turn. I bolted from the bed and made it just in time to throw up. There wasn't much in my stomach because I hadn't eaten dinner on my date. I laid my head on the toilet and waited for my tummy to settle.

Drew came in and handed me a glass of water. "Are you okay?" he asked, concern lacing his voice.

"Yeah, I probably just got the flu or something."

"Let's get you back in bed."

To my surprise, he hoisted me up under the arms, then walked me back to bed, making me take the side closest to the door in case I got sick again. I woke up several more times that night to run to the bathroom. In the morning, Drew brought me some crackers, a few bottles of water, and my phone. He made me promise to call if I needed him.

I spent the entire day in bed, making several more trips to the bathroom. I felt horrible. Every smell made me want to vomit. I hated getting sick because it always seemed to drag on for days with me.

Every time I ate something, I threw it back up. Drew called me several times to check in, but I told him I was fine. What would he do about it anyway?

By the fourth day, I was still in the same condition. I felt absolutely horrible and couldn't believe how this flu was dragging on. I spent more time in bed than out, and rarely felt well enough to eat anything. Because I had been sick so much, I didn't have the energy to do anything other than sleep. I hadn't been working on my book, and my editor needed me to finish the corrections for the final edit. Drew was starting to look at me with worry and insisted that this was more than a nasty stomach bug. I told him I would make an appointment to see a doctor the next morning, but I forgot again the next day.

CHAPTER 30

JACK

I HADN'T HEARD from Harper since I picked her up from her date. I was starting to get nervous that she was blowing me off because I waited too long to change my mind. I hoped to God that she was considering my offer, but I had to keep in mind that she might not want me back, and I would have to accept that. The stress of not hearing from her was killing me. I had texted her several times over the past few days reminding her that I was serious and I wanted her back, but she never responded. I tried calling a few times, but it always went to voicemail.

I was elbow deep in fixing a car when my cell phone rang. I jumped up to answer it and banged my head on the hood of the car. Swearing, I rubbed my head and quickly wiped my hands on a rag so I could answer my phone.

"Hello?"

"Hey, Jack. It's Drew."

I hadn't really talked to Drew very much since he moved in with Harper, so this was a little weird. "Uh, hey. What can I do for you?"

"I need a favor." There was a pause on the line, and I was wondering if he was going to ask. "Harper is going to kill me, but I need your help. She's been really sick this week. She keeps telling me it's a nasty bug, but she hasn't been able to keep anything down, and she doesn't even get out of bed. I made her a doctor appointment, but I can't get out of work today. I need you to take her."

"Of course I will. What time is the appointment?"

"It's in two hours at the women's clinic."

"Alright. Don't worry about it. I'll take care of her."

I heard Drew sigh in relief. If he was making her a doctor appointment, this must be pretty bad. "Thanks. Let me know how it goes."

"Will do."

I hung up the phone and practically ran to the office. I let my office manager know that I had to leave, and then went to talk to Sal. He had no problem taking over for me when I told him I had an emergency to take care of. I quickly went home to shower, then headed over to Harper's.

I knocked on the door, but no one answered. I called Drew and found out where the spare key was and what the security code was for the alarm system. When I walked upstairs, I called Harper, but she didn't answer. The bedroom was empty, and when I looked in the other room, steam practically shot out of my ears. There was no bed. It had weights in it, but none of Drew's stuff was in there. I peeked back in the other room and saw his stuff in the hamper. They were sharing a room. I couldn't deal with this now. Harper needed me, and I had to focus on that. I knocked on the bathroom door, but when I got no answer, I opened it to find Harper asleep on the bathroom floor.

"Harper. Hey, come on. Wake up."

Harper opened her eyes and looked at me. "I don't feel good."

"I know, honey. I'm gonna take you to the doctor and we'll see what they say. Come on. Let's get you cleaned up."

I had about forty minutes left before we had to leave. I ran her a bath and quickly washed her hair and cleaned her up. Then I got her out and dressed in some comfy clothes, and dried her hair. We were running a few minutes late, so I carried her out to the truck and drove over to the clinic.

"How are you doing over there?" I asked as we drove to the clinic.

"I've been better."

She was leaning against the door, and she was extremely pale. I hated to see her not feeling well, but honestly, I was a little scared that she was so sick.

"We're almost there. You can see the doctor, and then I'll get you back to your bed."

We arrived at the clinic with two minutes to spare. Harper didn't want me coming back with her, and I tried not to be offended by that. When she came back out over a half hour later, she was deathly pale. She was walking slowly toward me and she was shaking slightly. Shit. This must be bad.

I took her by the arm and led her to the door. We slowly crossed the parking lot to the truck and I helped her in, all the while she was completely silent. When I got in and closed the door, I turned to her. She was staring at her shaking hands.

"Harper. What is it? What did the doctor say?"

"Um, she said that it's just a really bad stomach bug, and she wrote a prescription for an antiemetic. She said that once I get the vomiting under control and I can hold down food, I should feel better. Would you mind stopping at the drugstore on the way home?"

"Of course not, but how about I get you back home and then I go for you so you can rest?"

"Okay. That sounds good." She leaned her head back against the headrest and kept her eyes closed the whole way home. I helped her back into the house and was going to take her upstairs, but she said she was too tired and would just veg out on the couch. I covered her with a blanket and got her a bottle of water, then headed out to the drugstore.

When I picked up the prescription, I asked the pharmacist if there was anything I needed to know.

"Hmm. Well, let's see. Is she sick?"

I looked at the pharmacist strangely. "Yes, that's why she was prescribed an antiemetic."

"No, sorry. What I mean is, does she have cancer? This medicine is primarily prescribed for patients undergoing chemo."

My world stopped. She was sick. That explained why she was so pale and was exhausted. I half-listened to the rest of what the pharmacist said, then walked out of the pharmacy, completely blown away. Harper was sick, not just a little sick. I felt sick to my stomach. What if I lost her? I was just about to get her back. I had wasted all those months without her, pushing her away so that we could get over each other.

I climbed in the truck and stared out the window. How had I gone from wanting kids with her to this? It wasn't fair. I glanced down at the medication. I needed to get that to her so she could feel better. I drove back to Harper's, but I sat in the truck for fifteen minutes trying to get myself under control. She needed me to be strong. It was obvious she didn't want me to know yet, so I would have to wait for her to tell me. It occurred to me that her appointment hadn't been very long, so I wondered if they had done blood work, or if she was scheduled to go back in for a screening or a biopsy. I had so many questions that I knew I didn't have any right to ask. I walked back into the house to see Harper staring at the television.

"Sorry about that. There was a line."

I went to the kitchen and got some more water for her, and handed her a pill. She drank it and snuggled into the couch. I made myself comfortable in a chair and just stared at her.

"You don't have to stay. Sitting here looking at me is kind of creepy and won't make me feel better."

"I'll stay until Drew gets home. I don't want to leave you alone."

"Do whatever you want."

She slept on the couch for a while, and when she woke up an hour and a half later, she asked me to make her some soup. I was so relieved that she was feeling better that I practically ran into the kitchen to get her soup and crackers. She didn't eat much, but I was pretty sure she was testing her stomach. She slept on the couch the rest of the day, waking periodically and drinking some water. I had the television on low, and tried to discreetly do some research on cancer. It was difficult because there were so many factors to consider, and I really couldn't research properly until I knew what kind she had.

When Drew walked through the door at five forty-five, I practically jumped out of my chair, looking at Harper to make sure she was still asleep. I had hated Drew for a while, was even pissed when I realized he was sharing a bed with her. But right now, I needed to tell him what was going on. I was just happy I wasn't alone with this knowledge anymore. I nodded toward the door and he followed me out.

"So, what did the doctor say?"

"It's cancer." Drew's face grew dim and he tried to school his features, but I saw the sadness there.

"I thought it might be something like that. She's just been so sick this week and...I'll get her to talk to me about it, and we'll go from there. I'll let you know as soon as I know something. I don't want to push her until she's ready to talk about it though."

I knew that was my cue to leave. I had no permanent place in her life right now. I stared at the door, wishing I could just tell him I'd sleep on the couch, but one look at him, and I knew that wasn't going to fly. I couldn't blame him. He'd been there for Harper when I wasn't. He sat with her when she cried. He held her in his arms when she was sad. And what had I done? I'd stayed away because I was afraid, because I made decisions without truly thinking about the consequences.

Nodding to him, I turned to go. "Please, just tell her to call me if she needs anything."

"I will."

Glancing back at the house one last time, I walked away. Driving away from her was the hardest thing I had ever done, harder than breaking things off with her. Maybe because this time, the stakes were higher.

Two days had passed and I still hadn't heard anything. I texted Drew, but she still hadn't said anything to him. She did have another appointment scheduled for tomorrow. I pulled the time out of Drew and made the appropriate arrangements at work. The next day, I arrived at the clinic a half hour ahead of time. I wanted to catch her before she went in so I could lend my support.

When Drew and Harper pulled up at the clinic, Harper looked shocked to see me there. She glanced at Drew and he gave her a sheepish look. She climbed out of the truck and threw her hands on her hips.

"Jack, what are you doing here?"

"I just wanted to be here for you."

"I already told you that it's just a stomach bug. This appointment is just to make sure that I didn't catch anything else."

"Okay, well, I'll go with you."

She ignored me and walked on shaky legs into the clinic to check in. I kept my hand out the whole way, like she would suddenly topple over. Glancing at Drew, I saw he was doing the same thing, just a tad more discreetly than me. She sat down in the waiting area and I followed her over there, sitting right next to her and grabbing her hand to hold. I had to touch her. I needed to feel her hand in mine and know that she would be okay. More than anything, I needed her to know that I was here for her. Screw it. I couldn't pretend like I didn't know. I wanted to go back to the room with her so that I could support her.

"I want to go back with you."

"Uh, Jack, this is a private appointment. I don't want you there."

The nurse called her name and she shook my hand off, standing to walk away. Every step she took away from me was torture. I needed to be back there with her.

"I know you have cancer," I shouted across the waiting room at her.

She turned beet red and I felt like a shit for embarrassing her, but the time for going slow had passed.

Glancing around the waiting room, she said, "Jack, I don't have cancer."

I walked over to her and lowered my voice slightly. "Sweetheart, I know that you don't want to burden me with this, but I want to be here to support you. The pharmacist said that the medication was used with people undergoing chemo."

"Did he also tell you that it's used for morning sickness?" I looked at her in confusion.

"I'm pregnant. That's why I've been so sick. I have Hyperemesis Gravidarum. That's why I needed the nausea medication."

I stood there stunned, and when I didn't say anything for a minute, she turned and followed the nurse. I stumbled on shaky legs over to my chair and flopped down, absolutely stunned. Then it hit me like a ton of bricks. We hadn't slept together since New Year's Eve. She had slept with someone else.

Drew looked equally as shocked, and I really hoped that it wasn't him that had knocked her up. As I looked at him further, I noted a hint of relief on his face. Of course, we both thought that she had cancer, so this was a good thing in comparison, but she had moved on. I had been pining over her for six months and had stupidly thought I could win her back. I turned to Drew.

"Did you sleep with her?"

He held up both hands. "I swear, we've never even kissed. As far as I know, she hasn't been with anyone. But...she was in England for three weeks."

He looked almost sad to be saying that. I had a feeling that he actually wanted the two of us back together, but I was too late. What chance did I have at getting her back now? She didn't want me with her, so I left the building in a daze and drove to the nearest bar and ordered a drink.

How could I have been so stupid? I actually thought that she hadn't been with anyone else since we broke up. I thought she was just as depressed over our breakup as I was. Here I was, ready to give her everything just to be together again, and she had gone and gotten pregnant.

I ordered a few more drinks, and after a while, it all seemed pretty funny. Pretty soon, I was telling funny stories from my time with her to anyone who would listen. I had the whole bar laughing hysterically about the turkey incident. Of course, they were all drunk, so anything was funny to this crowd.

I was in the middle of the football story from Thanksgiving when I felt a hand on my shoulder.

"Hey, man." I turned around to see Logan sitting at the next bar stool.

"Hey! It's Logan. How are ya? I was just telling the guys about how I hit Harper in the face with the football."

"Yeah, that's a good story."

"I know, right?" I turned back to finish the story.

"Drew called," Logan said. "He told me Harper's pregnant, and that you haven't been with her since you broke up."

I turned back to him and then ordered another drink. "Yeah, that was quite the shock. I followed her to her appointment because I thought she was sick, and I wanted to be there for her. She didn't want me in the room with her, so I stood up and shouted across the room, *I know you have cancer.*" I huffed out a laugh, shaking my head slightly. "The whole waiting room got really quiet and she turned bright red. Guess I don't always have the best way of going about stuff. That's when she told me that she didn't have cancer. She said she was pregnant, and I just stood there like an idiot. Then she went to her appointment, and I came here."

"That sucks." We drank in silence for a few minutes. "Do you still want to be there for her?"

"You know I love Harper, but I'm sure she's going to go be with the sperm donor. They'll meet up again, and she'll tell him she's having his kid. He'll take care of her. Who wouldn't want Harper? She's the best."

"So, if she's the best, why are you walking away before you even talk to her? You don't even know when it happened. Wasn't she over in England for a few weeks? It could have happened over there. She didn't sleep with any of the guys we set her up with. We made sure of that."

"Even worse if it's a Brit. They have those accents that the chicks love." I turned to him drunkenly. "What do you mean *we made sure of that?*"

Logan started laughing. "We all got together and made a plan to get you two back together."

I scoffed. "Well, you did a bang up job. See how happy we are together right now?" I said mockingly.

"You guys were on your way back to each other. It was working. This is just a minor hiccup."

"A minor hiccup? She's pregnant with another guy's baby. How is that minor?"

"Look, the way I see it, you have two options. You can sit here and drink and wallow in this new information, and live the rest of your life miserable and alone. Or, you can go home and sober up. Go visit Harper tomorrow and talk this shit out. You already told her you wanted a kid with her. Does it really matter if it's not your kid, as long as you have Harper?"

I thought about it for a while as I drank the rest of my beer. Did it matter if it wasn't my kid? I had been so lost without her over the past six months. My life was empty. My house was empty. Nothing in my life was right without her. No, it didn't really matter. I wanted Harper, whether the baby was mine or not. The kid thing was new to me, but since I hadn't planned on having kids, it was just an adjustment in the plan I had already made. I just had to be man enough to crawl back to Harper and beg her to take me back. I couldn't lose her now. We had been so close to getting back together. Hopefully, she still wanted that.

"Logan, I need you to take me home, and in the morning, take me to my truck."

"It's already taken care of. Do you really think I came alone? The guys are in the parking lot, waiting to drag your ass out of here, in case you decided to come to the wrong conclusion. We'll drive your truck home, and we're even gonna make sure you wake up thinking the same way. Cuz if not, we're gonna beat your ass."

CHAPTER 31

HARPER

I WAS DEVASTATED when I found out I was pregnant. Jack and I were headed toward a reconciliation, but Jack wouldn't want to be with me if I was having a kid with someone else. He didn't even want one with me. It took us being apart for a long time for him to realize that he was willing to have a kid. But this? This was too much. I had slept with someone else, and I didn't know if we could come back from that, even if we were broken up.

I hadn't been ready to tell anyone I was pregnant. Now, both Jack and Drew knew I was, and it wouldn't be long before all our friends did also. As I got dressed after my appointment, I remembered the look on Jack's face when I told him I was pregnant. He looked shocked and devastated. When he just stared at me, I turned and walked away. His anger was something I couldn't deal with at the moment.

However Jack chose to deal with this was on him, even though it pained me to think that way. I didn't owe him anything. We had broken up. We'd been broken up for six months. I hadn't cheated on him, and I had no clue that he would change his mind and want me back. If I had known that, I would have never slept with another man.

But I had other things to think about now. I was going to be a mother, and that meant putting my child first. When I was finished, I walked out of the room and headed back to the waiting room, and disappointment flooded me. Jack was gone. I knew it was too much to hope that Jack would stick around, but I had been expecting this reaction. Taking a deep breath, I walked over to Drew and gave a small smile.

"Everything okay?"

"Yeah, they just wanted to make sure the medication was working for me."

"What would they have done if it wasn't?"

"IV fluids," I grinned. "Doesn't that sound fun?"

"It wouldn't really matter, as long as you were feeling better."

"Well, let's just be thankful that the medication is working."

Drew and I walked out together and he was quiet the whole way home. I knew I needed to talk to him, but two brooding men in one day was just too much. When we walked in the door, the inquisition started.

"Why didn't you tell me you were pregnant?"

Sighing, I sat down on the couch. "I didn't want to tell anyone yet. As soon as I said it out loud, it was real. I just wanted a little time to process."

"What are you going to do about Jack?"

I blew out a breath and leaned back into the couch. "I'm pretty sure Jack isn't going to stick around. I had sex with someone else. This isn't his child. Why would he still want me?"

"Well, whatever happens, you have me."

"Drew, that's really sweet, but I'm going to be a single mother, and the sooner I get used to that the better."

A grin appeared on his face. "Does that mean you're kicking me out?"

"No. I just don't want you to feel like you're responsible for this child because you live here."

"What about the father? Where's he?"

"He was my one night stand in England, that I was so sure was a brilliant idea to get over Jack. I don't even remember his name. I don't have the first clue how to find him. Besides, after I slept with him, I started crying and he bolted for the door, so I'm pretty sure he would be perfectly happy to never hear from me again."

He pulled me against him, wrapping his arm around my stomach to slightly hold my belly. "You're gonna be a momma. I can't wait to meet this little guy."

"Why would you think it's gonna be a boy?"

"More like hoping. I think it would be cool to teach a little boy how to throw a ball and ride a bike. Let's just say it's wishful thinking."

We went to bed together like we always did, and Drew held me as I slept. I laid awake for a long time thinking about what life was going to be like from now on. I felt comforted being held by Drew, and for the first time since I found out, I was happy.

The next morning, I woke up to a queasy tummy. I got out of bed, and as usual, ran to the bathroom to be sick. When I had purged all I could from my stomach, I walked downstairs in my bathrobe and sat at the breakfast nook. Drew had my pill and some water waiting for me. I had to let the nausea lessen some or I would end up throwing up my pill. I laid my head on the table and waited. After a few crackers, my stomach felt slightly better and I took my medicine. It took about a half hour to kick in. Drew made me some toast and I slowly ate it, even though it tasted like cardboard to me. I took a cup of peppermint tea to the couch and sat down. I hated it, but it helped my tummy settle, so I drank it.

I was watching some television when a knock sounded at the door. I got up and answered the door, completely shocked to see Jack standing on my doorstep looking sexy as hell. He was wearing jeans and a white t-shirt, but that was how I preferred him. I looked down at myself, embarrassed to see that I looked like I hadn't showered in a week. My hair was pulled up in a messy knot on the top of my head, and my ratty bathrobe had crumbs from my toast on it. I knew I still looked deathly pale. It had become my new complexion these last couple of weeks. This was definitely not the way I wanted Jack seeing me.

"Hey. Can we talk for a minute?"

I stepped aside and let Jack inside. He walked in, looking around for Drew, but he had already left. "How are you feeling today?"

"Still pretty shitty, but the medicine helps."

"I know that you must be wondering what I'm doing here. I didn't react very well to your news yesterday."

"Well, I suppose I should have told you earlier when we were in private. I just didn't want you to know that I had...you know."

"Slept with someone else? I think I would have figured it out when you were walking around with a big belly. At the very least, when you were *carrying* a baby."

I smiled slightly. "I could have told you I ate too many Oreos and that I had adopted."

He smiled at that, and I felt some of the tension leave the room. "So who's the guy?"

"Jack, I really don't want to do this with you. What's done is done."

He held up his hand to stop me from saying more. "I'm asking because I want to know if he's going to try to get parental rights. I don't want someone coming in trying to take our baby from us."

"No, I don't know..." I stopped and frowned at him. Did he just say... "Wait, what did you say? Did you say take the baby from *us*?"

"Yeah, pretty girl. I did." He shoved his hands in his pockets and his face turned serious. "I know I was shocked yesterday, and I'm not gonna lie, it hurt to hear, but I finally saw reason after the guys threatened to kick my ass."

I kept frowning at him. I was so confused. "Aren't you wondering about the father? I mean, I slept with someone else. It was only once, but still..."

"I don't need or want to hear about that. It's in the past, and that's where it needs to stay. We were broken up and you were trying to move on. I can't fault you for that."

I was still shocked, but nervous that this was a knee-jerk reaction. What if he changed his mind once the baby was born?

"Are you sure you want to do this? This isn't something you can just back out of. Once the baby's here, I need you to be ready for this. I don't want you to do this out of some sense of obligation to me."

"Pretty girl, I don't feel any kind of obligation other than what a husband is supposed to do for his wife, and we will be married, as soon as possible. We're going to love this baby, and if we don't kill this one, maybe we can make another one."

My eyes grew wide. I hadn't even had this one and he was already talking about me having another? "How about we just start with one and go from there?"

"Sounds good to me, as long as we get to practice in the meantime."

Jack leaned forward and kissed me, but my stomach chose that moment to revolt. I shoved away from him and sprinted to the bathroom. I felt him holding back my hair as I vomited my toast into the toilet. It was so disgusting, but he didn't even flinch. Leaning against the wall, I closed my eyes and let the shaking subside.

"I'm going to assume that it was the morning sickness and not me."

I smiled slightly, my eyes still closed. "You could never make me vomit."

I felt him lean in, just inches from my face. "Good, because there's no way I'm ever letting you go, pretty girl."

He brushed a light kiss across my lips, then my forehead. "I love you so much."

I finally opened my eyes and looked at him. "I love you too."

He smiled, brushing back the sweaty hair from my face. "It's about time we both came to the same realization."

"What's that?"

"That I'm completely wonderful." I smacked him on the chest

and he laughed. "This was always meant to be. It doesn't matter what life throws at us. We belong together, and I'm not waiting another minute to start my life with you."

"That's really good to hear," I said, my voice filled with mock seriousness.

"Why's that?"

"My books were getting a little too violent. I think my editor was starting to worry about me."

The next few months flew by much the same way. I never puked on him, which was a good thing, but he spent all his time at my house, kicking Drew out of bed and forcing him to sleep on the couch. He didn't like my house, or the fact that Drew lived there, but he did like the fact that he had someone else there to gang up on me.

Harper, eat your food.

Harper, take your medication.

Harper, let's get fresh air.

Harper, get some sleep.

Part of me really wanted to move in with him, but the other part of me was scared. I was worried that at any moment he would change his mind. Wasn't it better to play it safe? And that was once again our argument after we got back from the doctor.

"Jack, I don't want to move in with you yet. I need more time."

"More time for what? The baby's going to be here in another few months. We have to get you moved in and get the baby's room set up. I don't want to leave everything to the last minute."

"I'm just saying I need more time. Can't you give me that?"

"More time for what? To make sure I don't bail on you? Haven't you noticed yet that I'm not going anywhere?"

I looked away. I didn't want him to see the uncertainty in my eyes.

"I'm not going anywhere," Jack said as he walked to the door.

"Except for right now. I have to get back to work, but I'll see you tonight. This conversation isn't over."

Jack never came over that night, and I had a hard time getting ahold of him over the next few days. I knew this would happen. It was getting too real and he was bolting. Drew came home from work and went right upstairs to take a shower. When he was done, he told me to go get dressed because he was taking me out. I ran upstairs and threw on a maternity dress. I was so excited to get out of the house.

Drew took me to a nice restaurant downtown and I devoured my food. Ever since the morning sickness let up, I had a great appetite, and I was making up for those months I couldn't eat.

"So what's the special occasion," I asked as I ate dessert.

"This is a goodbye dinner."

"What?" My fork clattered to my plate. "You're leaving? But you said you would be here. You promised me I would always have you." My voice was rising and was bordering on sounding hysterical. Jack wasn't talking to me, and now Drew was leaving. This couldn't be happening.

"I'm not leaving. You are."

"What?"

"You're going to live with Jack. Enough is enough, Harper. What more does the man have to do to prove that he's sticking around?"

"You can't order me out of the house. I'm on the lease."

"I'm not ordering you out, but if you go back there, you won't have any stuff. Anna and Luke came over to clear out all your stuff when we left the house."

"What," I screeched. "What were you thinking, Drew? You had no right to do this."

"I was thinking that my back hurts from sleeping on the couch."

"Traitor," I glared at him.

"Just come with me and let me show you something. If you still aren't convinced, I'll take you back home, along with all your stuff."

I glared at him, and he had the decency to look properly chastised. "Fine."

We finished our dessert and then Drew took me over to Jack's house. When Jack opened the door, the first thing I saw was a Christmas tree in the corner, fully decorated with the ornaments we had picked out the previous Christmas.

"It's beautiful."

He grinned. "That's not all I have to show you, pretty girl."

Jack led me down a hallway to the guest bedroom and opened the door. The bedroom had been converted into a nursery. It was painted blue with decals of diggers, backhoes, tractors, and various other machinery on the walls. There was a simple crib that had a mattress and fitted sheet already in it, and a dresser with a picture of Jack and me with a few small decorations. A changing table sat along another wall, fully stocked with diapers, wipes, diaper rash cream, pacifiers, vaseline, bibs, and burp cloths. Finally, in the corner, sat a cozy glider with a baby quilt on the back of the chair. There was a small table next to it, and a lamp behind it.

I walked around the room and took it all in. I opened the drawers to see several baby outfits, socks, sleepers, and sleep sacks. The bottom drawer had spare sheets and mattress protectors. It was the perfect room and he had thought of everything. I walked over to Jack and gave him a big hug.

"Alright, fine. I'll move in with you. I mean, my stuff is already here and moving is such a pain."

"I'm glad you see it my way. I was thinking if I could just get your stuff here, there would be no way you would want to pack and move back with Drew. Because I definitely wouldn't be helping you. Now all we have to do is get married."

"I am not getting married when I'm pregnant. I don't want my kid seeing pictures of our wedding day, thinking we had a shotgun wedding."

"As long as there isn't a shotgun at the wedding, it's all good."

I didn't even notice Drew slip out as Jack dragged me back to the bedroom and started kissing me. We hadn't had sex yet because I hadn't been feeling well until a few weeks ago. When he started taking me out, I always wanted to go back to my house, and Drew was always home. He had waited patiently for me, but now that I was back in our house, I knew he was going to take what was his. He ripped my clothes from my body and gave me a bruising kiss. Then he seemed to rein himself in.

He pushed me back on the bed, being extra careful with me. He was up on his elbows, not allowing his body to lay on top of mine. Enough was enough. I was tired of being babied.

"Jack, I'm not glass. I won't break."

"I just don't want to hurt the baby. What if I lay on you and he comes flying out of your vagina?"

"Really, Jack? That's not likely to happen."

"But are you sure? Have you researched it? Maybe we should google a little before we do this."

He got up and walked over to his laptop on his dresser and started googling. After a few minutes, he turned around and scratched the back of his head. "Um. It says it's not possible for me to push the baby out of you by laying on you during sex."

I snorted and really tried not to laugh, but it was just too funny. Jack leapt on the bed next to me, then began teasing me by running his hands all over my body, but never touching my most intimate places. I needed to feel his hands on me.

"Touch my boobs, Jack." His hands trailed up to each breast and massaged me, then he pinched my nipples. "Y-yeah. That's good."

"What else do you want, pretty girl?"

"I want...I want you to touch my pussy." His hand moved south, but instead of touching me, he trailed his hand down my leg and ran his fingertips up my inner thigh, around my mound, and down the other thigh. I was quivering with need and started to beg. "Please, Jack, just touch me."

"You've kept me waiting, and now it's your turn to wait." He got off the bed and walked around to the side where I was laying. He grabbed his cock and stroked it. "Open your mouth."

I turned my head to the side and opened wide for him. I started to suck on him, my pussy dampening with every lick. I loved to have him in my mouth. I moved into a new position, one where I could take him deeper. I gently tugged his balls with my other hand, and my core tightened when he groaned. His hand slid down my stomach to my pussy, sliding his fingers through my wet folds. His fingers pumped into my channel as his cock pumped in my mouth. My legs were quivering, and we both knew I was getting close. His fingers rubbed my clit, and I groaned as he pumped harder and faster. My legs clamped together as he rubbed me so hard that I came with a shout. He thrust one more time into my mouth and I felt warm liquid shoot down my throat. He stood there breathing deeply, and slowly pulled himself from my sore jaw.

"That was fantastic, baby. I'm gonna fuck your mouth a lot over the next few months."

"As long as you fuck my pussy too, I'll let you do whatever you want to my mouth."

His eyes darkened. "I'm gonna hold you to that."

CHAPTER 32

HARPER

"JACK, I think today's the day."

"The day for what, baby?" He rolled over in bed to see me sitting on the edge.

"To have the baby."

He stared at me for a moment, almost like he thought I was joking. Then he jumped up from the bed and ran to the dresser. He pulled his pants out and started to put them on, but changed course and started running to the bathroom. He got caught up in his pants leg and fell flat on his face. I watched in fascination as he struggled to get his pants on, then ran to the bathroom and was back out a minute later. I followed him as he ran into the living room and grabbed the car keys and the hospital bag. He was out the door in a flash, and I tilted my head, listening for the sound of the car. Smirking, I watched from the window as he pulled out and headed into town. When he was out of sight, I went to the kitchen and grabbed a bottle of water, then went back to the window to wait for him. About five minutes later, he was back and running through the door.

"I'm so sorry, honey. I was in such a rush to leave that I forgot you. Is that what you're wearing?" I was still in my bathrobe, drinking my water.

"I said today was the day, but it's not time yet. Besides, they won't let you in the hospital without a shirt and shoes."

He looked down at himself and chuckled.

"I still have a while before we can head to the hospital. The contractions are just starting."

I went about my morning of getting breakfast and taking a shower. Every time a contraction hit, Jack was standing next to me in case I needed him. It was getting on my nerves. The contractions started to get really painful, and every time one hit, I felt like I was going to black out. My vision would cloud over and no amount of walking seemed to help.

"Maybe we should call the hospital," Jack said worriedly. "What do I do if you pass out? Do I just pull the baby out?"

I glared at him hard. "If I pass out, you call an ambulance. This isn't rocket science, Jack."

"Well, how the hell should I know! This is my first time doing this."

"It's my first time too, but you don't see me pacing the floor."

"You were just doing that," he shouted. "You're walking back and forth constantly."

"Because I'm having a baby! I walk to help the contractions."

"That doesn't even make any sense," he scoffed. "We don't need to help the contractions. We need to help the baby!"

I groaned in frustration at his idiocy. Deep down, I knew that he was just scared and saying anything that came to mind. It didn't matter if it made sense.

"Maybe I should call my mom. She's been through this before."

"And you think the doctors don't know what they're talking about?" I snapped.

"I just want a second opinion. This looks like...really bad. You're on the verge of blacking out. That can't be normal!"

"Then just call the nurse line again," I snapped.

He called the hospital, but my contractions were still too erratic, so the nurse said they would turn me away if I showed up. About an hour later, I couldn't take it anymore. I called my doctor and they got me in to be checked.

"Jack, we need to leave now. The doctor can get me in to be checked."

"Okay, just let me go to the bathroom really quick."

"Alright, I'll make my way to the car." I headed out the door and twenty minutes later was still sitting there. Sitting made the contractions more painful, and I needed to go find him or I would end up having this baby in the driveway. Where was he? I walked back inside to see him doing the dishes. What. The. Fuck.

"Seriously? You're doing the dishes now?"

"I needed to do some cleaning up before we left."

"Jack. I told you I needed to go in. This morning you were in such a rush that you left without me, and now you need to do the dishes?"

"Well, I had to go to the bathroom, and then I didn't want to bring the baby home to a dirty house. We can't bring a baby around germs. What if the hospital doesn't let us bring him home?"

"Seriously, Jack, it'll be fine. Now, my contractions are getting closer, so unless you want to start wearing your balls as a necklace, can we please go?"

"Ya know, just once, I wish you wouldn't threaten to cut off my balls. There are other ways of making your point."

"But none so effective."

I made my way back to the car and we headed to the doctor's office. The doctor examined me and said that I was four centimeters dilated and we could head over to the hospital. She called ahead and let them know I was on my way, then apologized for the rude nurse on the phone. Hospital protocol was that you were checked, and if you were far enough along they admitted you, but if you weren't, they asked you to come back later. I never should have been told to wait it out at home, at least not if I was in that much pain.

We headed to the car, but I had to walk slowly. Now the contractions were coming every three to four minutes, and they were really painful. We pulled up to the hospital, but had parked at the wrong entrance and I had to walk over to the correct elevator. Jack was parking the car, so I decided to start making my way to the other side of the hospital. I figured that by the time I got there he would catch up. Every time I passed a hospital employee, they asked me if I was okay. Probably because I was doing my deep breathing and working through contractions the whole walk.

"Miss, are you okay?" Deep breath in, deep breath out.

"Yes, I'm fine. I'm just heading up to the maternity floor."

There was a group standing outside the elevators. The whole group got on, but there wasn't enough room for me. No one offered to move over and let me get on. I continued to stand there waiting for another five minutes, cursing the people that didn't have enough decency to let me on. Could they not see me trying to get through each contraction? Perhaps I should have started screaming in pain. Then they would have stepped out of my way.

"You still haven't gotten on the elevator?" Jack asked.

I turned and glared at him. "There was no room for me."

His jaw clenched hard, and when the next elevator arrived, anyone that started to get on with me received a withering stare. I was a little frightened too. I mean, not that I would be injured, but that Jack would take out anyone that came near me. His reactions today were giving me whiplash.

After checking in, the anesthesiologist arrived in no time, and soon I was feeling no pain. I laid there thinking about how my mother had once told me that she didn't remember any pain when I was born. She even told me that she slept while having contractions. I didn't see how that was possible. I had intense pain from about four hours on. Now that the drugs had kicked in, I finally dozed a little, but honestly, I was too excited to sleep.

A few hours later, the nurse came in to check me.

"How are you feeling, sweetie?"

She started checking my vitals, and I looked over at Jack, completely embarrassed by what I needed to tell her. When I didn't answer, she looked over at me with a stern expression.

"What is it?"

"Um..."

Jack jumped up from his chair, immediately grabbed my hand. "Pretty girl, what's going on? Is everything okay?"

"Can you give us a minute?"

He looked completely shellshocked. "You want me to leave?"

I could have laughed at the pitiful look on his face, but I didn't. Not externally, anyway. "I just need a minute to discuss something private with the nurse."

He narrowed his eyes at me. "I don't like it."

"I'm pretty sure that doesn't matter right now. Please, just give me two minutes."

Huffing, he walked out of the room, pushing hard on the door, only to have it slowly close. He flung his hands in the air, obviously pissed that he couldn't even take his rage out on the door.

"So, now that he's gone, what's going on?"

I blushed bright red, afraid to tell her.

"Honey, I've heard it all. There's nothing you could tell me that I haven't heard before. Is he not the father?"

I shook my head, ready to tell her that Jack already knew.

"So, you're worried he's going to come out brown and blow the surprise?"

"What? No, it's nothing like that. I mean, it's sort of like that, but not in the way you mean."

Her eyebrows furrowed.

"He already knows he's not the father. I am worried he might come out brown though."

"I don't understand."

I glanced back at the door. "I really have to poop."

She stared at me for a minute, and then burst out laughing. "Oh, honey. I take it back. That's a first for me." When she stopped wiping at the tears streaming down her face, she finally moved down by my feet. "That just means it's time to start pushing. Let's get you checked out. She lifted the gown to check me and gasped.

"Wow. That's a lot of hair."

I knew she was talking about the baby's head because Jack had just helped me trim myself. I didn't want to show up at the hospital with a full bush. No matter what people said, I wanted to be presentable to the people that would be so intimately acquainted with me. The nurse pulled out her phone and called the doctor.

"You need to come now. This baby is already on its way out."

The door pushed open just as she was finishing up that thought. Jack looked at me in panic. "What?" Jack rushed over, gripping my hand. "Hurry! Put your hands down there and catch it. If my baby falls and hits his head, I will sue your ass."

"Sir, calm down. The baby won't *fall out*. I didn't mean to worry you. I was just letting the doctor know that he is ready to be born."

Jack seemed to calm down when he heard that. I started laughing at him. He was being ridiculous. The doctor came in and gave me the all clear to start pushing. Jack started creeping down to the end of the bed, but there was no way I would stand for that. I didn't want him to see my hoo hoo all stretched out, even for the birth of our child.

"Jack! What do you think you're doing? Get back up here by my head."

"I want to see our baby being born."

"No. You are *not* seeing this. I don't want to, and I don't want you to either. Once that's in your head, you can never unsee it." Then I turned to the nurse. "And please clean him up before you put him on me. I really can't handle all the goop, and I don't want to throw up on my baby."

The nurse smiled and chuckled a little. "Of course. Now, get ready to push."

I pushed twice and my son was born. That was it. It didn't hurt and I wasn't sweating and panting as I laid in bed. There was no yelling or gripping Jack's hand so tight I might break it. Basically, anything you read about never happened. It felt a little anticlimactic. I felt like I was missing out on some really good stories.

Another nurse stepped in and took the baby, then placed him on my chest. I just stared at him with wide eyes. Not because I was amazed at the child I had just pushed out of a rather small hole, but because I had specifically asked for him to be cleaned up first, and now there was a bloody pile of goop on me. I was very close to panicking.

"Don't worry. Everything is fine with him. He's breathing."

Then I heard the baby cry and the nurse smiled. "See? He's fine." The other nurse stepped in and took him from my chest and cleaned him up. She must have seen the panic on my face when the other nurse hadn't taken him right to the incubator to be cleaned.

Jack leaned in and kissed me. "He's alright, baby. Don't worry."

"I'm not worried. I was looking at him and thinking *Why is this kid on me? He's all goopy.* not *Why isn't this kid breathing?*."

Jack looked at me funny. Yeah, he was probably thinking that I was going to be a terrible mother. I knew it sounded bad, but I really didn't want to hold him until he was cleaned. Hand me a worst mother of the year award for freaking out at having my gross newborn on me. The nurse finished cleaning him and handed him off to Jack, who was waiting eagerly next to the nurses. He smiled down at his son, and it was something I would always remember because he was standing under a light and it was reflecting all around Jack and my newborn son.

The way he was staring down at him made my heart melt. All these months, I had been so anxious that he wouldn't love my son. I worried that he would take one look at him and decide that he didn't want him. But looking at him now, I could see the love on his face, and I knew everything would be fine. We would be one very happy family.

"Meet your son, Harper," he said as he placed our son in my arms. "What should we name him?"

I stared down at my son with so much love. He was absolutely perfect and even though he wasn't biologically Jack's, I wanted to give our son his grandpa's name.

"Ethan. Ethan Graham Huntley."

ALSO BY GIULIA LAGOMARSINO

Thank you for reading Jack and Harper's story. It was my very first creation, and based on some comical events in my own life. I hope you enjoyed it. Need more? Check out the next book in the series Cole!

Join my newsletter to get the most up-to-date information, along with new content in the Reed Security series.

https://giulialagomarsinoauthor.com/connect/

Join my Facebook reader group to find out more about my obsession with Dwayne Johnson!

https://www.facebook.com/groups/GiuliaLagomarsinobooks

Reading Order:

https://giulialagomarsinoauthor.com/reading-order/

To find the individual series, follow the links below:

For The Love Of A Good Woman series

Reed Security series

The Cortell Brothers

A Good Run Of Bad Luck

The Shifting Sands Beneath Us- Standalone

Owens Protective Services

Printed in Great Britain
by Amazon